ENDURING PASSIONS

ENDURING PASSIONS

DAVID WILTSHIRE

THORNDIKE
CHIVERS

This Large Print edition is published by Thorndike Press, Waterville, Maine, USA and by BBC Audiobooks Ltd, Bath, England.

Thorndike Press is an imprint of The Gale Group

Thorndike is a trademark and used herein under license.

LIBRARY OF CONGRESS CATALOGING-IN-PUBLICATION DATA

Wiltshire, David, 1935–
    Enduring passions / by David Wiltshire.
        p. cm. — (Thorndike Press large print mystery)
    ISBN-13: 978-1-4104-0327-8 (hardcover : alk. paper)
    ISBN-10: 1-4104-0327-0 (hardcover : alk. paper)
    1. Police — England — Fiction. 2. World War, 1939–1945 — Social aspects — England — Fiction. 3. Social classes — England — Fiction. 4. Great Britain — History — George VI, 1936–1952 — Fiction. 5. Large type books. I. Title.
    PR6073.I47535E53 2007
    823'.914—dc22   2007034617

BRITISH LIBRARY CATALOGUING-IN-PUBLICATION DATA AVAILABLE

Published in 2007 in the U.S. by arrangement with Robert Hale Limited.
Published in 2008 in the U.K. by arrangement with Robert Hale Limited.

U.K. Hardcover: 978 1 405 64288 0 (Chivers Large Print)
U.K. Softcover: 978 1 405 64289 7 (Camden Large Print)

Printed in the United States of America on permanent paper
10 9 8 7 6 5 4 3 2 1

For Archie, Beth, Conrad, Guy, Marcus, Tom, and not forgetting Molly. May they never have to go through such a war.

Oh, Rank is Good, and Gold is Fair,
And High and Low Mate Ill;
But Love Has Never Known a Law
Beyond its Own Sweet Will!
John Greenleaf Whittier
1807–1892

ENDURING PASSIONS
PROLOGUE

It was a beautiful day, bright and very still when he got up, the lawn sparkling with dew, like millions and millions of diamonds catching the morning sun.

How Fay would have loved it.

At ten o'clock Mrs Howard arrived to clean the house and prepare the midday meal. He let her help him on with his coat — his old flying jacket — and hand him his cap.

'Are you sure you should be going out on your own?'

Testily he said, 'I'm not going alone, Alfie's coming with me.'

She rolled her eyes in despair at the mention of the Jack Russell. In doggy terms he was 84, nearly as old as his master.

With his cap pulled down over his wispy, white hair and Alfie waddling behind, he set off across the lawn to the gate that lead into the meadow.

She watched him until he shuffled out of view. Shaking her head she got on with her work. It was easy to see the poor man was heartbroken. He and Mrs Roxham had been one of the most devoted couples that she had ever known.

Slowly he made his way across the field towards the river he had once fished, until he got too unsteady on his feet. In the cold air his breath came in little puffs of moisture.

Alfie stopped occasionally to have a good sniff and cock his leg, before padding on behind his master.

By the river Tom Roxham paused, watching the shafts of light flashing in the rippling, bubbling water. Eventually there came the sound of a steam train, labouring up an incline. Across the valley amongst the trees of the forest he could see the smoke coming in almost continuous puffs, merging together before slowly dispersing in the foliage.

It did his old heart good to hear a Great Western locomotive still working in the tweny-first century — and on the other side of the world.

His grandchildren and their children and their children's children would be able to experience that wonderful sight and smell and sound of his youth.

On the way back to the house he heard the grand piano, Fay's grand piano. It was his daughter who was playing, of course, she had come to have lunch with him, did several times a week. She was obviously worried about him now that Fay was gone.

As he crossed the lawn he could see her through the french windows, and for one heart-stopping moment he seemed to be looking at Fay when he'd first set eyes on her a lifetime ago; same slim, lithe figure with dark shining hair cut to the nape of her neck.

Alfie reached the window and reared up on to his hind legs, scratching at the glass, his stump of a tail twitching furiously. She stopped playing the nocturne he'd first heard Dame Myra Hess performing at the National Gallery, and opened the door. Stooping, she patted Alfie, and scratched his muscular little body.

She stood up, holding out her arms, looking anxiously at him. 'Hello, Dad, how are you?'

Her voice even had the same tone as Fay's but, as nature decreed, she wasn't an exact copy, not a clone. Close up she was *of* Fay, but *not* her.

His throat tightened, but he managed 'Oh,

all right, darling, I'm getting by, don't you worry now.'

Brightening, she put her arm through his. 'Come on, let me give you all the news from the big city.'

They had a lovely lunch, Mrs Howard fussing around them, obviously delighted that he was enjoying himself. Finally the time came when his daughter had to go.

She looked at her watch. 'Just make it back before the family comes home.'

She went through the customary worry about him being alone, wouldn't he consider selling up and moving to a nursing home now that Mum was no longer with him?

Gently, but firmly, he reminded her once again that there was no way he would leave his home except in a box. No, he wasn't worried about burglars and the like, not after what he'd been through in the war, and in any case he'd got his old service revolver in his downstairs bedroom, wouldn't hesitate to use it if necessary, and to hell with the consequences. They could sort that out later.

Though he could afford it, he flatly refused a live-in-nurse, but allowed care assistants to get him up in the morning, and in the evening to make sure he was changed and ready for bed.

They also supervised his medication — he had to take up to nine tablets a day now, to control his blood pressure, diabetes and Uncle Tom Cobley and all.

Later that evening, nursing a large glass of whisky that would have been frowned upon by his medical attendants — if they'd known about it — he sat in his favourite winged chair before his other, acknowledged luxury — an open fire.

They'd left him enough wood to last the evening. Alfie was on his lap, snoring gently as his back was slowly stroked. He was listening to a CD playing beside him on the table. It was his favourite — Elgar's Cello Concerto.

He'd played a sax, in a dance band in the 30s, till the whole world had fallen apart.

It was Fay who had introduced him to classical music.

He took his hand from Alfie's back and picked up a much creased and faded black and white photograph from 1939 that he'd carried with him through the war years. That morning he'd taken it from an old wallet at the back of a drawer.

Laying it down again on the arm of his chair he gazed into the red and yellow depths of the fire with his rheumy old eyes, no longer afraid of his Gran's warning that he would go blind if he did.

He grunted at the memory, and let the music, the warmth and the flickering red corridors between the burning wood draw him from the present. Away from his feeble body, to a time when there were no morning tablets, no walking sticks, no stiff aching joints, no shortness of breath, no going to the bathroom every couple of hours.

But also a time when there was a way of life and a culture that now no longer existed: a class system that had died in the most terrible years of their lives.

That at least was a good thing. Except for those five years they'd had a good life, not like many friends who had never made it. But they'd sworn never to be parted again.

And they *wouldn't* now.

He'd thought about using his old service revolver, but the horror for whoever found him, to say nothing of his children's reaction had made him reject that. Anyway, he chuckled, his hands shook so much these days that he'd probably miss and shoot Alfie.

So it would have to be the other.

He'd kept it ever since he'd been issued with it in Burma with the advice — 'If the Nips get you, for God's sake get it down you whilst you still can.'

The cyanide pill.

Very quick acting they said.

He picked it up, turning it around, examining its every aspect. It looked so dull, so ordinary, but. . . .

It was a link to a terrible past, but also to the future — if there was one.

Either way, he would be with Fay again, his kindred spirit.

Unhurriedly he placed it into his mouth, bit down on it, then took a swig of whisky.

He just had time to whisper 'See you soon, Fay' and then his heart and lungs ceased to work.

Alfie's head came up as the whisky tumbler fell to the floor.

■ ■ ■ ■

PART ONE

■ ■ ■ ■

CHAPTER ONE

He took a last look in his mother's dressing-table mirror, adjusting one of the sides to get a better view as he used one of her ebony backed brushes to sweep back his Brylcreemed hair to perfection.

Straightening up he flipped his hand across each shoulder to make sure there was no dandruff present on the maroon double breasted blazer he was wearing. Satisfied, he picked up his saxophone case and skipped down the narrow stairs that ran in the middle of the red brick terrace house he shared with his parents and Gran.

The latter was standing in the scullery. He put the case down on the table in the dining room with its long black cast iron range at one end, the coals glowing brightly behind the bars, and went out to her.

'How do I look, Gran?'

He did a little jiggle.

His grandmother paused from sorting

through the washing and putting it in the galvanized tub with its gas ring beneath.

'Right handsome, my boy. Now you take care. There'll be a lot of drinking tonight — and there is always trouble where there's drink.'

He grinned and gave her a kiss on the forehead.

'Of course, but I'm in the band don't forget, and it's a really posh do.'

She shook her head.

'You got to come home, that's the time to be careful, tonight of all nights.'

He got his coat from one of the pegs in the hall. He was proud of the white trench-coat with epaulettes that he'd bought after he had seen Humphrey Bogart wearing one at the flicks a couple of months ago. He'd gone to the 50 Shilling Tailors saving up for three weeks before he could finally manage the down payment. He had a card now that was ticked off as he paid the balance at 2/6d a week. His brown trilby he placed at a rak-ish angle on his head.

With a last stop at the outside WC with its long bench-type wooden seat, he pulled the chain and snapped off the electric light. Dad had put it in himself — fed up with the oil lamp they had all managed on since the house had been built in 1890.

Although Cheltenham was Regency and known as the gateway to the Cotswolds theirs was a red brick terrace — one of many built for the workers. Their area was never featured in the calendars he'd seen in the bookstores on the Promenade, the wide, tree lined, fashionable shopping street of the spa town.

He closed the gate at the bottom of the garden and made his way down the unmade lane that ran between the rows of houses. It was dark and he nearly walked into Mr Ilsley's Austin Seven.

Out on Leckhampton Road he stood at the bus stop by the underground public lavatory. As a ten year old he'd accidentally gone down the ladies staircase and was so embarrassed that when he came up he'd never stopped running until he'd reached home.

He grinned inwardly. After the shock had worn off he'd been enthralled by the fact that there were no urinals — just doors to cubicles. Girls were obviously very strange and private.

The bus was packed, so he slid on to the bench seat just inside the entrance, giving his money to the conductor who plucked a ticket from his rack, punched the cardboard, and gave it to him, his shiny uniform back pushing against the saxophone case as he moved on.

When he reached the hotel ballroom the band was already set up, the maroon and cream plywood screens shaped like three opening sections of a fan, were placed before each player's position. Across the panel lettering announced 'Raymond Dean and the Serenaders'.

Raymond Dean was a large man with a head of thinning black hair, dressed in the same manner as the rest of the members of the band, or orchestra as he called it, except that he wore a custom-made maroon tuxedo with black dinner trousers. His shoes glistened in the light from wall lamps reflected in the revolving mirror ball hanging from the ceiling.

Apart from the dance area before the band, the rest of the ballroom was filled with round tables covered with crisp white cloths. Around them sat men and women, the men in evening dress with white ties, the women in full-length figure hugging silk dresses of various hues, with their hair set in the style of the time.

Balloons were held in nets above the dance floor. Everywhere was the rattle and chink of cutlery and glass as the waiters and waitresses served the nobs who had paid over ten guineas a ticket to see out 1938 and bring in 1939. Above it all was the growing volume of voices, men booming and the ladies tones tinkling with laughter as the champagne flowed. The oysters or paté course had been cleared away and now the waiters were serving portions of freshly caught Scottish salmon delivered that morning on the overnight train from Glasgow.

'Where've you been — you're late?'

Raymond Dean's beady eyes bore into him from beneath his dark eyebrows.

Tom shrugged. 'Sorry.'

Dean jerked his head. 'Your stand is already set up for you. We are going to start in five minutes.'

Hurriedly putting his coat with the rest of the band's he got to his seat and opened the case, the latches thumping up as he slid the buttons to one side. Lying in the contoured green baize interior was the shiny brass saxophone, with the mouthpiece in a separate recess. From the little box with a lid in the corner he took out his neck cord, and put it over his head, before lifting the body of the instrument and passing the hook of his harness through the eye at the back. Steadying it with one hand he took out the mouthpiece, checked the reed and blew it a couple of times to get the feel as it vibrated against his tongue and lower lip. He tightened the screws and tried again. Satisfied he pushed it firmly on to the neck of the instrument and gave a tentative blow and fingered a few notes before turning his attention to the sheet music on the stand. He'd only just got it sorted when Dean held up his baton, glanced around them all, then brought it down in a gentle stroke. The soft sensuous music did not even cover the growing clamour from the partygoers.

They played for another hour before they stopped for the refreshments they'd been promised. There was a ripple of polite applause as it became evident they'd finished and a lone pianist took over.

In a room off the kitchen was a table laden with sandwiches, mince pies and trifles. The band was soon tucking in — it was one of the perks of the job.

They chatted for a while, mostly about football. One of them turned to one of the waitresses as she passed through to the kitchen.

'Elsie luv, have you got something' — he nodded at the table — 'you know?'

Elsie grinned. ' 'Course, I'll get you a carrier bag — any of you others want one? What about you, darlin'?'

Elsie was in her mid-thirties, with a wedding ring on her finger, but her big brown eyes gave Tom an appreciative flash.

He nodded. 'Yes — please.'

He knew the others had large families, but a few treats wouldn't go amiss at home as well. The food piled on the table would only end up being thrown out for pigswill.

She came back with the folded-up bags, lingering a little longer near the well-built boy with the dark hair and blue eyes. She looked at him, hand on hip, as she said to them all. 'There you are — take what you want.'

He could feel his face going brick red, which seemed to please her even more as she handed out the bags. 'What's your name, luv?'

'Tom,' he stammered, acutely aware of the others' grinning faces.

'Tom, that's nice. Well, Tom — you can have *anything* you like.'

Fortunately the implication was lost on the others who were already gathered at the table sweeping up sandwiches, little trifles and sausages on sticks.

He took the offered bag. 'Thanks — it's very kind of you.'

She continued grinning, eyes bright under her large lashes, one pencilled eyebrow raised.

'Think nothing of it.' She gave a wink and turned away.

When she'd gone Tom took an extra large gulp of his mild and bitter.

He hardly had time to get his food before Raymond Dean was moving among them. 'Come on, gentlemen, your whistles must be well and truly wet by now.'

Whether it was Elsie's attentions or what, but he needed a slash and asked directions.

After several turnings he found himself in an elegant corridor with small side-tables and sofas, and large paintings in ornate frames on the walls. The Gents was at the end, through a scrolled Regency doorway.

Several people were scattered around, coming and going, all in evening attire. He realized as he edged past one crowd that he was probably in the wrong place. He'd never been near to such elegantly dressed women before, some wearing tiaras, and he was acutely aware of the heady, musky scent emanating from the silk and pale powdered flesh.

Inside the marble-floored lavatory was a row of urinals with great marble side stones. On the opposite wall was a row of hand-basins with an attendant waiting with towels, brushes and cologne. A dish was half full of coins, mostly shillings and sixpences and the odd half crown. Voices echoed in the tiled room, raised with the effect of alcohol.

One young man, eyes squinting against the smoke from the cigar clamped between his teeth as he wiped his hands, said.

'Damn me, I thought this place was for gentleman, that's what the sign says.'

Tom kept his eyes fixed firmly on the wall ahead, but he knew it was him that was the object of the remark — bloody toffs.

Another young affected voice said, 'Don't know what the world's come to since the Strike of '26.'

The first voice drawled on, 'Never been the same since the war, old boy.'

Tom had been feeling uncomfortable up to that point. But then his blood started to boil.

His father had been gassed in that blood-bath, and far from returning to a country fit for heroes he'd been treated shabbily after 1918, not only by the government, but by the landlord who had promptly put up the rent on his return. He was invalided out with lungs that would never work properly again.

His mother had taken in washing — still did — to make ends meet. The scullery seemed never to be free of steam and he had stood on a bucket when he was small to turn the big handle of the mangle as she fed in the wet clothing. The family reckoned that's where he got his broad shoulders from, that and the digging on the allotment that was his Father's pride and joy, source of all the fresh vegetables that fed them all. Only his Father couldn't dig, so the young Tom had done all the hard spade work for years.

It was while he was tending to the patch of earth, surrounded by grass paths that was their allotment, that he became interested in the railway line that passed down the side of the field. He watched the engines labouring out of the branch line station, pistons thumping; smoke beating in a continuous rhythm from their chimneys into the sky, only for it to slow and drift in lazy clouds across the fields as the carriages clattered past. As it finally evaporated only a sooty smell remained.

He got to know a lot of the drivers and firemen and now he worked for the Great Western Railway — but in a way he could never have imagined as a youngster.

He buttoned up his flies and turned for the sinks. There were just two of them — both taller than he, but only one was as broad shouldered, and he barred Tom's way.

They looked at him as if he had just crawled out from under a stone, but if they expected him to slink away with his tail between his legs they were soon disabused.

Tom squared up to them saying nothing. Seconds passed. It was something in the eyes perhaps, a steely glint, that could only lead to one thing — violence — this made the second one flinch and say as nonchalantly as he could muster, 'Jeremy, the girls will be getting concerned as to where we are, impatient for their first dance.'

He began to move towards the door.

Jeremy did not move, eyes locked in a duel as old as mankind. The attendant seemed transfixed with fear. Suddenly the door opened and several more men crowded in, breaking the moment.

'Jeremy — you coming?'

The man took a last slow draw on his cigar, eyes never leaving Tom's, and tossed the butt casually into a sink.

He nodded — not in agreement, more at Tom. 'Nothing to stop me here.'

He walked to the door, paused — 'Another time then, old boy?'

Tom nodded.

The door closed behind him.

Tom looked down at his bunched fists, let them relax, went to the sink, paused, conscious of the time and said to the attendant with a grin, 'I know where I've been — not like some,' and left.

Everybody in the band was ready, the male, and a female singer in a sparkling sequinned dress, were gathered at one large microphone, Dean at another. He shot Tom a glance of pure acid. No sooner had he sat down and picked up the sax than Dean announced, 'Lords Ladies and Gentlemen, Raymond Dean and the Serenaders are proud to perform for your pleasure. This is their big band extravaganza, as heard on the wireless, as we play out the old, and play in the New Year.'

With that he turned to the band and shouted out loud, 'One-two-three,' and brought the baton down in an exaggerated sweep.

They all kicked in with *Whispering.*

Soon the floor was full with circulating couples, some showing more elaborate footwork than others.

They played for three quarters of an hour, the lines of saxophones and trumpets taking it in turns to leap up and feature their instruments.

After every three dances there was a small break announced by Dean with, 'Next dance, please.' They rearranged their music, adjusted instruments — got rid of over-wet reeds and fluid in the tubes.

It was while they were at rest and he was sitting ready to restart that Tom suddenly saw a girl who quite literally — for a second — took his breath away, talking with a bunch of other girls just below his position on the platform. She was wearing a pale lilac silk dress that followed the contours of her slim body, showing off her tiny waist and cheeky little bottom, hugging her legs until it flowed out a little just above her knees. At the front he could see the slight curve of her belly and the jutting points of her hips. The top part was almost like one of those glamorous ladies nightdresses he'd seen in the films worn by Jean Harlow, the tiny straps passing over finely boned shoulders. But it was her face that struck him the most, high cheekbones, red lips forming a generous mouth, finely pencilled eyebrows and shoulder length hair with a glittering slide on one side. She was smiling, her eyes warm and intelligent.

He must have been staring so hard that she somehow felt it, for at that moment she turned and caught him in the act. For a few seconds their eyes met, then, as he felt the blood surge into his face, she looked away again.

31

She didn't look back.

The man next to him had seen the whole thing and leaned towards him.

'Don't get any ideas, sonny, you can't afford her and in any case she's not for the likes of you.'

He tried not to watch her as Dean called out, 'Ladies and gentlemen, a Paul Jones', but he could see her move into the centre where all the girls held hands in a ring facing outwards, as the men did the same, but facing inwards. They struck up the tune, both circles moving in opposite direction until at a sweep of the baton, Dean abruptly cut the music. There was a roar from the crowd, as whoever they stopped opposite, they had to dance with. Dean then restarted with a slow foxtrot — only to repeat the whole processi another four times.

He only caught an occasional glimpse of her in the throng. She never once looked in his direction, but seemed to be laughing and enjoying herself immensely with all her different partners.

But she *did* glance towards him — several times — but always when he was occupied.

The great moment came and piper appeared and a man dressed as Old Father Time, complete with scythe, as over the speakers came the solemn, reassuring gongs of Big Ben as it struck midnight. On the last one, to a tremendous roar from the crowd and the sound of party bugles, the band played a fan-fair and a young lady, scantily clad in a flesh-coloured body costume with wings on her back, waved to everyone from the floodlit balcony — the emblem of the New Year.

The cheering continued as the piper played.

He suddenly saw her — head back, being kissed, and to his crushing agony she seemed to be very happy. Utter dejection came over him. The balloons rained down, some being burst, as they struck up 'Auld Lang Syne'.

They played on, but for Tom there was no joy, only a bleakness in his soul, as the champagne corks popped, some bouncing into the band. He deliberately concentrated on the sheet music even though he could play most of the tunes from memory. There was no way he wanted to catch sight of her again — it was too upsetting. So he never did see the continuing surreptitious looks she flashed in his direction, over the shoulder of whomever she was dancing with, as she passed the band time and time again.

The programme called for carriages at four, with hot soup served from three o'clock onwards, but time seemed to stand still, the hour of his release always a long way away.

So when it came, he was utterly exhausted and fed up. As they cleared away, packing up their instruments and stands Raymond Dean moved amongst them, dishing out buff coloured envelopes with their names on.

When he got to Tom he glowered.

'I'll need to speak to you before we hire you again — your timing and commitment leave a lot to be desired.'

Tom just took his money, in no mood to tell him what he could do with his part-time job — there were plenty of other bands looking for good saxophone players and he could turn his hand to the clarinet and piano if need be. He found his raincoat and trilby, but on a whim of cussedness, decided to walk out through the hotel rather than a staff side door. He knew he was doing it on the off chance of bumping into her again.

It was as he turned a corner that he saw her — back against the wall, being leaned over by the same fellow he'd seen her kissing. And to make matters worse, he now realized, it was the jerk from the lavatory.

She seemed to be trapped, frowning and moving her head from one side to the other to avoid his face as he leant closer to hers, murmuring something.

For a slight second he was uncertain as to what to do, but then remembered the kissing. It really was none of his business. He was about to pass, but as he did so he heard her say, 'Please, Jeremy, I don't want to.'

Hearing her voice for the first time and seeing her distress made him shift the saxophone case under his arm making it bulkier and more difficult to pass them in the older narrower corridor.

He paused. 'Excuse me.'

The man straightened up.

'Well, if it isn't our little Bolshevik friend.'

Tom felt his temper rising, but controlled it enough to say, 'Excuse me, I couldn't get by,' made to move on, but Jeremy 'Jerk' had other ideas, obviously angry at the interruption. He sidestepped to obstruct his progress. Tom could also smell the alcohol on his breath.

'Where do you think you are going?'

'I'm leaving.'

'Not this way you're not — use the tradesmen's entrance.'

Tom ignored him.

'Excuse me.' He tried again but again found his way blocked.

'Jeremy — let him go.'

Somehow that made him really angry. Who the hell was she speaking about, as though he was some person who was beneath them, being bullied. Christ, it was she who had needed the help. What was the matter with the woman?

Maybe it was the training he'd received in restraint lately, but he was amazed as he heard himself say, 'That's right, let me go, Jeremy.'

That's what he said, but Jeremy seemed to think he was being funny.

'Why, you sarcastic little bugger.'

The blow came out of nowhere and struck him right in the eye in an explosion of stars and flashing lights. He stumbled back, dropping his saxophone and tripping over a delicate rosewood table, sending a lamp flying and collapsing in a pile of splintering wood. There was a tearing sound as his mac caught in a screw that had fixed the electric flex to the wall. It tore his coat from the side pocket right up to the armpit.

'Jeremy — that's enough — please.'

Her irritating voice sounded more cut glass than ever.

Tom looked at his mac, could have wept. Instead he got to his feet.

'You're going to pay for that, Jeremy.'

The latter sneered.

'Sorry, old sport, I haven't got any loose change left.'

That did it. As Jeremy assumed the classic boxers stance that had won him a house blue he was taken by twelve stone of bone and muscle, head down, that drove him back into the opposite wall, forcing every bit of air from his lungs.

Before he could recover, two great pile drivers to the guts and chin ended all knowledge of his New Year celebrations for the next twenty minutes. Tom's fight however had only just started. The girl's scream brought a host of men running, and seeing one of their tailed brethren unconscious on the floor, they asked no questions — it was obviously an assault on one of their own.

Ten minutes later the side door into the alley opened and a bloodied and torn Tom was thrown amongst the kitchen dustbins, his saxophone case crashing on to a metal holder, spilling the contents.

He lay for a while, tasting the blood in his mouth and the foul wetness of the concrete. In the doorway the girl made towards him, as if to help, but was pulled back and the door slammed shut.

It was daylight by the time he reached home. He was putting the kettle on the hob on the range when his grandmother appeared, hair in a net, feet in brown indoor bootees, plaid dressing gown wrapped round her ample frame. Her hands flew to her face.

'Oh my godfathers I knew this would happen.'

He grunted through fat lips, trying to see her through his one eye, the other swollen and closed.

'It's all right, Gran — just roughed up a bit. It's worse than it looks — honest. A couple of them won't look so pretty for a while either.'

She fussed over him.

'I'll get a bowl and bathe your face.'

He nodded. 'Thanks.'

His body ached. He knew it must be covered in bruises, and it hurt to breathe, a cracked rib was a possibility. Luckily he didn't have to work until the day after next.

'And your coat, darling, it's ruined.'

He looked at his ripped and stained pride and joy. There were still six instalments to go. He never found his hat.

'Take it off.'

He did as he was told, but could not help wincing as he did so.

Apart from creases and one stain, his maroon jacket was untouched. Ironic that, because he wasn't going to be playing with The Serenaders again by the look of it. His trousers were all muddy, and there was blood on his collar and shirt front. His tie was missing.

'My God, Son — who did this to you?'

Breathing carefully he managed, 'I told you, about three or four of them, no reason, just drink,' he lied. Outside the Norwood Arms.'

His grandmother's eyes blazed.

'They ought to be birched within an inch of their lives. They're scum.'

He didn't argue with that.

And if he could have got his hands on that young woman — stunning or not — she wouldn't have been able to sit down for a week.

It was next day when he found that there was a big chunk missing from the cover of the saxophone case, the white wood like a scar against the surrounding cloth-covered surface. Worse, he'd found that one of the lever mechanisms of the instrument was jammed. It would cost to have it repaired. He shuffled despondently down the stairs.

What a disastrous night. What a bloody way to start the year. It would have been better to have stayed at home and listened to the wireless — Henry Hall and his

Orchestra had been on.

His mum and dad were sitting at the large table, waiting for him to appear in the doorway. Gran was out, but had obviously told them what had happened. His mother stood up and held out her hands.

'Oh, darling, what have they done to you?'

'It's OK, Mum.'

His dad started to say something, but then went into a paraxym of coughing that went on and on. Anxiously, his Mother switched her attention from him to her husband, placing a hand on his back, rubbing and gently tapping to help get up the phlegm. When it was over she told him to stay quiet. 'I'll tell him.'

Tom mumbled, 'Tell me what?'

His mother smiled, transforming her pale drawn face, taking away the lines of fatigue and disappointment and revealing a bit of the happy young woman of another, earlier time, long since past.

'Your father has decided to pay off your coat — don't argue now, it's decided.'

'But Mum —'

'No, that's it.'

He felt wretched, and relieved at the same time. He would be able to pay for the sax's repair straight away and start earning some extra cash again.

40

He shook his head, but said, 'I'll make sure you get it back — I promise. It's just a loan.'

His father managed to speak, his voice hoarse and whistling. 'You're a good lad, never given us any bother, and you've helped us keep afloat this year. So take it — we want to help you for a change.'

A lump came into his throat, and a burning resolve that he would make something happen to help them have a better life.

But what? There wasn't much scope for immediate wage improvement in his day job, even though it was dependable, respectable and had good prospects.

But he'd start looking around — think of something. Meanwhile tomorrow, aching or not, he had to drag himself off to work.

The ringing was like a fire alarm exploding in the blackness of the room. His hand came down smack on top of the twin bells on the alarm clock, cutting off the murderous noise. He leapt from the bed. As the eiderdown was thrown back it crackled with the icy film that had formed during the night from his breath.

He reached for his underpants, pulled free the tie in the white cord of his pyjama bottoms, stepping out of them and kicking them away.

His collarless shirt was soon on, hands fumbling at the buttons. In seconds he was into his trousers, pulling the braces over his shoulders, wincing with pain from his beating, before tucking the shirt tails around his bottom. He didn't do his flies up straight away, getting the chamber pot from under the bed.

Downstairs, his face in the pitted mirror, he applied a thick white lather as he soaped up with brush and stick. He used a Gillette safety razor, not like his father who still used a cut-throat, but even so he managed to cut himself under his chin.

When he was satisfied he cupped his hands with water and splashed his face several times to try to remove all the soap. He finished the job, dabbing with the towel.

Teeth cleaning came next. He rotated the brush head in the flat tin of Gibbs paste, the metal showing through in the middle.

His hair was the last thing to be tackled. He scooped up some Brylcreem and spread it on the palms of his hands before vigorously attacking the crown of his head, finishing with a comb, making a pencil sharp parting on his left side, and sweeping the gleaming black hair almost straight back.

He checked his appearance. Everything

seemed in order. He regarded his nails. Clean. He rinsed his fingers and palms. After a struggle he fixed his collar and stud, and then his tie. Between sips of tea he did up his waistcoat, careful to leave the bottom button undone.

With his loose change stowed, handkerchief in pocket, wrist-watch checked — his father had wanted him to have Grandad's Albert but it looked too old-fashioned for his taste — he was finally ready. And, as he wasn't coming back that night, he had packed his little brown overnight case.

There came a creaking of floorboards above his head. Tom finished his tea just as his mother came in, wrapped in her thick woollen dressing-gown.

'Darling, are you sure I can't get you a hot breakfast?'

He flung his arms around her, then regretted it as his ribs ached.

'Mun, I'm going to have breakfast on the company.' He gave her a big kiss. 'Go back to bed, the room will be warm in another half-hour. See you tomorrow — home about six.'

At the bottom of the garden he got his bike out of the shed, swung his leg over the saddle, and pushed off. It was all downhill, thank God.

Later, after a mountainous fry-up, he began to feel better.

CHAPTER TWO

The maid paused at the door, shifted the tray to one hand and tapped the door with the other. She opened it a fraction, then entered the darkened room, setting the tray down on the bedside cabinet.

'Good morning, miss. It's ten o'clock.'

She went to the heavily curtained windows and allowed some light in. All that could be seen of the occupant of the bed was dark hair spread on the pillow; when she turned she heard a groan.

'Thank you, Brenda.'

The maid knelt at the small, black grate, and used some rolled up newspaper balls and kindling to start a fire. It was soon crackling and smoking.

'There you are, miss. Fire's going. I'll draw your bath in ten minutes, all right?'

A muffled sound that she took to be 'yes' came from the bed. Just to be on the safe side, using her apron to protect the cord from her slightly dirty hands, she drew the curtains back a further few inches.

Another groan came from the bed.

Grinning, she said as she left, 'It's your aunty's wish that breakfast be finished by eleven o'clock today.'

When she'd gone the figure stirred, and slowly pulled herself up into a sitting position. With the bloom that only youth gives, Fay Rossiter was stunningly beautiful even in disarray. Her black hair was awry, one strap of her silk night-dress down over her shoulder and eyes full of sleep, but still large and clear and unpuffy.

She sipped her tea, watching the flames spread up the wood to the lumps of coal.

The fire was taking root but still no warmth came from it as she slid her feet into her slippers and drew on her silk dressing-gown with its Chinese pattern — a gift from an aunty in Singapore.

After she'd used the lavatory down the hall she made her way to the bathroom, with the big claw-footed bath in the centre of the black and white marbled floor, and a large aspidistra in its brass pot near the window. She tested the water, and turned on the hot tap for more as she slipped out of her dressing gown and night-dress.

With the water temperature just right she

stepped in and sank down. She began to soap her flannel, thinking about yesterday. She'd had another miserable night because Daddy had rung to wish them all a Happy New Year and Aunty Cynthia had told him about the fuss at the hotel.

She winced. When she'd gone downstairs to the elegant hall of the Regency house and had taken the receiver he'd given her an awful wigging. 'Why hadn't she stayed in Cirencester? Gone to one of the many house parties like previous years? It had been a dreadful idea to go to a public do, she had to think of her reputation.'

She'd rolled her eyes at the grandfather clock.

It was useless explaining that they had all wanted something livelier this year — it wasn't *just her* idea, everybody in her set had wanted it, including that idiot Jeremy who had started the whole thing.

Her aunty only knew because her friends had come home all excited about it, laughing and talking. Jeremy had had to be helped in, still groaning and holding his jaw; he'd lost a side tooth. As she dressed, choosing a dark tailored frock after turning side to side, trying it up against her petticoat, she remembered the incident the previous evening and the man who had been involved, the one she had caught staring at her in the ballroom.

Fay felt the same unsettling shiver run up her back as she did at the time. He had been so obvious in his approval of her that she had been quite taken aback, then frankly a little frightened.

Those intense blue eyes beneath black hair were quite something.

Then she remembered the appalling violence, ending when the other men had set on him like that. She had tried to go to his aid, but had been restrained and ushered away. She wanted, somehow, to meet him. Maybe she could find out more through the band — the hotel would have a contact number. As she packed, she thought about it further, resolving to make enquiries on Monday. She was always organizing events — that would be her excuse.

Later, she pulled the draw rope beside the fireplace to call for her aunty's chauffeur to collect her cases. They were all getting the same train back to Cirencester so he was using the old Rolls Royce for the luggage, in addition to the two taxis that had been ordered.

While she waited, she ran a hand over her tummy, it felt like lead and ached abominably. The Curse had started that morning, which explained why she had been so tense and edgy before.

When Jeremy had kept on pestering her for a silly kiss, she had said no, and dug her heels in, even though she had let him do it before. It was the fact that he was tipsy and completely different from normal, all bullying and overbearing.

Fay really couldn't understand men. At nineteen she had a general idea about life, but decidedly no experience of it. At Cheltenham Ladies College, where she had boarded, there had been smutty stories and, as a horsewoman, she obviously knew how animals came into the world, but *men* — they were exasperating at one moment, mysterious and exciting the next.

There was a knock on the door. When she opened it the chauffeur stood there.

'Come for the bags, miss.'

Fay stepped aside. 'There we are, thank you.'

She drew on her long cream coat with its high collar, pulling the belt tight. She already had her small hat on, the top adorned with feathers, a small net covering her face to below the eyes.

They were all waiting in the drawing-room so she sat on the arm of the sofa, one leg swinging.

Aunt Cynthia beamed. 'Haven't forgotten anything have you, my dear?'

'No, it's all packed.'

'Give my love to your mother.'

A maid came from the hall.

'The taxis are here, madam.'

With much taking of farewells and 'thank yous', they crowded out into the hall, Aunt Cynthia calling oit, 'See you all for Gold Cup week.'

The taxis were two large black Austins. Fay ducked into the leather and wood-smelling interior and sank back into the deep seat by the far window. To her irritation Jeremy's large frame thumped down alongside her, his weight making her fall against him.

'For heaven's sake, Jeremy.'

'Sorry.'

Fay straightened herself up as the taxi driver slammed the door. It was a short ride to St James's station but the streets were becoming increasingly crowded with cars. There were Humbers, Jaguars, Morrises and, of course, buses and bicycles. Quite a few horse and carts were moving among the other traffic, some with pneumatic tyres, as they clip-clopped their way along, occasionally leaving little piles of dung.

The new Regal cinema had been built on

the end of Imperial Terrace, behind the Neptune fountain, which looked very sad today with icicles hanging like bogies from the sea god's nostrils.

A 'coming this year' poster for a new film called, *Gone with the Wind* showed a determined looking Clark Gable lifting Vivien Leigh in his strong arms and bending her backwards about to kiss her. The boy who had caused all the trouble last night looked vaguely like him, at least around the eyes, but he didn't have a moustache. God, what was the matter with her? Was she going to have these ridiculous fantasies all the time? But as Vivien Leigh disappeared from view, Fay put her head back, ostensibly looking at the roof but, in reality, copying the star's position — with that boy bending over her in her imagination.

At Cheltenham's main railway station he entered the modest, stone-flagged concourse and proceeded down one red-bricked side and under the glass canopy with its filigree woodwork that ended at the platform edge.

The office he was making for was at the far end of the station. When he entered it, his nose was assailed by a smell of old coal gas from the now redundant wall lights mixed with years of smoke and steam. A single electric light under a dirty celluloid cover still glowed in the high roof. Facing him was the large, white-faced clock inscribed, 'GWR' that clonked out the time. The railway time that had brought unity to the whole country. He was a few minutes early.

He was proud of being a detective constable, albeit a temporary one, and knew that at his age having this position was due to a combination of events. Firstly, the Great War; then the influenza epidemic in the twenties; and more recently, the retirement of those who had survived those catastrophes.

Tom Roxham had only just finished checking himself and gone back to the outer room when Sergeant Whelan came in. His hair was parted neatly down the middle of his head, swept equally and exactly away from it just like draped music hall curtains. He had a moustache, waxed and turned up at the ends, steel-blue eyes above pock-marked cheeks and a nose that had seen more action than Tom's which, in comparison, seemed quite normal.

He towered over Tom, all six feet four inches of him; his uniform immaculate, with a chrome whistle chain neatly showing, black leather belt exactly horizontal, all befitting a man who had been an Irish Guardsman in the war. Some said he had been with Rudyard Kipling's son, who had been posted missing, presumed killed in action. They had never found his body.

'Well, so there ye are. What time do you call this?'

Tom glanced at his watch. 'Five minutes to eight o'clock, Sergeant.'

'What's that funny thing you're using, boy?'

'It's my wrist-watch, Sergeant.'

'Don't be cheeky with me, son!'

The booming voice made Tom flinch involuntarily, even though he knew something like that was coming. It was always the way with Sergeant Whelan. He seemed to expect that the world, his little world at any rate, always needed a shake up in the morning, even if there was nothing wrong.

'*That's* a timepiece.'

Tom found a large Victorian pocket watch with its lid open in front of his eyes. He said nothing. Whelan looked at it, then snapped it shut and put it away. The fact no more was said meant that Tom was correct, he had been asked to muster at eight, and eight it was.

Whelan went smoothly into routine.

'Present your appointments.'

Tom offered his warrant card and then displayed his short truncheon and his handcuffs.

Whelan nodded, took a stroll around his constable, checking. In fact he was pleased with the lad, but sniffed. 'Your shoes could be polished better — see to it next time. And what happened to your eye, boy?'

'Fell over, Sergeant.'

'Hmmm.' Whelan didn't believe him for a moment, but it had been New Year and boys would be boys. Whelan turned to the office desk, not seeing the sigh of relief as Tom returned his appointments to their rightful place. Although it was not wise to get on the sergeant's wrong side, he was well known to have a heart of gold where his men were concerned. He would back and protect them with a fierce loyalty that had no doubt been in his heart at birth in Carlow in Ireland, but had been seriously tempered in the flames and blood and mud of the Western Front.

'Now then, you are going to Cirencester Watermoor today, staying overnight?'

'Yes.'

'Tomorrow, I want you to get off at Leckhampton on the way back.'

Surprised, Tom asked, 'Why's that,

Sergeant?'

Whelan picked up a folder from his desk. 'The station master telephoned me. Said there had been an unpleasant incident — a passenger assaulted on the platform.'

Sergeant Whelan ran the back of his finger along his moustache, first one side, then the other.

'It's a nice day to have a leisurely journey through the Cotswolds — you're lucky.'

Tom didn't disagree.

Impatiently Whelan gestured towards the door. It was clear that the orders had been issued and the troops were dismissed.

The station was busier now, with cars and taxis swinging into the cobbled forecourt to unload hurrying passengers.

They flooded on to the platform, where the chocolate and cream-coloured coaches of a Great Western Railway Express stood waiting; wisps of steam rising from the couplings and vacuum brakes, and drifting over the platform. In the dining-car white-coated staff were moving down the aisle laying cutlery on the white tablecloths complete with little lamps next to the window.

Out of sight around the curve of the platform, smoke drifted almost straight up from an engine. But he made for a side platform and a local train.

The taxi turned in under the glass canopied entrance and rolled to a stop on the cobblestoned forecourt of the red-brick station. St James's was a small terminus, the starting place for the famous 'Cheltenham Flyer' that went via Gloucester and then non-stop to London, the fastest scheduled train service in the world as the GWR posters proudly announced.

Porters with their barrows appeared and gathered around the cars.

'Which train, sir?' asked one of them. Jeremy said, 'The one for Cirencester.'

They moved on to the small concourse with the buffers, where the lines ended.

A newly arrived engine was standing hissing gently, the air above its squat copper chimney shimmering with heat. The driver, a grizzled older man in a blue tunic and a black oily looking peaked cap was leaning out of the cab looking down, eyeing them all up as they went past.

She noticed with pleasure the engine's name — Codrington Hall. Daddy had been pleased when they had been invited to include their house name in the Railway Company's new class several years ago.

To reach their train they had to walk to a short side platform, where there were several coaches and two horse boxes as well as the guard's van.

They were walking along looking for the first-class compartments when, for a split second, she thought she was seeing things; her mind flew back to her reverie about the cinema poster.

It was Jeremy who made her realize she wasn't dreaming.

'Good God, look who's coming towards us. If it isn't the little bugger from last night.'

Tom Roxham was equally stunned. He'd been up to see the engine out of interest and was walking back to the guard's van.

CHAPTER THREE

He took a deep breath, guessing that, dressed as he was they would not realize he was on company business. But he was in no mood for niceties, not with this bloke. But frustratingly he couldn't stop himself shooting a glance at her. She was wearing a cream coat with a high collar that framed her head, her eyes and lips made even more alluring by the net veil of the hat. The madness this woman seemed to engender in him *had* to come to an end. With supremely professional effort he managed, 'Good afternoon, sir.' He looked at her and touched his cap acknowledged her with, 'miss' and kept walking.

'Well, I'll be damned.'

Jeremy watched his retreating back.

'Must have had enough.'

A still stunned Fay finally pulled a face. 'Don't be silly, Jeremy, he's not afraid of you.'

That seemed to annoy him. He gave her a funny look. 'What's the matter with you?'

Fay carried on walking, relieved to see Tom was all right — apart from the shiner. She hoped he was looking at her as she found the first-class carriage and started to board. She gave a quick glance in his direction, and was disappointed to see he was talking to the guard. Inside she walked down the side corridor, following the sound of laughter to find their compartment. She settled into a cut moquette seat with a generous arm rest and a white antimacassar, resolving to find out about him somehow.

It wasn't long before the guard's whistle gave three shrill blasts and with a jerk the coach started to move. The sound of the engine's laboured puffs increased then died back, to repeat again as they picked up to walking speed, and lurched over the points.

Jeremy drew the sliding door shut, closing off the racketing echo of the wheels in the long corridor.

'Soon be home, eh, I fancy a drink already.'

He brought out a hip flask and offered it to her.

Fay shook her head. 'Not for me,' but there were plenty of takers. When he'd had another swig he screwed the top back on.

'You taken a liking to Mellors?'

Fay frowned. 'Mellors?'

Jeremy lounged back with a dark grin on his face as the other men shared in his mirth.

'*Lady Chatterley's Lover* — he's the gardener.'

'Jeremy, what are you talking about?'

'Don't you know the book? I read it in Paris — unexpurgated.'

She began to lose patience and turned to look out of the window.

He said, 'It's all right by me, my darling. I'm a man of the world. Every girl should be allowed to have her day — as long as what's sauce for the goose is sauce for the. . . .' His voice tailed off.

Fay vaguely began to perceive what he was hinting at.

'Jeremy — that's disgusting.'

The others laughed and to her extreme annoyance she felt her cheeks reddening.

She stared fixedly ahead, looking at a sepia-tinted view of Weston-Super-Mare. All the other scenes on the carriage wall above the white antimacassars were views of seaside resorts served by the GWR — she could not have cared less.

Her mind stayed on the boy — somewhere

on the train behind her — and what Jeremy had hinted at.

They rocked gently along, the smoke and steam of the engine becoming trapped in the depths of a narrow cutting and clouding the window. Later it lifted away to roll across the open fields. After ten minutes there was the squeal of brakes as they lurched to a halt at Cheltenham South — Leckhampton Station. Somewhere a door slammed. Surreptitiously she looked out of the window as one or two people passed. To her relief he wasn't one of them. Rattled by her reaction she looked around. The others didn't seem to have noticed.

The train laboured on its way, through fields and hills and woods, the tiny stations a roll call of Cotswold beauty spots. Finally, Cirencester was the next stop. Although Fay couldn't be sure, he didn't appear to have got off the train.

They began to slow down on a gentle curve into the station. Everybody stood up chattering and making tentative dates.

Eventually a platform slid into view, backed by a wooden picket fence. A Camp Coffee sign went past, then the station building itself appeared. With a final squeal of brakes they ground to a halt. Doors opened and slammed shut as a porter shouted 'Cirencester — Cirencester Watermoor.'

A girl jumped up and down, waving. Beyond the station, Fay could see cars lined up on the forecourt and Wilson standing beside the Alvis.

The corridor was crowded with people getting off. Fay stepped down on to the platform, Jeremy, supporting her arm, said, 'I'll organize the luggage.'

They walked towards the back of the train where porters were already stacking cases and trunks on to the platform and then on to barrows as members of their party pointed them out.

Fay had just spotted her three when she became aware of *him,* standing in the doorway to the guard's van, right on top of her.

Even though she had been on the lookout for him, the unexpected closeness came as such a shock, that Fay found she couldn't breath properly. He looked into her eyes, for the first time close to. Something passed between them, something that had not been there before. They were like that for what seemed seconds before Jeremy snapped, 'You again.'

Tom dragged his eyes from her. 'I might say the same about you, *sir.*'

There was no escaping the sarcasm.

'Now just a minute you. Who do you think you're speaking to?'

Tom stepped down on to the platform and moved right up to him. Although Jeremy was a few inches taller he flinched slightly — remembering the last time. The face in his said, 'I suggest you get your luggage and be on your way, sir. The train needs to leave.'

Jeremy's lip curled.

'Since you are obviously a railway employee you can help us with our luggage.'

Slowly Tom turned back to her. Their eyes locked again. Fay still seemed to be having trouble with her breathing, her chest rising and falling with the effort, but she managed to say, 'That would be very helpful — I'm Fay Rossiter. You'll find my name and address on the labels.'

The voice was softer than he remembered, but still with a posh accent.

And suddenly he realized what she had done. From those red lips below the net, she had given *him* her name and where she lived — *intentionally.*

With a rush of adrenalin that overcame his shyness, he nodded.

'It will be a pleasure, Miss Rossiter, I'm Tom Roxham based at St James's.'

Jeremy frowned. 'Now look here . . .'

Excited and unnerved by what had just

happened, Fay moved towards the exit.

'Come along, Daddy's waiting.'

Tom found her bags, picked them up. There were enough of them. Struggling, he suddenly noticed the grinning guard. Tom jerked his head.

'Blow your whistle and get out of here.'

The man nodded. 'You'll be lucky, that's Lord Rossiter's daughter.'

Irritated, Tom humped the heavy suitcases away. The man was right, of course, what on earth was he doing — even thinking about?

But somehow it made no difference. He followed them through the wooden floored booking-hall with its fire glowing in the grate, and out on to the forecourt, eyes never leaving her slim figure.

They stopped by a two-tone car, with sweeping wheel arches; the bottom half burgundy, the top black. A tall distinguished man in a camel-hair coat and wide brimmed felt hat greeted her with open arms. 'Darling, welcome home.'

'Daddy.' She lifted up her face.

He put his arm around her and gave her a kiss on both cheeks, before extending his other hand to Jeremy.

'And you, my boy. Thank you for looking after her. So what's all this about some trouble?'

Jeremy turned and glowered at Tom, who had just struggled up.

'Well, sir,' but Lord Rossiter interrupted him. 'Ah, the bags, put them in the boot please, Wilson will show you.'

He turned back to Jeremy but a shocked Fay heard herself say in a voice that Tom could hear, 'Oh Daddy, could I go back to Cheltenham next week? I can stay at 15 Imperial Square — Aunty says so. It's just that a wonderful new collection of clothes is coming into Cavendish House that I don't want to miss.'

Her father frowned but his attention was distracted again as the boot lid slammed shut. He always kept change in his pocket and found a tanner which he slipped into the man's hand.

'Thank you for your help.'

Tom looked down at his palm, then up at Lord Rossiter who had already turned back to Fay.

'Cheltenham? Well, I'd hoped you would come with your mother and I to Lady Woods's soirée in London and then the next day we could see the latest Noel Coward play.'

Fay looked past her Father and met Tom's eyes. 'Oh Daddy, that would have been lovely — but you and Mummy will have a much better time just the two of you. And in any case, I have been invited to a dinner party Lucy Bates is giving — you remember, she was in my class at school? I said I would be around after the shopping.'

Her Father grinned. 'Ah, that's the real reason is it? You going too, Jeremy?'

Jeremy opened his mouth to say 'no', but Tom tapped Fay's father on the shoulder.

'Excuse me, sir. I am not a porter. Very kind of you, of course.' With that he gave the sixpence back to a bewildered Lord Rossiter, looked meaningfully at Fay and gave a slight nod, then turned on his heel. The older man watched Tom's retreating back.

'I'll be damned — who is he?'

Jeremy gave her a scowl, but held his tongue when he saw the warning flash in her eyes, and said dismissively, 'Just somebody who was on the train, sir. He was travelling in the guard's van. A bit rough — he's got a black eye somebody gave him — you can understand why, can't you?'

Lord Rossiter paused as the chauffeur held the rear door open. 'I certainly can. What a strange fellow. In you go, darling. Can we give you a lift, Jeremy?'

Fay sat in and slid across the leather seat,

joined by her Father as Jeremy leaned in.

'Thank you, sir, but I'll walk.'

He looked across at Fay. 'I'll speak to you soon, Fay. We have things to discuss.'

She raised one eyebrow. 'Have we, Jeremy?'

He nodded. 'We have.'

He turned his attention to Lord Rossiter as he closed the door. 'Goodbye, sir.'

The car moved off.

Her father looked at her, smiling, and asked, 'My dear, is he going to pop the question?'

Fay pulled her chin in and said simply, 'Good heavens, I certainly hope not.'

Disappointed, Lord Rossiter frowned.

'He's very eligible, my dear, a nice enough chap, you could do a lot worse. Oh, I know he's not titled, but the family is solid county stock and they are very comfortably off.'

She looked away, her mind utterly in turmoil about quite another man.

Fay was glad she was sitting down, because her legs felt weak at what she had just done — giving her name and telling him where he might find her next weekend. Something about Tom Roxham, she savoured the name, deeply attracted her. There was a strength in his blue eyes — an intensity that seemed to go right into her.

He was broad shouldered and rugged and she knew he was capable of violence — at least when provoked. If he wanted to kiss her when they met she wouldn't be able to stop him — he would be far too strong for her. So she wouldn't resist, would she?

She shivered, and despite the warmth of the car pulled her coat further round her as if to protect herself against her own silly fantasies. They were totally alien to her and filled her with guilt.

She came out of her reverie to find her father looking at her.

'Sorry, Father, what did you say?'

He sighed.

'I see you were dreaming again. I asked you to give some thought to the future. Your music is important, but a marriage would give you a secure base, and a family is the best thing in the world for a woman. It's her anchor in a cruel world.'

'Very well, Father.'

It was difficult to imagine anything more opposite to what she had been thinking about. Her body was afire with something far more elemental than thoughts of a good marriage.

The car turned past the Lodge and drove along the tree lined drive. Codrington Hall stood in the weak winter sunshine; the light reflecting from the leaded Tudor windows set in the warm limestone walls.

Here she felt secure. Inside, her mother would almost certainly be in the sewing-room doing her latest piece of needlework, and Fay could soon be seated at the grand piano in the music-room. In a way it would be the perfect antidote to the fires raging in her body.

But what about the weekend?

What did she think would happen?

Oh God, the delicious weakness came over her again.

Tom watched the car disappear out of the yard, his notebook in his hand, ink still wet from what he had hastily written. Fay Rossiter, 15 Imperial Square, plus Codrington Hall, Bagendon, Cirencester.

'Fay' — he savoured the name.

What the hell did he think he was playing at? She was upper class. There was no way she was going to take him seriously.

But she had given him her name, there was no doubt about that and the address. What did she want of him? What was it all about? He was normally painfully shy, utterly lacking in experience of girls, except for childish kisses and fumbles behind the bike sheds at school when he was a kid.

Had he gone mad? Taken leave of his senses? He felt immensely excited — and at a complete loss. She was incredibly beautiful and with the hat that she had been wearing — eyes and long lashes behind the net and her red lips unguarded beneath its edge, she had started a raging storm that had made a tidal wave of his hormones.

It was only as he made for the station master's office to begin what he was there for that he realized he'd left his brown weekend case on the train. By then it was just a plume of steam and smoke as it made its way to South Cerney. He ran to the office, tapped on the door and went straight in. He found himself confronting the startled station master.

'I'm sorry to burst in on you — Detective Constable Roxham.' He waved his warrant card under the man's nose. 'I think you are expecting me?'

The elderly man had just taken off his silk top hat — a tradition he continued from the earlier part of the century when the station master was a person of some note and had to receive and send off nobility and other important people. He was due for retirement soon — thank God — standards were slipping and he didn't take lightly to young men bursting in. He flicked the tails of his coat and sat down. 'We wondered where you were. Then the head porter said you were carrying bags for Lord Rossiter.'

'That's right.'

The station master took out his hunter and flicked open the lid, checking it against the clock on the wall.

'Since when did the GWR Police Service carry out porter's duties and deny them their tips?'

Tom winced. 'It was something special, sir — a personal favour to Miss Rossiter.'

'Know her do you?'

There could be no doubting the sarcasm in his voice.

He shifted his feet.

'No, sir — not very well. Anyway, I have forgotten my overnight case and wondered if we could phone South Cerney? It's in the Guard's van.'

The hunter was snapped shut.

'That will do you no good.'

Crestfallen, Tom managed, 'No?'

The station master relented, opened a drawer and took out a bottle of brandy — given to him that Christmas by Lord Rossiter, and two tumblers.

'Like a drop?'

Tom didn't drink much and never on duty, but after everything that had just happened, well his nerves cried out for help. He nodded. 'Under the circumstances, thank you. Why won't it help?'

The man nodded to a corner of the room. When Tom looked round there was the brown cracked overnight case standing in a corner.

'The guard put it off. Here —'

A small glass much smaller than the generous portion the station master had poured for himself, was pushed across the highly polished surface of the desk.

'Now, let's get down to business. About this break in. . . .'

Fay met her mother exactly where she thought she would be, busy with her needle-point. Immediately Lady Rossiter dropped what she was doing and came forward, arms outstretched. 'Darling, you're home.'

The two women embraced, Fay taller than her Mother who was rather petite, her dark hair with threads of silver, still cut short in the earlier style of the twenties flappers. Because of Lady Rossiter's youthful looks they could have been sisters.

'Did you have a wonderful time, Fay. Are you glad you did what you did?'

Arm in arm they made for the drawing-room, Lady Rossiter saying over her shoulder to a maid. 'Tea now, please Edna and we'll take luncheon in the orangery.'

'Yes, Mummy, it was great fun — so unstuffy.'

'Good.' Her mother had a twinkle in her eye. 'Did you dance much?'

She squeezed her mother's arm.

'I did, Mother.'

'What were the other people like, were they decent?'

'Yes, of course. It's Daddy, isn't it? He really is an old fogey. This is 1939, nearly the forties. Times are changing, Mother.'

Lady Rossiter pulled a face.

'Your father is just naturally cautious dear, after all, he went through a lot during the war and he says it was only the thought of home and family that kept him going. He doesn't like change. Anyway — what was the trouble Aunty told him about?'

Fay was as dismissive as she could manage.

'Oh, it was just Jeremy being Jeremy.'

Still arm in arm, her mother studied her.

'There's something you're not telling me, Fay?'

She felt her cheeks going red.

'No, honestly, Mother. By the way the orchestra was terrific, they played all the latest numbers. You should have heard them.'

Her mother had been a great one for dances in her youth.

'Sounds marvellous.'

But she was under no illusion. Her daughter had just changed the subject. She could wait — Fay would tell her what it was all about in her own time.

But she would put money on it — there was a boy at the bottom of all this.

The 'boy' she was speculating on was at that moment writing up his report in a meticulous hand — nothing less would pass muster with Sergeant Whelan who would send it on to Swindon.

His pen scratched as he finally got to the end and signed his name with a flourish.

His digs for the night were just across the road in rooms above the Railway Inn. He took his leave and crossed the lines on the wooden sleepers — there was no footbridge. The pub doors were locked, but his repeated knocking finally brought the sound of bolts being drawn.

A large woman in a Dutch apron filled half of the double door that was opened.

'Yes, what do you want?'

He explained and she relented, stepping aside.

'Right. We didn't expect you until later. Come in.'

He followed her into a stale beer-smelling public bar, past pumps covered with a stained tea-towel, the sawdust on the floor scuffed into the sides. She opened a green painted door. A steep flight of wooden stairs lead directly up to a lino-covered corridor.

At the top, breathing heavily she nodded to the end door.

'That's the lavatory — this is your room.'

She opened the door in front of her. There was a single bed with a green candlewick bedspread that had cigarette burns on it, the headboard a dark brown scrolled affair. There was a wardrobe of the same design and colour, and a free standing wooden towel rail beside a small white sink with a mirror over it. He set his case on the bed.

'Can I get something to eat later?'

She was already on the way down the stairs, pausing to say, 'When we're open I'll do some bread and cheese all right? If you want anything more there's a café near the town centre that's open till eight o'clock and a fish and chip shop round the corner.'

When she had gone he crossed to the sash window, and tried to open it a crack. Cold or not he needed to get fresh air into the damp-smelling room, but it wouldn't budge. It had been crudely painted. He leaned on it. Suddenly it crashed down, the rotten rope spilling out, snapped. Try as he might the window wouldn't stay up. Cold air flooded into the room. Desperate, he looked around for something to prop it up. There was nothing, until his eyes fell on to his weekend case. Emptied, it shut the window to within an inch of the top.

Satisfied, he wondered what to do next. In the end he removed his shoes and trousers, got into bed and pulled the clothes up over his head to keep warm and thought of her.

Tom Roxham had never felt like this before.

Was he going mad?

CHAPTER FOUR

The cause of his madness was, by this time, sitting by the fire in her room, dressed in the floral silk dressing-gown, one graceful hand playing with a curl on her forehead, neglected book at her side, as she stared into the glowing embers.

What was she doing? What did she think would happen when she went on her own to Cheltenham?

Paradoxically she was both excited and terrified at what had come over her. She knew nothing about the boy — and yet was hoping to meet him without any friends or anybody with her at all — something she had never done before. Fay gave a little shudder at the thought of her reckless behaviour, and for a fleeting moment thought about backing out, then just *knew* that that was *not* going to happen. Her Mother had readily agreed to the trip so Father would be all right — as long of course there was not a whiff of the real reason. Jeremy was a worry. She'd never told so many white lies to her parents before.

What on earth had got into her?

Timmy, her cat, leapt up on to her lap. Fay lifted the orange and white bundle of fur to her face and gave it a kiss. Timmy settled down, purring deeply as his mistress gently stroked his side. She'd wondered about her future from time to time, but today, listening to her father going on about Jeremy and marriage and feeling as unsettled as she did, she realized that things were coming to a head. She was an accomplished pianist and if the plaudits she received from the many distinguished house guests were anything to go by, she had a future in music.

Several singers, particularly of German Lieder had intimated their interest in her playing. She seemed to have that intuitive feel that made a good accompanist.

First thing in the morning she would phone Sir Nigel Travers the conductor, and set things in motion. Daddy might have some objections, of course, something along the lines of wait till after marriage, but Mummy would be supportive, after all, she had been quite an accomplished singer in her time.

She stroked Timmy for another few minutes before placing him gently on to the carpet, where, back arched, tail swishing in annoyance, he stalked slowly away in a huff.

Fay stood up, and pressed the bell for her maid, Julie. Dinner was in half an hour, and although it was only family, her Father always insisted they dress appropriately. She undid her dressing-gown and let it fall to the floor. In the full-length mirror she looked at her reflection, regarding it in a way that she had never done before. She was wearing the latest brassiere and matching french knickers, in midnight blue and trimmed with little pink bows, her silk stockings held up by her garter belt. Even though she was alone she blushed all over at the thought of him, *Tom,* ever seeing her like this. Heart thumping in her chest she began to daydream, pretending it was her wedding night — until a worrying thought struck her. In the sudden excitement of the moment she had done her best, but did he feel the same way?

Then she recalled the look he had given her. That was why she was standing like an idiot in her underwear, thinking things that were the stuff of schoolgirls' dreams.

When there was a knock at the door and Julie entered she physically jumped.

'Sorry miss. Did I startle you?'

Fay turned away so that the girl couldn't see her embarrassment.

'No, not at all, Julia, I think I'll wear the green dress tonight.'

As the girl crossed to the large wardrobe, Fay took a last, quick glance at herself in the mirror. Was the weekend going to be a terrible anti-climax, or a huge embarrassment or, God forbid — *worse?*

Her father wasn't in the dining-room when she entered, just her mother sitting on the side at the far end of the long mahogany table with its silver candelabra. She sat down opposite her, thanking the butler, Wilson, who moved her chair gently into place. She glanced at the empty chair at the head of the table.

'Where's Father?'

Her mother nodded at Wilson who went off to get the soup tureen.

'He's still on the telephone dear, calling his secretary. Mr Hitler has said or done something; it was on the wireless, and he's been agitated ever since.'

Nervously Fay took a sip of water, suddenly conscious that her mother was going to say something, probably about the weekend, and she said, 'I'd like to go hunting tomorrow — is that all right?'

Lady Rossiter raised an eyebrow. 'Of course, you don't usually ask, so why — ?'

Just then her father came in, looking thoughtful, hands in dinner jacket pockets, thumbs sticking forward. 'I'm sorry, my dear.'

Frowning, he sat down. He reached out his hand and covered his wife's. 'Do you mind if we go off on Thursday — I need to attend a meeting, a group of us want to have a debate when the House resumes sitting.'

'Of course not, George. Fay, will you be all right?' Her mother looked at her with what Fay thought was suspicion. Feeling guilty she swallowed, took a deep breath.

'Yes, of course.'

Lord Rossiter clipped the top of his napkin to his white shirt front and murmured 'Good, good.'

Fervently, for the only time in her life, Fay silently thanked the German Chancellor.

Tom had come down the stairs into a room thick with smoke from the wooden and clay pipes of several men gathered around the bar and fire. Their sudden roar of laughter and voices with broad Gloucestershire accents coming up through the floorboards had woken him up. The woman who had shown him in earlier was pulling a pint, the handle clonking back on each release. She seemed to be in no better mood than before. All the men fell silent and looked at him. He gave a weak smile and a nod, 'Good evening.'

There were a couple of grunts.

The landlady, work on the tankard finished as froth flowed down the sides, called out 'You want that bread and cheese now?'

He shook his head. 'I'm going out to eat.' She wiped her hands on the same tea towel he had noted that afternoon.

'Suit yourself. Don't forget we lock up at eleven on the dot.'

He nodded and edged past them and out into the fresh night air. It was only a short walk to the market square, dominated by the church. A couple of cars were parked outside a hotel. Down a side street he found a café but somehow he didn't fancy sitting there for the next hour or so on his own. It took a while, but eventually his nose led him to the fish and chip shop. There was a little queue, and a couple of youths, sitting astride their bikes as they ate their penny worth of scraps.

He had rock salmon and chips, with plenty of vinegar and salt, wrapped in one layer of grease paper and then two sheets of newspaper.

Cold or not, he found a seat and picked a hole through the newsprint and then into the hot succulent depths, pulling out a chip first, then breaking off lumps of battered fish fried in lard.

Tom knew of no finer food in the kingdom.

He started to think what he was going to do. Would he just hang around outside the house in Imperial Square? That seemed stupid. Inadequate. The answer when it came, seemed simple. He would write a letter to her at Codrington Hall. It would give her his address, and suggest a time and meeting place for the Saturday. He only hoped she wouldn't be offended, or that in some way she would get into trouble. But it was the only thing he could think of to do.

The morning was cloudy, threatening rain. He stood on the platform waiting for the train to Cheltenham. In one way it felt sad, leaving her, but it was also a day nearer to the weekend. Tom strolled past milk churns on trolleys, to the end of the platform where it sloped down to track level. A water tower with a canvas pipe dripped steadily on to the ballast.

He checked his watch, looked down the track to the gasworks beyond the station.

Several people were gathering, some sitting on the benches, but mostly standing or in the waiting-room. Beside him were a group of small boys — trainspotters, with their books, sitting on a parked handcart by the wooden fence, squabbling over something.

For a brief moment he wondered if she would appear on the platform, but knew it was wishful thinking — she knew nothing of his movements, but still. . . .

The rails started to give out a faint hum, his eyes drawn to where the track curved away out of sight. A signal clonked down. The humming increased. The boys stopped fighting and gathered near him.

And then, in that exciting moment that he saw the children still experienced, around the bend in the distance came a black smudge. Spurts of white steam flickered at its wheels, and smoke flowed away from its chimney.

It grew in size until he could see that it was an old MSWJR engine now in GWR colours.

When it finally got to the other end of the platform it had slowed right down, and by the time it reached him it was moving at a walking pace. With a surge of steam it ground to a halt.

He nodded to the driver and walked away down the length of the train until he found an empty third class compartment. Drawing down the solid metal handle and stepping up into the interior he slammed the door behind him, released the leather strap from its stud and dropped the window. Tom put his head out and surveyed the platform, just hoping. There was only one person standing there, talking to someone on the train. The porters slammed doors, the guard raised his green flag, holding it out so that it could clearly be seen by the driver. He blew his whistle. Disappointed, Tom drew his head in and hauled up the window.

Imperceptibly they started to move, slowly gathering pace, easing out through the town into the countryside.

He rested his brown case on his knees and got out his notebook. It was time to compose the letter to her. He would copy it out at home on to notepaper they kept in the top drawer of the sideboard, beneath the wooden biscuit barrel with its metal lid.

But as he found a blank page, nothing seemed to come. Could he say 'Dear Fay'? Really, he didn't know her at all, it seemed presumptuous — rude even. No, it had to be 'Dear Miss Rossiter.' The other was just wishful thinking.

So using his fountain-pen he started with his address. After several attempts he came up with:

Dear Miss Rossiter,
I hope you don't think me rude, but I wonder if we could meet at the Cadena Café on the Promenade on Saturday, at, say, eleven o'clock for coffee?
I will understand completely if you are otherwise engaged, and will not bother you again.

Yours sincerely,
Tom Roxham.

He read it over and over again, nearly forgetting to get out at Leckhampton Station. Sergeant Whelan would have had his guts for garters. As it was he wouldn't get home until quite late, and would probably miss the last post. So, feeling frustrated, and with only one thing on his mind, he struggled to concentrate on his work.

Fay had had a good day. She was letting Jenny, her dapple grey mare walk home at her own pace. They were both splattered with mud and it was all over her white breeches and black jacket. The chase had been exhilarating and, whether it was the

86

emotional state she was in, or the post period euphoria, but she had galloped harder and jumped higher than she had ever done before.

Now she was thinking once again about the weekend and her meeting with Tom Roxham.

Would he be a gentleman with her? Fay shuddered at the risk. Jenny picking up the movement through Fay's knees, shook her head and snorted. She tried to take her mind off the possibility by wondering what they might do especially if the meeting continued to be awkward, or they were bored.

The *Gloucestershire Echo* would be delivered that evening, it might offer some ideas.

Another rider, in hunting pink, suddenly appeared alongside her. She knew who it was even before he spoke.

'Fay, you've had a good day?'

It was Jeremy. She stiffened.

'Yes, have you?'

'I should say so.'

They walked on, only the sound of the horses and their jingling harness breaking the silence for a minute, before he said: 'Fay, this fellow — you do know what you're doing?'

She bristled, 'Of course.'

Jeremy snorted. 'The man's a thug and way beneath you. I'm sorry for what I said before — I was cross and jealous, but now I'm worried about you. I really think I should tell your faither — for your sake.'

'Jeremy' — her voice was like ice — 'if you do that I will never speak to you again — ever. Is that perfectly clear?'

He said nothing, and she didn't say anything else. When they reached the end of a lane where they would part company they reined to a halt.

Fay looked across at him, broke the silence.

'Well?'

He didn't know it, but her heart was in her mouth.

Jeremy found he couldn't say, 'all right', but he couldn't say, 'no', either.

Scowling, he touched the peak of his hat with his whip and swung away, leaving her to sag in the saddle. God, what was he going to do?

But then she calculated that he wouldn't be able to see her father now, at least until after the weekend, and by then it would be too late.

Whatever that meant.

She handed Jenny over to the groom, gave

88

her a scratch and a kiss and made for a hot bath.

Julie helped her off with her boots then bustled away to run the hot water. Fay had taken off her hat, now she reached up and released her hair from the strong net that had contained it through thick and thin all day.

When the maid came back she had already stripped and put on her dressing-gown.

'Julie, can you see if the *Echo* has come? I'll have it in the bathroom if it has.'

She was immersed in soapy water when a knock came on the door and Julie entered.

'It's here, miss — and a letter for you marked "personal". It came in the second post.'

She dried her trembling hands then took the envelope. It was postmarked Cheltenham. Tummy churning, she didn't recognize the neat careful writing.

'Anything else, miss?'

Hardly able to contain herself she just managed to nod at the wall heater. Whether it was fear or excitement she didn't know but her shoulders seemed suddenly cold.

'Turn on the heater, please.'

As soon as Julie had gone she tore open the envelope and read the letter. It took several attempts before she finally managed to calm down enough to realize that he would be at the Cadena in Cheltenham at eleven o'clock, and that seemed very polite and proper. She gave a sigh of relief, read it once more, noting his address, and the way he signed *Tom Roxham* with a bit of a flourish. She put it on to the cork-topped table beside the bath.

She just lay there for a long time, almost dazed by the speed of the events, then remembered the *Echo.*

It would be a good idea to have some suggestions of what they might do — *if* she stayed.

She took the paper up and turned the pages until she came to the entertainments and features section.

It hit her almost immediately. The advertisement carried a photograph and an article on the event. If they went to it, it would give them all afternoon to find out about each other, and she could duck out of the evening if it was a disaster. That made her feel better.

And it sounded fun.

She let the paper drop the floor and submerged herself to her chin.

And if he was *'all right',* what then?

Despite the heat of the bath water, she

shivered.

It was becoming a familiar sensation.

CHAPTER FIVE

It was lucky that, in their household, Friday night was bath night. Tom had considered going to the municipal baths, where, for sixpence, you could have a sumptuously big tub of hot water and a small bar of coal-tar soap. But then his mother and father would have got suspicious if he hadn't joined the family in their weekly ritual.

The long galvanized bath that hung on the outside wall of the scullery had been brought in and placed before the range in the living-room. Hot water from the boiler, which was used in the week for the laundry, was poured in by the bucketful. Mum went first, then Gran, followed by Dad. Tom brought up the rear, sometimes lucky enough to have some of the used water baled out and the odd fresh one or two bucketfuls added. Now, in his winceyette pyjamas and warm in bed, his mother came to kiss him goodnight. He rolled on to his side and again thought about tomorrow. Would it be a fine, sunny day? His gran said 'yes'. There had been a red sky that night and the bladder-wrack seaweed from Barry Island hanging out by the WC was flat — he thought. He could never remember whether that was good or not.

Tom knew what he was going to wear, his Harris Tweed jacket with grey flannel trousers and his Oxford brogues. Of course, as soon as they all saw him dressed up like that they would know something was up.

Restless, he turned over, punched the pillow, and tried to get to sleep.

But it was impossible. His heart was racing, he could feel his pulse in his ears. All of a sudden he had just the faintest of faint ideas what it must have been like for his father, in the trenches waiting to go over the top.

Fay, he would never have guessed in a million years, had also gone to bed nervously at her aunty's, as restless as he was about what the morning would bring. His letter in her handbag, read and reread. She had arrived by taxi that afternoon, to be received by a delighted Aunt Cynthia, who, having lived alone since 1917, hadn't had so much company for years.

After supper they had sat in her Regency drawing-room playing gin rummy and drinking pink gins. Aunty had insisted Fay join her in one 'pinkie' and she had ended up having three. Normally Fay only drank sherry as an aperitif and wine during dinner, apart from the odd stirrup cup. But tonight? She knew why, of course. Her nerves had been playing up all day. Since the morning, when she had packed her cases with Julie; then on the train as she headed, alone, to what? She had read his letter for the hundredth time.

And now to cap it all, she had a headache.

Fay felt very lonely, very vulnerable, very foolish and *very* excited.

Gran was right, it was a nice day. Tom walked to town rather than going by bus. He wanted to get away from all the snide remarks his father was making as soon as he had seen him spruced up.

He was tense and worried. Had she received his letter? And if she had was she coming? There could be many reasons for her not showing up; from a simple one that she just couldn't make it, through to the one that hurt him the most to think about — she was showing it to her friends and laughing at him. Perhaps she had only ever been teasing him.

He knew he was early, but that was only proper. It was her right to expect him to be there first.

He reached the Cadena. As he approached he looked out for her among all the bobbing heads and faces of the walkers, but she was not there. As he entered the café his nostrils were assailed by the smell of the freshly ground and roasted coffee from the machine in the window.

It was busy, but there were still a few tables free. He made it obvious that he would not be alone, by ostentatiously checking his watch and looking around.

A waitress came over to him. Tom had intended to leave and wait outside, but it dawned on him that that was a pretty silly thing to do. She would simply enter to find him.

'A table, sir?'

'Yes, please — for two.'

He followed her and sat down as she placed a menu card on the table.

'Coffee?'

'I'm expecting a lady. Can you come back in a few minutes?'

She smiled knowingly. 'Of course.'

As she bustled away he took a long look around the room. It was noisy, filled with chattering women in hats and fox furs and men smoking cigars; their Homburg hats hanging from the stands dotted among the palm trees. Cups rattled on saucers and the small string trio were playing a medley of popular songs at that moment from *The Merry Widow.*

Suddenly there was a crash as a tray was dropped, cups and saucers breaking and bouncing on the parquet floor.

For a brief moment there was a hush while only the orchestra continued, then, with a rush of renewed talking and laughter, the moment passed.

The poor red-faced girl, his waitress, was helped by the head waiter and another girl with a dustpan and brush. Tom felt for her and was pleased to see that the head man was treating her decently.

The orchestra finished its piece.

'Hello.'

Astounded, he looked up at her. She seemed to have just materialized out of thin air. He took in the slim figure in a herringbone coat, tightly belted at the waist. Her hair falling straight down to curl inwards near the corner of her red lips. She wore a small black beret set at a jaunty angle, a red bobble matching her lipstick. Her eyes were even warmer and more intelligent than he remembered.

Hardly daring to trust his voice, he got slowly to his feet, and held out his hand.

She offered her gloved hand, which he took. 'Thank you for your letter.'

For a moment they remained like that — the first time he had touched her. He didn't want to let go.

She had been disappointed — worried even when he wasn't waiting outside. Tense, Fay had taken a deep breath, and pushed open the door. It didn't help her nerves when, as she had stepped into the large room there was a terrific crash of breaking crockery.

Everybody had looked in that direction. She saw him instantly over by the wall. He was as handsome and exciting as she remembered — better even. Her blood raced as she had made her way unnoticed towards him.

Finally he let go of her hand, stepped to her chair and held the back. She ran her hands under her coat as she sat and he eased the chair into the table, feeling that everybody in the room must be looking at her.

Fay started to take off her gloves, as he sat down opposite. Hesitatingly, he said, 'I didn't know if you would come.'

She finished with her gloves and raised one eyebrow.

'Why not?'

He pulled a face, 'well. . . .'

Fay Rossiter said matter-of-factly, completely hiding her inner turmoil, 'Here I am.'

He nodded his head in agreement.

'It's wonderful.'

There was a pause, broken as the waitress came over.

'Can I take your order, please?'

Tom Roxham licked his dry lips.

'Coffee?'

'Yes, please.'

The waitress scribbled in her order book, said without looking up.

'Anything else, sir?'

He glanced enquiringly at Fay. Her thick hair swished as she shook her head.

'No, thank you, I've just had breakfast.'

He also shook his head at the woman who tore the top copy of the order and left it on the table as she bustled away.

There was another awkward pause. She dropped her eyes to her lap.

'I hope you didn't think it terribly forward, what I did?'

He blurted it out without thinking. 'I was going mad. I wanted to meet you — but under the circumstances. . . .'

She looked up worriedly.

'What do you mean?'

Embarrassed, he just had to say it, it had weighed so heavily on his mind.

'Well, to put it bluntly you wouldn't normally meet somebody from my background, would you?' A fire suddenly stirred in his eyes. 'But I'm proud of my family — they are the best.'

Fay glanced away, across at the orchestra who had just started up again. She bit her lip.

'I'm sure they are, and you're right. This is unusual. It's the first time I've ever done anything like this. I don't know what came over me.'

'What do you mean?'

She smiled shyly.

'I've never met anybody for coffee — or anything. I only go out with a crowd normally. You see — this is very special for me — it's my first — what do they call it in the American films?'

Somebody seemed to be standing on his chest — 'Date?'

The tip of a pink tongue moistened the red lips.

'Yes' — but an anxious frown passed over her face.

'That's what it is, isn't it?'

Unfortunately the girl was back with the coffee, setting the pot down, placing the cups and jug of cream, as they sat like wooden dummies looking at each other.

When the waitress got back to her station she said to her colleague, 'Those two are so love-struck over there — they can't talk.'

But Tom Roxham just had.

'Yes.'

They both started to grin wider and wider. Fay took in the boyish features, the warm generous eyes and felt comfortable, safe and, paradoxically, somehow freer.

He saw only eyes that sparkled, that made him feel terrific. Nothing in his existence had made him feel so good about himself. It was as though he was seeing things in the new Technicolor.

They started to giggle, with sheer relief and an excitement of something new in their already changed lives.

'So,' she hesitated, '*Tom* — have you any idea what we are going to do?'

He was bowled over hearing his name coming from those lips.

'We could watch the rugby — Cheltenham are playing at home today, and perhaps the cinema tonight?'

'That's fine. I'm quite prepared to do that,

but I did find something rather exciting, going on today and tomorrow.'

'Yes?'

She picked up her handbag and started to root in it, at last finding the page she had torn out of the *Gloucester Echo.*

'Here we are.'

She handed it over, saying, 'Is Staverton very far?'

He read the article with growing trepidation at the possible cost.

'You want to do this?'

Fay's excitement was overwhelming.

'Yes, wouldn't it be fun?'

There was a picture under a heading, which read: *Flying Show at Staverton Aerodrome.*

The picture showed a large passenger biplane with two engines and a cabin, the pilot's open cockpit set on a higher level. It looked to Tom Roxham like a converted bomber from the war. It was called 'Queen Hunter' and was to give flights to members of the public piloted by Sir Allan Cobham the famous aviator and entrepreneur. There were to be displays of aerobatics, wing walking, and bombing using confetti.

'Well?'

He looked up at her expectant face and knew that whatever the cost he wasn't going to disappoint her. He had two big, white fivers taken from his savings account in his wallet that he hoped to pay back in after the weekend; plus three pound notes, a ten shilling note in the second compartment and seven and six in his back pocket.

'Yes, let's go. The bus station is just over there.'

'Bus?'

For an instant she was bemused, thinking only of taxis, then remembered that she was with *him* and that's all he could afford. Besides, she thought, it might be fun. The last time she had travelled that way was when they were hired by the school for outings.

Puzzled he asked, 'Well, how else are we going to get there?'

She grinned. 'Of course — silly me. Are you sure? You don't have to go if you're not interested?'

'I think it's a great idea.'

He looked at his watch. 'We've got plenty of time.'

Fay sat back, holding her cup in both hands.

'That's great. I can't tell you how excited I am. I've always wanted to go flying.'

His jaw dropped. He hadn't thought he was going to be leaving the ground.

'You're actually going to go up?'

'Of course. Don't you want to?'

He certainly didn't want to appear unmanly.

'I've never thought about it much — but I'll give it a go.'

Fay's face lit up with pleasure.

'Then it will be a first time for *both* of us.'

Somehow that pushed all trepidation aside. He was going to do something with her that nobody else had ever done before. From that moment on it became almost a sacred duty.

When they finished he picked up the bill. Fay wondered about offering something, then thought better of it, suspecting that any offer to pay her way would hurt his feelings. But she was determined to help somewhere during the day.

Outside he waved in the direction they had to go.

'We're over there.'

She fell into step beside him, noting that she hardly came up to the level of his shoulder.

As they crossed the Promenade and made their way to where he said the bus would be, she said, 'You work for the Great Western Railway then?'

He took her elbow to help her across

another smaller road.

'Yes. Been with them for two years now.'

Fay, conscious of his grip on her arm, said, 'What do you do? Other than play in the orchestra?'

At the pavement he stopped, released her. 'Don't you know? I thought you did.'

Mystified, she shook her head.

'No — are you in the accounts or something?'

He wondered if what he was about to say would count against him.

'I'm in the police, the railway police, acting detective.' He left out the constable bit.

Fay looked amazed.

'Really — how exciting. Do you track down thieves and things?'

Tom shrugged. 'Yes, among other things.'

He decided of to tell her about the Saturday night drunken punch-ups he had to attend on rotation at Paddington & Bristol. Or the pickpockets, card sharps and the scams he had to look out for. Instead he said quickly, 'And you, do you do anything?'

As soon as it came out he realized it sounded patronizing.

'Sorry, I mean. . . .'

She cut him off. 'It's all right and it's true. I have been slow to do something with my life. I play the piano — there might be a future as an accompanist, I've got to look into it.'

He was genuinely impressed. 'That's wonderful.'

'Oh, I don't know about that.'

They chatted about music and his playing in dance bands, arriving to find the bus they wanted just about to pull out.

'Come on.'

He grabbed her hand and ran. The driver in his cabin beside the engine saw them and slowed right down.

Tom gently pushed her on and followed, waving his thanks.

She sat by a window and he lowered himself into the seat beside her.

With a roar of the diesel engine and a crash of gears, they were off. Eventually, the conductor came bumping down the aisle with his ticket board.

'Going to the air show?'

'Yes.'

When he'd finished giving them their tickets he said, 'You wouldn't get me in one of those things. If God had meant us to fly he would have given us wings.'

With that he crashed his way to the next passengers, leaving Tom thinking he was right. But Fay chuckled and, mimicking his voice, said, 'And if he'd meant us to float on water he'd have given us boats as feet.'

Still chuckling she looked out of the window, at the passing Regency houses.

'Cheltenham is very beautiful isn't it?'

He pretended to be looking as well, and said, 'Yes.'

In reality he was gazing at her reflection in the glass. Several moments passed before he suddenly realized that she was looking back at him, had been for some time. She turned and their eyes met — the closest they'd ever been.

She smiled.

Sheepishly, he smiled back.

The bus cleared the outskirts and entered rolling countryside. In the distance were the hills of the Cotswold escarpment.

The conductor rang the bell for the driver to stop at the next fare stage. Over half the bus passengers had already stood up.

'Staverton — for the air show.'

Tom got up, stood aside to let her go first down the aisle. When he reached the conductor, the man pulled a mournful face, 'Good luck.'

There were a lot of people walking up the lane and in the distance they could hear the sound of aero engines.

Fay fairly skipped ahead.

'Come along, I don't want to miss a thing.'

She held out her hand. Tom took it, marvelling at what was happening, when a massive roar sounded overhead and a dark shape right above made them duck instinctively. It was gone in a flash, leaving a fleeting impression of a leather helmeted and goggled figure, sitting in the cockpit of an upside down biplane, silk scarf flying in the slipstream.

It flashed away, revolving upright as it did so and pulling up into a steep climb.

'It's a Gypsy Moth,' shouted Fay, 'just like Amy Johnson's,' and pulled on his arm to hurry.

Tom was amazed that she should know what it was. At the entrance to the field was a gaily striped tent where tickets were being sold. Pennants were flying at its corners. Fay went first, already reaching into her handbag. 'Here, let me do this.'

Tom was not having it.

'No.'

His voice came out louder than intended and the sudden dark look on her previously dazzling face made him frightened that it was the first thing that had gone wrong all day.

He pleaded, 'Please, it's my place to.'

Fay relented.

'All right, but promise me I can treat you

just once today, it's only fair. It's what I'm used to.' It was a lie — a white lie. Jeremy and the likes would have laughed at the idea of a woman paying for anything. But that, in its way, was irritatingly condescending.

Eager to make up, Tom nodded. 'If you want.'

'I do.'

With the tickets finally purchased, they entered the field. She was so happy that Tom felt over the moon. What a wonderful bit of luck that it was on that day.

They came to a row of parked aeroplanes in bright colours, crowds around each one.

She actually jumped up and down with excitement.

'Look at them. They're Hornet Moths and the other two are Tiger Moths.'

Puzzled he asked, 'How come you know so much about aeroplanes?'

'My Uncle Sidney has one. He came for lunch with Aunty Pat last summer and landed in the park. Gave the sheep a rare old scare I can tell you.' Her face fell. 'Daddy wouldn't let me go up for a ride — said it was too dangerous.'

He swallowed. It was another world and a nasty reminder of the fact that he was not part of it and never would be.

'Come on, I want to see everything.'

She burrowed into the crowd and was soon talking to a man in a leather coat and breeches by the machine's wings. From there they moved successively along from one to the next until they'd reached the last one.

'Look!' Fay, cheeks rosy with the cold and excitement, pointed as a plane came in to land, its wings wobbling in the breeze, engine pop-popping. It touched down on the ground — bounced — came to earth again and stayed down.

It was a monoplane, the pilot inside the small cabin wearing a trilby hat.

'That's the future I suppose, but I love the open cockpit, don't you?'

Tom sniffed, beginning to feel the cold of the winter afternoon, as the time approached two o'clock.

'Looks more comfortable.'

She gave him a despairing look.

'That's not the attitude that built the Empire. Come on, it's my treat now.'

It wasn't the big converted bomber in the advert, but a De Havilland Dragon biplane with twin engines that could carry several passengers in two rows in a cabin in the fuselage. His heart sank. Did he have to go? Then he saw her shining eyes and knew there was no way out.

There was a table with a sign saying 'Joy Rides 5/-'

Fay was there before him.

The man sitting at the table looked up. 'Sorry, miss, the last flight's already fully booked.'

'Oh, no.'

Crestfallen, Fay groaned.

'Please, there must be a way? I've been looking forward so much to this.'

'Sorry, miss.'

Tom stepped forward.

'If it's a matter of only one seat, I can wait for another time?'

She was about to protest that she wanted them both to go, when a man who had been standing beside the table talking to two others turned, and flicked a finger along his small moustache. He was dressed in a flying suit. 'I'll take you up. Just going myself, before it gets too dark.'

Jealousy was something that Tom had not experienced before, at least not like the tidal wave of it that hit him now.

'That's very good of you, but we can wait.'

Fay looked at him and despite her longing to go, realized with bemused pleasure what was the matter. She took his hand to show that they were together.

'Mr — ?'

The man smiled, 'Captain Black, miss, ex-Royal Flying Corps, not this new fangled RAF.'

He managed to make RAF sound less than desirable.

Fay nodded. 'Of course, Captain Black. Anyway we both —'

Another younger man stepped forward.

'I'm going up, too, I'll take you. Captain Black here can bore the pants off this gentleman with the formation of the RAF — twenty odd years ago. Newfangled, indeed!'

Tom was caught by the pleading eyes of Fay. He swallowed.

'Well, in that case —'

'Fine.' Captain Black took him by the elbow and joked, 'He always gets the girl.'

Tom struggled with his jealousy. She was going with the young one — even worse. His fears were suddenly assuaged, however, by a very pretty girl who came over and spoke to Fay.

'Are you going flying with my husband?'

Fay nodded excitedly. 'Is that all right?'

'Of course.' The woman held out her hand. 'I'm Joan Hayes. We're about the same size. Would you like to borrow some overalls and a helmet? It's cold up there.'

Fay took her outstretched hand.

'That's awfully decent of you. I'm Fay Rossiter.'

She looked at Tom.

'See you back here.' She turned to Joan. 'How long will we be?'

'Half an hour no more.'

She squeezed her husband's arm. 'He's taking me out to dinner tonight aren't you, John?'

John grinned at them both. 'If we don't crash.'

Tom was given a large overcoat and a spare helmet by the garrulous Captain Black. They walked across the grass to a biplane with two open cockpits.

'You ever flown before?' Black enquired.

With his mouth suddenly as dry as a board, Tom Roxham had to clear his throat before saying, 'No.'

'Always wanted to I bet?'

'Well —'

But Black pointed to the back cockpit.

'Get yourself in there while I go through my checks. I'll strap you in. Only stand where it's marked on the wing, otherwise you'll put your foot through the fabric.'

Tom was left standing, feeling like an overdressed idiot — a rather apprehensive idiot at that. He'd set out that morning

tingling with excitement and anticipation —
never imagining he was going to do this.
Something he would never have done in a
million years left to his own devices.

As in a trance he stepped up on to the
wing, then lowered himself into the small
cockpit. His senses seemed to be height-
ened. He could smell oil, dope and even a
vague odour of sick. Tom sat there, blankly
looking at the dials, when nearby an engine
burst into life.

He watched as a similar biplane began to
wallow forward, the grass flattening with
the wind from the propeller.

The figure in the back cockpit started
waving like mad in his direction. Tom waved
back, suddenly realizing it was Fay. His
heart was in his mouth as he watched the
machine turn into the wind, and pause,
engine roaring.

Captain Black reared up beside him,
blocking the view.

'Now, let's get you strapped in. Sorry I
don't carry parachutes, but you wouldn't
know how to use it would you?'

He began pulling the tough canvas straps
over Tom's shoulders, drawing them painfully tight, so that he couldn't move an inch.

'Can't have you falling out during the
demonstration.'

'Demonstration?'

Tom felt his heart come up into his mouth.

Captain Black grinned.

'Yes — your lady friend is in the "enemy" plane, we are the good old home team.' He disappeared, just in time for a stunned Tom to see Fay's aircraft lifting off and climbing away beyond the wind sock, wings wobbling like a see-saw.

Black hauled himself up and then slumped down into the front cockpit. When he'd finished with his straps he gave a thumbs up. A man on the ground two-handedly pulled down on the propeller. It flicked around once. Nothing happened. The process was repeated, this time there was a cough and a cloud of black smoke. On the next pull the propeller suddenly flipped round and kept going as the engine coughed and coughed, then roared into life, the propeller disappearing into a blur.

Wind blasted his face.

'Chocks away.'

They began to move forward, bumping and creaking over the grass. Tom could see nothing ahead of them, as the nose was pointing upwards, but Black kept swinging the tail from side to side, so that he could see where he was going.

They braked to a halt. A voice crackled

into his ears, 'Revving up, checking our Ts and Ps and the magneto, then we'll be off.'

The noise of the engine increased to a deafening roar.

The plane shuddered and strained against the brakes.

The voice called again.

'Here we go.'

Tom Roxham didn't know what to expect, knowing only that Fay was already up there in the air somewhere ahead of him and that he wanted to be near her.

They started rolling, bumping and creaking and thudding, gathering speed. Suddenly his seat rose, the nose dipped and he could see ahead, at the grass racing towards and under them. Then all of a sudden the vibration and shaking ceased and they were higher and he realized they'd left the ground.

Tom gazed over the side at the dwindling earth and the tiny people; like hundreds of ants milling around the tents and aircraft. Beyond them lay the green fields of England.

Later, swooping between great mountains of cloud, down into valleys and soaring over peaks as occasionally, Fay's aircraft flashed into view and then was gone, plunging into the face of some cloud chasm, something grew in him and became stronger as Black climbed and dived and flew upside down above the heads of the admiring humanity. It grew until he knew that he wanted to do this — *had* to do this. He was destined to fly.

It seemed only a few minutes before Black's voice was telling them that they were coming into land.

The smoothness of the movement through the air gave way to a crashing thump, then smoothness, followed again by another thump and shaking as earth reasserted its rattling, vibrating hold. They finally rolled to a halt.

Tom Roxham climbed down. As his foot touched the ground he knew he was changed — for ever.

CHAPTER SIX

They met halfway between the aeroplanes. Her face was alive with excitement.

'Wasn't that just beautiful? A fleeting glimpse of heaven.'

Tom took both her hands in his.

'Without you I wouldn't have done that.'

She started to protest, but he shook his head and cut her off.

'No. Listen, I'm being serious. There are no words to describe that experience. I want to learn to fly now more than anything in the world.'

She laughed, released his hands and wrapped her arms around his waist in a big hug.

'Me too.'

Tom raised his hands to her back and drew her close to him. Her hair, just beneath his nose, smelt wonderfully fresh.

It happened so naturally. Without thinking, he kissed the top of her head.

She pulled away and looked up at him.

'Tom —'

He brought his lips down to touch hers gently. They stayed like that, motionless, until he slowly pulled back, realizing the enormity of what he had just done. What would she think of him?

'I — I'm sorry, I —'

Her fingers gently touched his lips, stopping him.

'I've wanted you to do that since I first set eyes on you.'

He was stunned, speechless.

She grinned shyly. 'I feel so light-headed, like I've been drinking champagne.'

Tom had never tasted the stuff in his life, but he knew what she meant — he was still tingling from the experience.

She put her arm through his. 'Come on, I'm famished and I've got to give this coat back to Joan Hayes.' He waited while she chatted to the woman, watching the last joy ride by the De Havilland Rapide take off. He noticed she pointed to him while she was talking. He wondered what she was saying, but forgot to ask.

Back on the bus they sat close, hands clasped.

She asked, 'Where shall we eat?'

He'd worried about that.

'Well, there is a restaurant in the town that serves very good food, but it's not plush.'

She squeezed his hand.

'That's fine. What do we care — nothing matters down here — does it?'

The place was a rather ageing café, that had seen better days. It was patronized by young couples and families before they queued at the cinema around the corner, to see the latest picture.

They had limited means, as did Tom, and he'd agonized over where to take her and decided this was the best he could afford.

Walking from the bus with Fay on his arm felt terrific. When they entered the restaurant with its table lit by little red lamps, it seemed rather busy.

A man came towards them dressed in a dinner jacket, his black hair parted down the middle and brushed straight back.

'Can I help you?'

Tom asked for a table for two.

'And the name, sir?'

Puzzled, he said 'Roxham — Tom Roxham.'

The man ran his eye down a list he was carrying.

'I'm sorry, sir, there isn't a reservation under that name. You did book, didn't you?'

Crestfallen, he said, 'Well, no, I didn't

know you had to.'

The man gave a supercilious smile and boomed out for all to hear, 'We're always full on a Saturday. You obviously haven't dined with us before.'

His tone was dismissive. Tom wished the ground would open up and swallow him.

Fay, aware of Tom smarting from the arrogant dismissal, and angered at the man's attitude, said in a loud exaggerated voice, 'Darling, come along, we'll get Lord Rossiter's usual table at the Queen's. Daddy won't be using it — he's up at the Savoy.'

Tom was amazed by her cut glass accent: much more pronounced now than the voice he had become used to during the day. But the effect on the man was instantaneous.

Blustering, he ran a finger down his list.

'I didn't say we couldn't do something, madam. As a matter of fact we do have a table free due to a cancellation.'

Fay turned to Tom.

'What do you think, darling? Shall we stay?'

He looked at her, realizing that she had stepped in and taken control, but was now handing it back to him.

'Yep, let's give it a go.'

When they were seated and the head waiter had fussed around, giving them the typed menu cards, taking their order for wine before bustling away, she leaned forward, 'Sorry about butting in, but that sort of person gets my goat.'

He smiled lamely.

'I'm not very used to this — must be pretty obvious.'

Fay placed a reassuring hand on his.

'Tom, it's easy for me, I've had a privileged upbringing.'

He sat back and sighed.

'And I haven't.'

Anxiously, she asked, 'Is it a problem?'

He swallowed, 'It worries me. I mean —'

He found it difficult to say, but she said it for him.

'That you're not good enough for me, is that it?'

Sadly, he just nodded.

Fay Rossiter's eyes flashed.

'Now, you just listen to me, Tom Roxham. Stop putting yourself down. I've never had so much fun — *ever.*'

'But —'

She made a chopping motion with her hand.

'No buts. All the men in my "posh" circle don't attract me one bit — so there.'

He blinked and said nothing as the waiter arrived with their wine.

'Will you taste it, sir?'

Almost imperceptibly she nodded, so he said crisply, 'Of course.'

The waiter poured a small amount into his glass. Having no idea what to do Tom picked it up and drank it straight down in one gulp.

'Tastes fine.'

The waiter gave him a funny look, but poured Fay's glass then refilled his again before leaving them alone.

Fay had a hand to her face to hide her grin, but he could see that she was amused. It no longer worried him.

'What did I do wrong?'

She shook her head, 'Nothing really, except you're supposed to sniff and sip the wine to see if it is corked.'

'Corked?'

'Bad wine tastes of the cork.'

'I see.'

He played his fingers on the glass. 'Do I?'

She put her head quizzically to one side. 'Do you what?'

'Attract you?'

Her eyes were as wide as he had ever seen them as he waited in trepidation for the answer.

Finally she whispered, 'You know you do. Is the reverse true?'

He smiled shyly. 'Of course.'

Fay took her sip of the red wine for support.

'I knew it almost straight away. I didn't believe things like that happened in real life.'

He felt the same, but felt compelled to say, 'We've only been together a day — you hardly know me.'

She nodded. 'True, but it doesn't matter — does it?'

He slowly shook his head. 'No.'

Radiating happiness she pulled off her beret, hair swishing freely. 'Good, that's settled.'

Later, as they left the restaurant he asked, 'What time have you got to be in tonight?'

Fay put her arm through his, 'No time really. I've got a key, though Aunty won't go to sleep until I come in. I'm supposed to be at a friend's all-day birthday party, but I conveniently forgot to give her a telephone number — so what are we going to do?'

'How about the pictures?'

'Do you know what's on?'

He'd checked the *Echo* in advance in case they might want to go.

'Well the newly opened Regal has Errol Flynn in *The Adventures of Robin Hood,* the Gaumont's showing *Boys Town* with Spencer Tracey and Mickey Rooney and the Daffodil has Carole Lombard in *Nothing Sacred* for a second time.'

She squeezed his arm.

'Oh, I'd love to go,' then she frowned, 'but you must have seen it already.'

He lied. 'No, but we'd better get a move on.'

They stepped out briskly, Tom listening to the wonderful sound of her heels tapping on the pavement.

Breathless she asked 'Will we be in time for the programme?'

'Not all of it, we'll miss a bit of the first film.'

The woman on the ticket kiosk reminded them of that fact as she pressed the button and two tickets issued from the counter top.

The usherette led the way in the dark cinema, showing them to their seats with her torch. They pushed past people who had to stand up to let them go by, apologizing as they went, seats creaking as they lowered them and sat down.

They were halfway through the first film — a comedy series that he liked called *Blondie,* with a character by the name of Dagwood Bumstead who made him laugh with his characteristic wild exit out of the home. His wife, Blondie and children lined up at the door with his hat, coat and brief-case.

The lights came up. Queues started to form for the ice-cream girls, picked out in spotlights with their trays supported by neck holders.

He got two, one vanilla and one straw-berry. Fay chose the strawberry. They sat digging in with the little wooden spoons.

'Tell me, Tom, are you going to take flying lessons?'

He grimaced. 'I want to desperately, but the cost, well,' he shook his head resignedly. 'It will be a few years yet, but I'll do it.'

She scraped the bottom of her tub before she spoke again. 'I might be able to help there.'

'No.'

He knew he'd done it again — over-reacted. Apologetically, he laid a hand gently on her arm. 'Sorry.'

She put her empty tub on the floor under her seat. 'Tom, I wouldn't dream of insult-ing you by trying to pay for you — even if we did it together.'

'Oh, what did you mean then?'

'That chap I flew with, Mr Hayes, he keeps a machine at Staverton, although they actually live in Cheltenham. His wife was very nice — said he'd be only too pleased to take you up anytime and give you a lesson if he's free.'

'Me?'

'Yes. I made it clear that it was for you. She said he would love to — he's always keen to help anyone who takes an interest in his passion. Be at the hangar on any Saturday or Sunday morning and introduce yourself.'

'Are you sure?'

'Yes. Absolutely.'

He couldn't believe it. 'You did that for me?'

She lowered her eyelashes. 'Yes.'

'Will you be coming as well?'

She sighed. 'Afraid not. I doubt if Father will ever let me become a pilot, so I'll have to wait and do it myself when I can. And even if he did I'd have to go somewhere nearer. There is a small flying club just outside Cirencester.'

Disappointed, his face fell.

'I'm sorry to hear that.'

After a while he asked, 'Why didn't you tell me earlier?'

She rolled her eyes in mock exasperation. 'I meant to but you suddenly kissed me — remember? I was not myself.'

He blushed. 'Fay, thanks for doing that.'

The house lights dimmed making the

'exit' lights stand out. Then a spotlight split the darkness, focussing on an area just before the stage. At the same time a large Wurlitzer organ lit up and a man in a dinner jacket, light flashing on his spectacles, began playing as the whole structure rose up.

There followed ten minutes of popular melodies before it began to descend. The audience clapped, the man turned and waved, and carried on playing until the spotlight went out.

There was a pause during which Fay took off her coat, folding it on to her lap together with her beret.

With an audible click, the curtains started to open, the Pathé News's crowing cockerel projected on the last of the rippling material.

The first piece showed the *Queen Mary* docking at Southampton and a famous American film star coming down the gangway lost in a huge, silver fox fur. She was to stay at the Ritz before attending a society wedding.

The next item was the launch of a new warship at Clyde Bank by His Majesty King George VI. A bottle of champagne broke on the bow as the ship started to glide towards the water. Tom was fascinated by the huge chains dragging behind the hull, breaking its speed of entry into the water.

The scenes of cheering crowds, of men in cloth caps waving union jacks, were accompanied by a stirring commentary that the Empire relied on the safe conduct of its mercantile marine.

The bulletin concluded with the latest football news, players running around on foggy pitches; the black and white film making it difficult to know which team was which, and then the cockerel was marking the end of the news. The flickering light from the projector caught the rising clouds of smoke from cigarettes as people lit up before the main feature film came on.

Hesitantly Tom put his arm across the back of her seat letting it lightly touch Fay, enough for her to know it was there. As the beautiful Carole Lombard came into view she snuggled up nearer him and he dropped his arm around her. It was all so unbelievable. He had never felt so good.

She was just a natural, beautiful girl, and with a spirit that made her fun to be with. And for the first time in his life he felt complete, as though up until then he hadn't been truly alive.

With Tom she felt at ease, his arm around

her shoulders was both protective and cosy, not in any way oppressive or threatening. And he was, it seemed strange to say it, a friend. Someone she could talk to — like another self.

But there was something else, a physical attraction that had stirred her blood the moment she had set eyes on him.

She tilted her head until it touched his. In the darkened cinema, with the glamorous world portrayed by Hollywood before them, all their troubles just faded away. But they knew, all those around them, that real life would return the moment they stepped back out on to the dim street. Fay breathed out quietly, and for a second or two ignored Carole. Although their bodies had known instantly when they'd first seen each other, it had taken these few hours for them to realize they were truly meant for each other — kindred spirits. Her hand found his and squeezed.

After the film they walked slowly to her Aunt's, arms wrapped around each other. At the top of the street she stopped. 'I'll tell her I shared a taxi and got off here.'

She turned into him, arms around his waist, face to one side on his chest.

'I don't want to leave you.'

He just held her tight, saying nothing.

After a while they kissed. The taste and feel of her was the most wonderful thing to him, her powder, her lipstick, her scent, her smoothness, her hair — *everything*.

They stayed for a long time, cheek to cheek, just content to breathe so closely together.

Eventually they kissed again, becoming bolder each time their mouths met.

He murmured, 'When can I see you again?'

He felt her tense.

'It's going to be difficult, Tom. My parents — well, they won't understand.' She shook her head. 'I'm sorry, that's a humiliating thing to say.'

He smiled sadly. 'No — I guessed that much. But when?'

She thought for a while. 'Can you get to London easily?'

That took him aback.

'Well, yes, I suppose so. I can use my warrant card, pretend I'm on the job. Why?'

'It's easier for me to be up in town doing various things than to be continually coming over to Cheltenham.'

'You say when, I'll be there.'

Frowning, she said 'It can't be next weekend, I've got a charity ball to attend.'

The jealousy rose in him again with the

same unstoppable force.

'Oh.' He couldn't keep the emotion out of his voice.

Her face was caught in the light from a street lamp as she looked up at him.

'Darling, there is nothing to worry about — it means nothing — honestly.'

'Who are you going with — that Jeremy fellow?'

She gave him a playful shake.

'Now stop it. Jeremy will be in the crowd — we always do things together — a whole bunch of us. If I suddenly stop going everybody will be suspicious, Daddy and Mummy especially.'

He tightened his hold, stopping her shaking him again.

'Sorry.'

They stayed hard together for a second or two, then he looked sternly down at her. 'You behave now — or else.'

She raised one finely plucked eyebrow. 'What?'

He remembered a film he'd seen recently. 'I'll put you over my knee.'

Fay felt positively weak at the thought, but said with a pretend toss of her head. 'Huh, you could try.'

Laughing, they moved a few more paces,

knowing that the time to part was upon them.

He tried to sound as matter of fact as he could muster. 'So, the weekend after next?'

She nodded. 'Absolutely. Can you make late Saturday afternoon?'

'Yes.'

'Paddington — by the destination board, at about five o'clock?'

He nodded. 'I'll be there.'

They shared a last kiss, then she broke free. 'I've really got to go.'

Incongruously she stuck out her hand. 'Thank you for a lovely day, Mr Roxham.'

He took it, grinning. 'My pleasure, Miss Rossiter.'

'Until the next time?'

'Indeed, yes.'

She turned away, stepping out down the ill-lit street as he watched her go, waiting for her to turn. Just when he thought she wouldn't, she did, waving and blowing a kiss.

Then, as she went up the steps of the house, she became obscured by the ornamental railings leading to her Aunt's door.

He waited until a shaft of light fleetingly illuminated her once more as the front door opened.

When it closed he felt like the loneliest

man in the world.

On the walk home he looked at the stars, wondering about the future.

Chapter Seven

The car was waiting for her at the station and soon she was at the entrance to Codrington Hall. Her mother greeted her in the drawing-room.

'Darling, have you had a good weekend?'

'Wonderful, Mummy.'

'Who was there. Anybody we know?'

'Oh, a couple of girls from school and a lot of people I didn't know.'

She changed the subject. 'And you, Mummy, did you and Daddy enjoy yourselves?'

Her mother finished adjusting the flowers cut by the gardener from the greenhouse. 'The show was very good indeed. Unfortunately Daddy was kept late. Didn't get there until after the first act.'

Fay winced. 'Oh dear, more trouble?'

Her mother nodded. 'He's upset by the way things are going. You know how he worries. You'll find him in his study, darling,

I'm sure he'd love to see you.'

Fay gave her mother a peck on the cheek.

'I've got something to ask him, Mother. I've decided to try to develop my piano skills as an accompanist. Do you think he'll approve?'

Lady Rossiter smiled. 'Oh, that's wonderful Fay, of course he will, and he can help so much. Go on, quickly.'

Fay gave her mother's hand a squeeze. She hurried across the hall and down a side passage. At the study door she paused. Taking a deep breath she gave a knock and waited. She heard her father's muffled, 'Come in'. Fay opened the door. He was behind his huge mahogany desk with its green shaded and brass reading lamp and silver inkstand.

The walls were full of leather bound books on the law, politics and history. Her father had gone to Harrow and Oxford, where he had taken a double first in PPE. From there he had gone straight to the Western Front. Now he was a junior minister in Mr Chamberlain's government, though in the House of Lords.

As soon as he saw her, he stood up, removing his half moon spectacles.

'Fay, darling.'

He came round the desk and embraced her.

As she hugged him she could feel he'd lost weight.

'Daddy, I am just back. Sorry to interrupt you, you look busy.'

'Never too busy for you. Did you have a good party?'

Again she lied. 'Yes, it was good to see some old school chums and a lot of new people.'

Her father returned to his seat, Fay noticed he seemed to have acquired a stoop as he said, 'That's good, that's good.'

He asked nothing further.

Relieved at his preoccupation, she pressed on. 'Daddy, I've been thinking. I'd like to try to be an accompanist.'

He positively beamed. The tiredness almost disappeared from his face.

'That's excellent, my dear, excellent. Would you like me to see what I can do — a few choice introductions?'

She nodded. 'That would be nice. It's what I hoped you'd say.'

'Well consider it done.'

She clenched her hands together in excitement.

'I'm going up to town the weekend after next,' she lied, 'to a Myra Hess concert. Perhaps it would be possible for people to see me then, I am staying overnight?'

'I'll make some telephone calls. I'm delighted, Fay, I really am. I was getting a little worried, you seemed to be drifting. It's wonderful — wonderful.'

Fay decided it might be a good time to mention flying.

'Daddy, all the girls were talking about getting pilot's licences. Could I have lessons as well? Amy Johnson started when —'

Frowning, Lord Rossiter stopped her then and there.

'Fay, no. It's far too risky and in any case it's not something a lady should do.'

'But Daddy, the Duchess of Bedford —'

'No Fay, that's an end to it. Look what happened to her. The world is a dangerous enough place as it is.'

She knew the finality in her father's voice only too well. It would be useless to pursue it any further at the moment. But fly she would — one day.

Meanwhile she was going to see Tom again in two weeks.

Up in her room Fay went to the window and sat in the casement seat, looking out across the lawn to the cedar tree and beyond, to the parkland. Behind the glass of the lattice window the sun was warm.

It all looked so lovely, so peaceful, like her life before she had met Tom, but now?

Wrapping her arms protectively around herself, she thought once more of his hard body when he had held her, and gave a little shiver. It felt like she was on the edge of a storm that was about to break.

Unknown to Tom, his mother and father had noticed a change in their son. He seemed to dream a lot if left alone and took a little more care with his appearance. They knew he'd been out with a girl and had poked gentle fun at him, but he didn't seem to mind. But he wouldn't tell them anything about her, and there was no suggestion of bringing her home.

The only thing that Tom Roxham did wax lyrically about was his trip in an aeroplane and how he was going to be a pilot.

His father had had a coughing fit trying to ask him about who was going to pay for such a mad cap idea.

Tom worked hard all week, ending up shadowing a gang of thieves on a train to Bristol Temple Meads station where the group of three, two men and a woman had been arrested, not without a little excitement. One man broke free, jumped down on to the tracks and made off up the line. Tom had pursued him for nearly a mile, dodging clear of moving trains and around

138

all the locomotives and rolling stock in sidings before cornering his quarry in a dead end.

The man pulled a knife and eyes wild, chest heaving, faced him, beckoning him on with his other hand.

'Come on then, copper.'

Tom took out his short truncheon. 'Don't be silly. We know who you are. Now come along quietly.'

Suddenly the man lunged violently forward, bringing the knife up in a vicious thrust —

He woke up in the casualty department of Frenchay Hospital. They dealt with his broken arm later, after assessing his concussion.

Tom signed off and travelled back to Cheltenham. He crossed the passenger bridge at Lansdowne Road station, suddenly enveloped in steam from a southbound goods train headed by a rumbling Collett 0-6-0, and left through the classical columns of the entrance.

After his supper and then the bath he read the *Daily Sketch* and listened to Arthur Askey on the wireless. He kissed his mother goodnight at nine o'clock.

'Early for you, son. Are you all right?'

He yawned. 'Busy day, Mum, goodnight.'

'Say your prayers now,' she called out.

Halfway up the stairs and out of sight he rolled his eyes and called out, 'I will.'

When he was tucked up in bed he did say the Lord's Prayer, then he added a plea of his own about Fay.

When he woke up at seven it was still dark, but he could just see the odd star through the window. It looked as if it was going to be a fine day.

His sheet and blankets were all in a twisted pile half off the bed and his shoulders, despite the winceyette pyjama top, were freezing. He found his tartan dressing-gown and shoved his feet into the felt carpet slippers under the bed.

Quietly he went downstairs, keen not to wake his parents. He got the fire in the range going with kindling without too much raking and noise and put the kettle on. Letting himself out of the scullery door, he stood shivering in the cold of the lavatory.

By the time he heard his father coughing, the kettle had boiled and he had made a pot of tea. He got the wooden tray with the picture of Weston-Super-Mare inlaid in its centre, and took them up two cups and some biscuits, knocking on the door before he entered.

'You working this morning?' His father asked.

His father was sitting up in the brass bedstead, holding the basin that he kept handy to spit into when he got the phlegm up. There was the faint smell of urine in the cold air coming from the chamber pot under the bed.

'No dad, I'm going to Staverton Aerodrome. There's the chance of a flight.'

Leaning over, his father put the bowl down on the floor by his side as his mother stirred. He grumbled, 'You're daft. Waste of time. Costs hundreds of pounds something like that. You'd be better off going to the football and I don't mean that funny highfalutin game with a pointy ball that you took up at school. I don't know what the council thinks it's doing. Bloody Cheltenham.'

His father who came from Gloucester, always found Cheltenham stuck up and pretentious. Tom had played rugby at school and occasionally supported the town's team, much to the disgust of his father, who supported 'The Robins' football team.

Tom backed out of the door. 'Well I'm going all the same. Probably be back in time to go to the game with you.'

He turned around and faced the door to

his grandmother's room, knocked and went in.

His mother elbowed his father in the side. 'Leave the boy alone, Father. It's got something to do with this girl.'

He got his bicycle out of the shed and opened the back gate, just as a figure in sailor's uniform with a kit-bag on his shoulder did the same.

'Morning, Tom.'

He put his leg over the saddle as he nodded and replied.

'Morning, Jimmy. Leave over?'

It seemed a daft thing to say, seeing as he had on his uniform and carried a kit-bag.

'Yes. Going to be on the train all day — worse luck.'

'Where to?' Tom was interested in the journey.

'She's up at Scapa Flow. All the way to Bonnie Scotland for me.'

'Well, all the best.'

He stuck out his hand and Jimmy took it. 'And you.'

The bag was swung up on to the shoulder, nudging Jimmy's cap. He straightened it so that the name band was in position. It was a source of local awe and pride that he was on the famous battle cruiser, HMS *Hood*.

The only thing moving in the street was

the milkman's horse and cart, with its three large galvanized churns with taps, and a measuring jug on a chain. The horse plodded gently along, munching from his nose bag.

Soon Tom was opt in the country, Churchdown Hill coming into view. He turned down an unmade lane, standing up and pumping the pedals as he climbed up a bank to a bridge which spanned the four lines of the railway running between Gloucester and Cheltenham. Down the other side the aerodrome was clearly visible. Compared with the other week it was all quiet and empty. There were two hangars tucked in near the embankment. He coasted down the approach path and saw an MG sports car with its canvas roof down despite the cold. It stood outside one of the hangars which had two huge double doors open. Inside he could see three aeroplanes, including the one he'd been in the other day. The engine covers were off the one he'd been taken up in, and a mechanic was whistling as he delved into the engine bay. Somewhere else metal was being hammered.

He dismounted and leaned the bike against the fence, then took off his trouser clips. Hesitatingly he approached the open door, stood there. The general smell of aeroplanes assailed his nostrils, the petrol, oil and distinctive aroma of doped canvas.

He must have been there for a good few minutes taking it all in.

'Ah, so this is the young man who wants to fly?'

Startled, he turned to see the pilot who had taken up Fay.

'Yes, yes sir.'

The face before him broke into a grin.

'Well, good for you. What's your name again?'

'Tom Roxham.'

The man held out his hand. 'And mine's Paul Hayes. Your young lady gave my wife a call — Miss Rossiter of Codrington Hall, is that right?'

Surprised, Tom nodded. He didn't realize Fay was going to do that.

Paul Hayes gave him a quizzical look. 'Where did you two meet, may I ask?'

Tom coloured. 'At a dance, at the Queen's Hotel.'

'I see.'

Tom sensed that the man was bemused that he could know the likes of the Rossiters socially, let alone be on familiar terms with them.

Perhaps Hayes sensed his resentment because he clapped his hands.

'Right, come on, let's give you a first lesson. You'll need a bit of kit. I've got together a few bits in the office.'

Having equipped Tom with a helmet, goggles and a pair of gauntlets and dressed him in a thick lambswool jacket, Hayes led him to a yellow biplane.

'This is a Tiger Moth.'

Tom followed him around as he checked and explained various things, then, leaning over the cockpit together, Hayes showed him the controls and what they did.

'This is the joystick — pull it back to climb, forward to dive, left and right to turn. You use it in conjunction with the rudder bar — there.'

Tom didn't realize he was going to be so thoroughly instructed. Paul Hayes was telling him about airflow over the wings and various surfaces. They stepped back down on to the concrete.

'Right, let me show you how to put on a parachute.'

'Parachute?'

Paul Hayes grinned. 'If you have to jump out, count three and pull that big ring.'

It took five minutes to put it on then he stood feeling awkward, with a large pack hanging off his bottom.

Hayes led him to his aeroplane.

'Get in the back cockpit, I'll strap you in.' Clumsily, Tom clambered aboard and sat on the pack.

Later, with the help of a couple of mechanics, Hayes pushed the machine outside into the bright morning sunshine, then climbed into the front, as the mechanics put the chocks on. The propeller was swung, and finally with a roar, the machine burst into quivering life.

Over the speaking tube Hayes called out, 'Off we go — at last.'

It all came back then. His blood raced with anticipation as they bumped across the grass, turned into the wind, ran up the engine.

When they began to move everything rattled and juddered as the wind blasted past his face. Suddenly all was smooth, and Tom knew that they were airborne. Through his goggles he watched the earth recede, and the sense of speed vanished as they climbed into clear blue sky. Spread out below them looking like a patchwork quilt were the fields of England.

Hayes's voice came down the tube. 'Beautiful day.'

Tom answered, 'Yes, it is.'

The head before him continually turned, looking left and right and up and down as he continued: 'Put your hands gently on the controls and follow me as I put her through a few manoeuvres — then you can have a go.'

To begin with Tom was too heavy with the stick and rudder and Hayes told him to relax. And then he began to get the feel of it, turning and climbing and descending with ever increasing confidence and precision.

Before they finally returned to earth Hayes took back control and finished with a few rolls and a loop. They taxied back to the hangar. In the silence when the engine was turned off Tom Roxham sagged back against the seat feeling utterly exhausted. Hayes led the way to the back of the hangar to a portioned off area that served as an office.

'Come in, have a seat. Like a drink?'

Tom nodded, assuming it was tea, but Hayes bent down, opened a drawer in his roll-top desk and produced a bottle of whisky and two tumblers.

He didn't say a word as Hayes poured out the light straw coloured liquid and said, 'Single malt. I love it after I've flown — helps me to put up with being down here again.'

He handed a glass to Tom.

'Cheers.'

They clinked the tumblers. Tom took a sip, his first ever of malt whisky and found it agreeably smooth, though it warmed up as it went down.

Hayes sat back, watching him. 'Still want to be a pilot?'

'Yes — very much.'

Hayes nodded. 'Good, because you're a natural.'

Tom blinked. 'What do you mean?'

Hayes took another sip. 'Just what I said. You've got it in you — a natural talent — good co-ordination.'

Tom felt a thrill run through him, like an electric current. It was so unexpected. 'Really?'

Hayes nodded. 'Really. Now how are you going to go about it — it's not cheap?'

Crestfallen, he took a gulp of his whisky. 'I don't know.'

His voice tailed off. He was disappointed because he thought Hayes was going to take him on. The latter drummed his fingers on the desk as he contemplated the suddenly miserable fellow before him.

'You're welcome to come here once a week, by arrangement, and I'll teach you the basics — no charge.'

Tom's heart leapt.

'Gosh, that's terrific. What can I say —

I'm really grateful.'

Smiling, Hayes nodded. 'I can see.'

Looking serious, he leant forward. 'But you need more than that — *deserve* more. I'm only an amateur instructor — fine to start off with, but you're good enough to need professional training, and *regularly.*'

Tom's jaw dropped. 'That's all very well, but I can't afford it.'

Quietly, Hayes asked, 'Ever thought of applying to be a volunteer in the Royal Air Force Reserve?'

Bewildered, Tom shook his head. 'No, to be honest this all happened so suddenly. I've got a regular job.'

Rubbing his jaw, Hayes picked up the bottle and poured two more small shots into the glasses.

'Well, there is another way. With all this talk of war, they've expanded pilot training everywhere. There's another scheme called "The Civil Air Guard", they train people to fly at aero-clubs' — he nodded out the window — 'like the one across the other side at a cost of about half a crown an hour.'

Tom was staggered and celebrated by downing his glass. 'I'll go over and apply — do you think they have places?'

Smiling, Hayes nodded.

'Oh yes, I can guarantee that, but there is a snag.'

'Yes?'

Shuffling amongst the papers on the desk, Hayes found what he was looking for.

'You sign a document undertaking,' he read, ' "to accept service in any capacity or rank, in connection with aviation in this country in the event of an emergency arising from war, or threat of war".' He threw the paper aside.

'They're after a last ditch of reserve of pilots in case the balloon goes up.'

Tom didn't know what to say, except that whatever the implications, he was going to do it. 'I'd better get over there.'

They stood up and shook hands.

Hayes said, 'Meanwhile, come over any weekend if you want.'

With his clips on, Tom waved and, straining at the pedals he started up the incline.

When he'd gone Hayes returned to his desk and, lifting the phone nearer, picked up the receiver and dialled. When he got through, he spoke to the Secretary of the Flying Club.

'Ted, I've just sent one Tom Roxham over to you — to enrol in the Air Guard scheme.'

There was a pause as he listened and then said, 'I understand, but you're going to like this one — he won't be chopped I can tell you. He's good, very good. He'll train up quickly.'

CHAPTER EIGHT

Fay could hardly concentrate on what was going on around her on Saturday. All morning she desperately wondered how he was getting on with his lesson and was envious to the point of hurting.

Once, she imagined she'd heard an aero engine and had gone running out into the garden, startling one of the young gardeners, convinced it was him flying over.

But there had been nothing in the sky. It must have been a motor bike or lorry on the main road a mile away.

As she stood there all she had heard was the faint rustle of the breeze in some conifers. When she returned, her father was standing by a window. He'd been looking at her the entire time.

'Fay, what were you doing out there?'

She faltered. 'I thought I heard an aeroplane.'

Her father raised a quizzical eyebrow. 'I

know you have a new found passion for all things aviation, but really.. . . .'

He pulled out his Hunter, flicked open the lid and looked at the time. 'Coffee, I think? Will you join us, my dear, I've got something to tell you.'

Fay wondered what was coming. 'Of course, where are we taking it?'

'It's such a nice day, let's have it served in the Orangery.'

They were seated in the wicker chairs, when the maid came in carrying a wide tray and set it down on the glass topped table.

While she poured out the coffee from a silver pot into bone china cups, Fay flicked through the latest copy of *Riders and Driving* noticing that a new centre had opened near Burford.

'Cream, miss?'

Fay lowered the magazine. 'Yes please.'

A plate of biscuits was offered. She took one. Her mother was talking to her father about the situation in Europe and it was moments before she realized that he was saying something to her.

'I'm sorry, Father, my mind was far away.'

He smiled. 'As it has been for most of the week, Fay. You tell us it's because you want to be a pilot but I don't think that's quite all — is it, my dear?'

Stunned, Fay didn't say anything, so her mother prompted. 'Is there a young man, Fay, a pilot? Did you meet him at the party?'

She was speechless and aware that her cheeks were colouring. Eventually, she stammered, 'It's not like that, Mummy. He's only just starting. He's a beginner.'

'What's his name?'

It came out before she had time to think. 'Tom Roxham.'

Shocked, but thrilled at the same time, her mother brought her back to earth and its dangers.

'Roxham? Do we know the family, my dear?'

'No.' It came out too forcefully, so she repeated more softly, 'No, Mummy.'

But she persisted. 'Where do they live?'

Fay was going to say she wasn't sure, which was the truth, but they wouldn't believe she didn't have *some* idea.

'Beyond Marlborough, some village or other.'

Her father frowned. 'Is that where he went to school?'

Relieved that she had inadvertently picked somewhere that killed two birds with one stone, she said, 'I believe so. He certainly wasn't a boarder at Cheltenham.'

That *was* true at least. She was feeling

pretty pleased with herself, when her mother grinned and asked slyly, 'When are you going to see him again?'

Fortunately they seemed to take her inability to answer as shyness. She finally mumbled, 'I don't know, nothing definite.'

'He *did* ask to see you again, did he, Fay?'

Strangely, it was her father who was being persistent.

'No, not really. I expect we may bump into each other in the coming months. I seem to remember he was going to be at a couple of events.'

Her mother sipped her coffee as elegantly as ever and asked sweetly, 'Will he be there tonight?'

She was already irritated that one of the reasons why she couldn't see Tom that evening was because of the stupid ball.

'Most definitely not.'

'And what does Jeremy think about all this, or doesn't he know?'

So *that* was it. She faced her father.

'Jeremy? What on earth has it got to do with *him?*'

'I rather thought that you and he had an understanding.'

'Daddy, I've told you before. Jeremy is just one of the crowd.'

'Well, he certainly thinks he's more than

that and I must say —'

'Please, I thought I'd made it plain that I think Jeremy is a nice, dependable boy but,' she looked for help to her mother — 'he doesn't excite me.'

Her father's face darkened. 'Stop being so juvenile, Fay. Life isn't like those stories in ladies' magazines you know. A woman should think of security and position. They're more important than notions of idyllic love. It's a cruel world out there, young lady.'

Fay bristled. 'Surely you and Mummy were physically attracted?'

Lord Rossiter was shocked. 'That's a little impertinent, Fay. You should apologize to your mother.'

'I'm sorry, Mummy.'

Her mother was looking uncomfortable. 'Well, of course, I fell madly in love with your father, Fay. I remember seeing him for the first time at my coming out ball. He was so handsome.'

Lord Rossiter frowned. 'Oh really, Eleanor . . .'

Fay leapt in. 'That's it, Mummy — you *knew,* didn't you, straight away?'

Lady Rossiter smiled, realizing that her daughter had played a cunning hand.

'Yes, I knew.' She glanced at her husband.

'But it took awhile before he noticed me.'

'That's not fair, Eleanor — and you know it.'

Eager to get away Fay stood up. 'If you'll excuse me . . .'

Lord Rossiter called after her, 'Don't forget what I said, young lady. Think of your future. Think with your head, not your heart.'

When she'd gone he turned to his wife. 'That girl is as strong willed as ever,' he grunted, 'even more so.'

The girl with the 'strong will' started to get ready for the charity ball that evening. She sat in front of her dressing-table carefully applying lipstick before dusting her neck and shoulders with a powder puff and thinking of the slip she had made in letting out Tom's name. It was worrying, because, knowing her parents, they might start making enquiries. Her thoughts turned to that night. Normally she liked the ball held in several heated marquees in aid of the NSPCC. It went on until the early hours, with more than one orchestra, several servings of supper, and various entertainments, conjurors, fire-eaters and the like.

But she would have swapped it all for an evening with Tom. Still, in six days she would be up in London — alone with him.

She stood up, dressed in lilac cami-knickers as Julie brought her the gown for the evening.

In the middle of the week Tom had had his interview with the Civil Guard people and was generally surprised by how easy it all seemed to be. They asked him about his keenness on being a pilot and how long had he wanted to be one. Worried that, being a new found passion, it might count against him, he was delighted when they seemed to suggest that it was probably better that way.

There were two of them, the owner of the flying school, whom he had seen last Saturday and made the appointment with. A thin wiry man with a neat military style moustache was also present. He had come down from London, a Squadron Leader Mayhew, though he was not in uniform. They sat in the flying school office, walls adorned with charts and silhouettes of aircraft, desk piled with papers and a flying helmet. On the floor in the corners were bits of engines.

The owner of the flying club, a Mr Trubshaw, said, 'Normally we would have given you a test flight before this stage, but Mr Hayes speaks highly of you and he's a top notch man himself — so what better recommendation could we have?'

Tom was pleased, but tried to contain his reaction.

'Thank you.'

'Tell me, Tom, what do you think about the international situation?'

It was the man from London, Squadron Leader Mayhew, who posed the question.

'Well . . .' Tom faltered. In truth he knew generally of the goings on with Herr Hitler, but he had been far too consumed by his job and rugby to really follow in detail.

'I know there was a problem, but Mr Chamberlain has fixed that, hasn't he?'

The two men looked at each other and Tom's heart sank. He was unprepared for this sort of thing. He thought he was just going to go up in the air again, hadn't realized there was to be an interview, as if he were applying for a job.

'Hmmm.' Squadron Leader Mayhew pulled a sheaf of documents from his brief-case.

'Mr Roxham. It is possible that another war might come along sometime. The object of this course of flying instruction, you have applied for, is to make sure we have a reserve pool of aircrew in case of such an event.'

Tom nodded, trying to look serious, as the man continued. 'If we do decide to take you on board for what is an extremely subsided course of instruction you do realize we, the government that is, expect to get something back for it. It's not just a cheap way of learning to fly for your own amusement.'

Tom frowned. 'Of course. Mr Hayes said something about that.'

'Good. Because I have a contract here. It means that in the event of any type of emergency that the government declares, they can call you up for full-time duty in any capacity, at any rank, in any aviation service of their choice.'

He lowered the paper. 'Now, is that perfectly clear before you sign it?'

Amazed, Tom's jaw dropped. 'Are you offering this to me?'

The two men looked at each other again. Trubshaw actually smiled.

'Yes, Tom, sign it and we'll start your training immediately.'

He took the proffered fountain pen from Squadron Leader Mayhew and wrote his signature where the latter indicated with his finger on the official looking document.

'Well done, young man.' Mayhew, with one hand on his shoulder, pumped his hand with the other, followed by Trubshaw.

The Squadron Leader picked up his

briefcase and made to go.

'Got to get off. Need to be in Bristol by five o'clock. Two more possibles down there.'

Trubshaw showed him to the door.

Out in the hangar, Mayhew said softly to his colleague. 'I wonder how many of these boys really think they are going to end up in the service of the country?' He shook his head sadly.

'See you next week, Ted.'

When Trubshaw came back into his office it was to find Tom Roxham, flushed and excited, looking for all the world like a schoolboy who had just been picked to captain the first eleven.

'Right then, Tom, let's get you kitted up.'

But for once, thanks to the tone of Mayhew's voice, the flying school boss didn't feel as enthusiastic as in the past.

Fay was in a turquoise silk ball-gown that floated from her waist to the floor. She carried a matching clutch bag, with her grandmother's small natural pearls in two strings around her neck. Her hair was swept up and held with a comb made of mother of pearl.

Jeremy was bowled over by her appearance and a radiance that he'd never noticed before.

'Fay, you look stunning,' he had managed when she had come down the stairs to the hall.

Now they were dancing a foxtrot. His arm encompassed her tiny waist, his large hand on her hip feeling every movement as they swung around the floor. Jeremy was conscious of other men's eyes on her. It made him feel proud and possessive all in the same moment.

The group of three dances ended and they made their way back to the table, where the others sat, talking and drinking, champagne bottles in ice buckets all around the tables.

'More shampoo, darlings?' One of the company, Monty Dytham, white tie undone and hanging down, waved a bottle at them, cigarette in the other hand.

'Not for me, Monty.'

Fay reached her chair and sat down. Jeremy found his glass and accepted a top up before Monty wandered off, his lanky frame looking even longer in his penguin suit.

Jeremy spun a chair and sat down, arms resting on the top, legs straddling the sides.

'Fay, where were you last week?'

She sipped her bubbling drink, playing for time. 'I've told you, with a friend I used to know at school.'

'Who?'

Fay started to get annoyed. 'Nobody you know.'

Even Jeremy detected the resentment.

The sound of the orchestra starting up again, caused many of the couples to get up and move in the direction of the wooden dance floor, leaving them alone on their side of the table.

'What about next weekend Fay, I thought we might go to Southampton? The *Mary's* docking from New York and the Pearlmans are on board. We could welcome them with a party — should be fun?'

At least Fay had a real excuse to hide behind. 'Oh Jeremy, that sounds wonderful but unfortunately I'm up in town — got some interviews with several singers.'

Disappointed Jeremy frowned. 'Meetings? About what?'

'Daddy is setting them up — wants me to get on with looking for a real job — says it's about time.'

Downcast, he asked, 'Does that cover the Sunday as well?'

'Afraid so. I shall be far too tired, and there might be a follow up call.'

'Which hotel are you staying at, I could come up and —'

'Jeremy *no*. I'm far too involved and in

any case I've got plans.'

Why on earth did she have to add that?

'I see.'

He looked so glum that Fay took pity on him.

'It was very sweet of you to ask me. I'm sure it will be fun, so do it all the same. Take Audrey, or Pam.'

Jeremy frowned. 'It's *you* I'm asking, Fay, not them. And what are these other plans?'

Thinking quickly she said, 'I might go to a recital if there's time.'

He couldn't stop himself. 'On your own?'

Her eyes flashed. 'What exactly does that mean, Jeremy?'

This conversation was not going as he wanted at all.

'Sorry, just being inquisitive.'

He refreshed his glass to the brim.

They lapsed into a strained silence, listening to the sound of the dancers and the music — saxophones and trumpets underlining the soft crooner singing 'Blue Moon'. Everybody seemed to be having a gay time which made it worse.

Jeremy broke the strained atmosphere by downing the last of the champagne in his glass and standing up. 'Right, I'm going for a pee.' He staggered off, bumping into a chair.

After a few moments Fay got up herself, fed up with the whole evening. If she could, she would have left right then and there, but decided to go for a walk around the inter-connected marquees, just to see the sights. In one area there was a jazz band, all dressed up in green striped waistcoats with boaters on their heads, belting out traditional noisy jazz, in another, people were dancing the Valletta to an old time orchestra.

The last marquee held the variety acts. A crowd was watching a man doing card tricks, whilst in the far corner Alfonso the Great was passing swords through a box containing his beautiful assistant Nina, cheered on by the cream of the Cotswolds. She stood for a while, enjoying the spectacle, but eventually drifted away to the all-night buffet provided extra to the supper they had enjoyed. In the middle of the long bar opposite was a multi-tiered champagne fountain, with a noisy bunch around it.

Somebody pushed a glass into her hand.

'Come on, enjoy it while you can — you never know when the train's going to hit the buffers.'

She frowned. What was the idiot talking about? But she swallowed a generous measure of champagne all the same.

On the way back to their table she was suddenly conscious of the fact that this year there seemed to be more heavy drinking going on than ever before, and a wildness in people. All the party were back at the table, one of the girls sitting on her escort's lap, giggling as she traced his lips with a finger dipped in champagne.

Jeremy glanced up as she approached. 'Where the hell have you been?'

Fay flinched at the harshness of his tone and then felt her temper flaring. 'I beg your pardon?'

He looked around at them all.

'Seems you prefer the company of others to being here with us.'

Fay stamped her foot. 'How dare you. You left me with an empty table, don't forget.'

The others stopped chattering and looked at them. He appeared to be about to say something aggressive, then changed his mind.

'I was worried — thought you might have gone home.'

From the look on the faces of the others she knew that was a lie.

Just at that moment a group of men, arms outstretched, ran around one behind the other weaving between the tables making aeroplane noises. Women were screaming with laughter and goading them on. Several bottles of champagne were shaken and aimed as they 'flew past'. When one of them was hit by a flying cork he pretended to be shot down, making a howling engine noise before 'crashing', throwing himself bodily on to the table, sending drinks and bottles everywhere.

He rolled on to his back yelling, 'crash and burned, crash and burned'.

A woman then threw herself on top of him. Under their combined weight the table collapsed.

In the ensuing uproar, as the staff rushed to help, they were hindered by staggering and laughing men and women who seemed to have lost all sense of decorum.

But Fay had stopped worrying about what had taken hold of everybody.

All she had ringing in her ears was 'crash and burned.'

A sudden irrational fear for Tom's safety took hold of her.

CHAPTER NINE

Tom Roxham watched the countryside slide past effortlessly at eighty miles an hour as the train raced across the flat land on the approach to Reading. The telegraph poles flicked by, the wires strung between them rising and falling, rising and falling.

The engine was No. 408 *Windsor Castle* that had backed on to them at Gloucester, still in pristine livery after royal duties the year before.

With each passing mile he felt the excitement rising. It had been a long week. Hardly a waking moment had passed when he hadn't thought of her.

With a blast of its whistle, the train slowed to forty miles an hour through Reading Station. The wide platforms slid past with glimpses of people, advertising hoardings, luggage trolleys, the W.H. Smith Newsagent kiosk, waiting rooms, a covered footbridge, station-master's office, left luggage and milk churns, until finally the platform narrowed, tapered away and was gone.

The carriage lurched as they went over points, then the clickety-click of the wheel bogies on the track started to increase in frequency as they picked up speed, heading for London.

With a sudden roar they crossed a road bridge with a brief glimpse of a main thoroughfare with red trolley buses. Soon they were out in the country again. Every now and then, as they rounded a curve, he could see their locomotive, steam spurting from its cylinder, the connecting rod on the three, big driving wheels moving rapidly up and down, up and down, smoke from its bronze chimney streaming out to roll lazily away across the meadows. They were fairly rattling along. He looked at his watch. They would arrive right on time.

He wondered how Fay was getting on with the singers. He'd had a quick note from her. He took it out of his wallet to read yet again. It was the opening and closing bits he liked.

Dear Tom and ending with *all my love, Fay. X*

It was the X that got him.

She had warned him that she had three auditions, and she couldn't say definitely when she could get away, but please, did he mind waiting?

He'd have waited until the end of time, when Paddington Station was being excavated by some future civilization — his white bones still holding what remained of the note.

He chuckled out loud, making the lady opposite look up, frowning, from her latest Agatha Christie novel.

Fay had come up the day before, taking a taxi to Claridges. Daddy had already booked a suite for her. The top-hatted commissioner had opened the car door and directed a boy from porterage to transfer her suitcase. She selected a ten shilling note and told the driver to keep the change.

In her room she pulled off her gloves as she looked around. It was tastefully furnished with a large sofa and two easy chairs.

Fresh flowers had been placed on a small table together with the latest editions of *Country Life, Picture Post* and the *Illustrated London News.* Doors led through to a separate bedroom and bathroom.

'Anything else, madam?'

'Thank you, no.'

She tipped again, giving the porter a florin. When she was alone she removed her hat and coat and took off her shoes, pushing fingers into her hair as she looked into the dressing-table mirror.

Fay picked up a magazine and lay with her feet up on the sofa. Later, she would be meeting Aunt Constance for dinner in the restaurant. In the morning at ten o'clock, she was going to the Queen's Hall for the auditions. The first was Terence O'Neil, the Irish Tenor, whose speciality was Celtic-type ballads. Later she was being interviewed by Sir Trevor Keynes, the baritone, who needed an accompanist for his tour of Australia and the Far East. The time abroad was something that worried Fay, now that she had met Tom, but it was a splendid opportunity. Finally, in the afternoon Kathleen Schroeder was giving her the chance to show how good she was at the unique skill of the accompanist. For Fay, all of them were a worrying challenge — at least they had been. Now, all her excited thoughts were on meeting Tom, being with him again for a whole evening in the bright lights of London Town. She flicked through the pages of the *Illustrated London News* hardly taking in the beautiful big sepia photographs.

The last week had been awful. So it was wonderful to lie there and not have to mislead her mother and father and put up

171

with guilty feelings about Jeremy. All she had to do was think about Tom — without a care in the world. Well, one. Had she dreamed it all last week? Would he really be there tomorrow? It was just so unbelievable, *being in love.*

With a start she suddenly realized that was the first time she had used the expression, even in her thoughts. She was in love.

She was in *love.*

Fay bit her lower lip. Was it just a girlish crush? She swiftly discounted that. What she felt for Tom was much more. It was a calmness of mind: perversely a contentment as well as excitement, a sense of security, a sense of oneness. And he *was* good looking. Not for the first time she wondered just what he saw in her. It wasn't as if she was that beautiful or anything.

Fay tried to imagine how his week had gone — how much flying he had done. Her heart positively ached to be with him; just the two of them high above the clouds, alone in the universe.

She set the magazine down and decided to ring Aunt Constance to make sure that she wasn't going to get in the way of tomorrow night. Her aunt would no doubt be encouraged by her parents to chaperon her where possible.

The hotel operator answered.

'I'd like to be connected to Speedwell 4359 please.'

'Certainly, madam, one moment please.'

After a delay the voice of her aunt's butler came on the line.

'Lady Greenwood's residence.'

'Good evening, Harberry, Fay Rossiter here. Is my aunt available?'

'Oh good evening, miss. Yes, she was expecting you to ring. I'll just put you through.'

There was a clatter as the heavy bakelite phone was put down.

She knew her aunt's hall well and imagined it now, with the telephone lying on the gold veneered wall table with its ornate framed mirror above, the white and black squares of the marble floor with the scattering of Persian rugs. She could hear the grandfather clock striking the hour and the tap tapping of her aunt's silver-topped walking stick sounding long before the phone was picked up.

'Fay dear, is everything all right?' The slightly tremulous voice came down the line.

'Yes Aunt, just wanted to let you know I have arrived safely and it's room 203.'

'Oh thank you, my dear, that's very considerate of you. We are meeting at eight o'clock in the dining-room, is that right?'

'Indeed. I'm looking forward to it very much and I am so sorry that I can't meet you again tomorrow night, but I've already booked to hear Myra Hess with a' — she had a sudden rush to the head — 'young man I met at a friend's party the other week. I hope you understand?'

'I see, well, of course, Fay.'

The elderly woman chuckled. 'You're only young once. Is he handsome, dear?'

'Very, Aunty — you'd like him.'

'Do you have a photograph of him? I'd love to see what he looks like.'

Fay said, 'No.'

They ended the call by saying how much they were each looking forward to seeing one another that evening.

Thoughtfully, Fay replaced the receiver. What her aunt had asked set her thinking. Perhaps they could have one done while they were together.

All of a sudden it became a burning urgency. She picked up the telephone again and got through to the desk.

Yes, they could arrange for a photographer — at what time? She asked for around six o'clock next day.

'Very well, madam. When you are ready can you come to the desk at your convenience and we will show you to the room we usually use?'

Fay replaced the receiver and wandered to the window, looking down on the street below. It was dusk now, and she could see the limousines and taxis drawing into the kerb, disgorging women in lavish furs, wearing hats of all shapes and sizes. After the cloche-type of the twenties the fashion now allowed for an enormous range of textures and designs.

In the bedroom she slipped out of her dress and pulled on a silk dressing-gown. She studied the row of dresses in the wardrobe the hotel maid had unpacked for her, selecting one for that night. She still couldn't make up her mind what to wear tomorrow.

The meeting with her aunt in the pillared and palm fringed restaurant was hugely enjoyable. The elderly lady was as jolly as ever, still with a twinkle in her eye and had teased her about this boy she had met.

With a sinking feeling Fay realized Constance's memory was as good as ever. After she had seen her on her way, Fay went to bed early and after a restless night was up and bathed by eight o'clock. She had her breakfast in her room, then, at 9.15, she took a taxi to the Queen's Hall, to be met by the agent of Terence O'Neil.

He showed her to the piano which had been tuned for that night's concert, to be conducted by Sir Thomas Beecham.

They went through the music for the popular tenor, who appeared twenty minutes later dressed in a grey double-breasted Savile Row suit and sporting a large carnation. He seized Fay's hand and clasping it in both of his, gave it a kiss.

'Miss Rossiter, it's a pleasure to meet you.'

Later when she went to remove her jacket he was there in a flash helping her. Fay sat at the piano, uncomfortably conscious that O'Neil's eyes were on her the whole time.

When the session was finished, he enthused over her performance, but his agent was more circumspect. She was told that there were others to audition.

Fay spent the next hour sitting in the stalls, listening as his other pianists performed with him. The whole process was repeated again for the eminent Sir Trevor Keynes, a tall imposing man who hardly smiled. Fay was asked to play some difficult Lieder and felt she had been a little slow in coming in — especially in Schumann's Liederkries.

There was a break for lunch which she took near Liberty's. Kathleen Schroeder was punctual, and at 2.35 Fay was free, with promises from all three agents of a decision by post early in the week.

Fay was exuberant. She would be at Paddington to meet Tom in plenty of time. Instead of taking a taxi she decided to go by the underground — something she had never done before.

The whole journey was exciting, with the rushing of warm air as the train came crashing into the station, the hiss of air pressure as the doors opened and closed, then the dark tunnels with cables rising and falling outside the window as they clattered around unseen bends. For Fay loved watching her fellow passengers, some strap hanging, others sitting staring blankly straight ahead or with heads buried in newspapers, it felt liberating, like being a girl in London with a job.

She had to change lines, walking with the scurrying crowds as they went their various ways, through archways or up escalators. She finally boarded an older bigger train, in a tunnel with twin lines and not very deep. It trundled along, a sudden burst of noise and the flashing lights of a train going in the opposite direction making her jump. The name Bayswater slid by on the white tiled walls as the train squealed to a halt. Only one more stop to go. Fay looked at her watch. She was an hour early.

The train had slowed to a steady pace as they started to slide through the brick canyons and short tunnels of the suburbs of West London.

Now they were down to a crawl, passing under great gantries of signals and traversing multiple points as rails weaved and criss-crossed on the approach to Paddington: locomotives waited in The Roads, being coaled and watered, or turned around on tables, ready to be signalled in to the platform, reversing tenders first, to be coupled to their coaches.

They finally drew slowly in under the great canopy of Brunel's masterpiece.

The light dimmed as the grime from the daily assault of steam and smoke turned the glass panes opaque. Almost imperceptibly they came to a halt, but even before they had stopped, doors were being opened and people were stepping out on to the platform.

Tom took his time, knowing that he was early. As he wandered down the platform *Windsor Castle*'s safety valve opened. A blast of steam under pressure roared up into the vast space beneath the vaulted glass roof.

The fireman had climbed down and was

checking the sand box while the driver leaned out and watched him. On the main concourse Tom checked his watch. She wouldn't be there for some time yet. He went to the gents, then washed his hands and combed his hair. Outside again, he crossed to the large model of a King class locomotive in a glass case. When his coin dropped the wheels turned and the piston and coupling rods worked. When it finished Tom looked around and decided to wander over to the arrival and departure board that dominated the gates to the platforms. It was where they had agreed to meet.

It was a few seconds before he realized she was standing a few feet away, turning, as he recognized her, to see him at the very same instant. With a rush they met, Tom sweeping her off her feet and swinging her round as they kissed and hugged, grinning like a couple of Cheshire cats.

Fay whispered, 'Darling, you're early.'

He set her gently down, 'Look who's talking. How did it go?'

She shrugged. 'We shall see.'

With arms wrapped around each other they just stood there, beaming at each other, until he asked, 'What would you like to do?'

She looked at her watch.

'Tom, I hope you don't mind, but I want

179

to have a photo done of us.'

He looked down at her, grinning. 'Have you got a box camera?'

Shaking her head, she said, 'I want a photo of us *together*. I've arranged an appointment with the photographers at my hotel. Is that all right?'

He squeezed her, feeling her lithe body against his.

'Of course, where's that?'

'Claridges, at six o'clock.'

'Claridges!' He relaxed his grip on her.

She looked worried. 'Is there something wrong?'

Tom shrugged. 'Expensive place, I'm not dressed very well.'

Fay stood back, took in his Harris sports jacket and flannels. 'You look just fine. Really.'

'Come on, we'll go there straight away and have some tea — treats on me. Then we've got the whole evening to ourselves — your choice.'

Full of misgivings he reluctantly let her lead him by the hand across the concourse to the side of the terminus where the road came down from Praed Street. A line of taxis stood waiting.

The deep snort of a locomotive broke through the noise of a motorized chain of luggage trolleys. They had to wait for it to pass before they could reach the first vehicle. Fay leant into the driver's window which was open.

'Claridges, please.'

'Very good, miss.'

Tom opened the door and she got in, sliding across the seat. He couldn't help but notice her legs and trim ankles, before stepping in after her, slamming the door shut behind him.

Studiously they sat in opposite corners, his hand in the strap beside him as the taxi swung in a tight circle and headed out into the bustling streets of London. He didn't tell her that this was the first time he had been in a taxi.

Now as they weaved amongst the red double-decker buses towards Marble Arch he felt a heady excitement. He glanced across at her, at this girl who had changed his life. She sat demurely looking out of the window, until she turned and became conscious of his interest. Her face broke into a warm smile. She gave the tiniest of nods of understanding. He did the same. There was no need for speech. With Park Lane behind them they entered the streets of Mayfair. Tom didn't know what to expect but the unassuming red brick building was not what he'd imagined. Everybody knew about Claridges — heads of state stayed there. The uniformed commissionaire stepped forward and opened his door. Tom got out, turned and helped Fay.

'Thank you.'

She made to pay but Tom had his wallet out, conscious of his masculine dignity.

'I'll do this.'

He watched as his ten bob note was taken and he waited for his change. When he turned around it was to catch Fay giving the commissionaire something, who touched the brim of his top hat.

As they entered he whispered to her, 'I would have done that.'

Fay realized he was feeling sensitive and clung to his arm, saying dismissively, 'It was for something he did for me this morning.'

The main doors were opened for them.

Feeling a little uneasy, he took in the opulent foyer with its paintings, china vases and the all pervading smell of cigar smoke — the sight and smell of wealth. A group of elegantly dressed women passed by as he followed her to the room where afternoon tea was being served.

They settled down into deep luxurious armchairs, a pianist in white dinner jacket playing gently in the background.

He looked around, realizing not for the first time that they came from different worlds.

After she had ordered tea and a selection of cakes she leaned forward excitedly.

'Now tell me, how's the flying going?'

Tom forgot the whole intimidating atmosphere as he filled her in on his luck at being accepted so quickly into the Civil Air Guard Scheme.

Her face clouded when he explained what it was all about.

'Oh dear, it means you might be called up then?'

He shrugged. 'That's not going to happen is it, and if it did, well. . . . ?' He pushed out his lower lip. 'I'd have to go like everybody else. Anyway the flying has been terrific, but it's a strange old business, sometimes everything goes well, at others nothing goes right. I can manage straight and level pretty well and some banks and turns, but for the life of me I can't keep it straight on the ground — I swing all over the place. So I've yet to master a good take-off.'

As he continued, telling her about spinning and stalling, Fay listened in rapture, but, in the end, her expression dissolved into glumness.

'I do so envy you, Tom. Daddy won't help

me at all — positively forbids it.'

He felt her disappointment keenly, as if it was his own and reached out a hand.

'You will, don't you worry. If, *when,* I get licensed, I'll take you up and teach you myself.'

She bit her lower lip. 'Is that a promise?'

'It is.'

Fay got up and came around the table and kissed him on the cheek and ruffled his hair.

Tom Roxham felt so tall that nobody in the room mattered one bit. He was on top of the world.

The waitress came back and set out a china tea pot and cups, a small milk jug, tea strainer and bowl and another with sugar cubes and tongs. There was a plate with lemon slices, and finally an ornamental cake stand, the waitress slowly turning it to allow them to make their choices. She poured tea into their cups then with a, 'Please call if you need further assistance,' they were left alone.

Fay offered him the milk jug, then took the lemon bowl and placed a slice in her cup. She raised the bone china to her lips and took a sip.

'What are we going to do tonight?'

He looked down, stirring his tea having put in three cubes of sugar.

'I wondered if you'd like to go to a Metropolitan in the Edgware Road — Arthur Askey and George Formby are playing there?'

Fay nodded her approval. 'But can we get in without booking?'

He drank his tea. 'I think so, but we might have to queue, is that all right?'

'Of course.'

And then they just lapsed into that comfortable silence that had happened before — being physically close to each other was all that they seemed to need.

The pianist tinkled gently in the background, coincidentally playing, 'I only had eyes for you'. When they'd finished, Fay asked for the bill. Tom started to reach for his wallet again. 'No, let me —'

She cut him off. 'Tom, I'm signing for it — let Daddy pay.'

With his thoughts on the tickets that night, he smiled. 'Fine.'

In the foyer, Fay turned to him.

'Would you mind waiting while I change my clothes, this suit is not what I want to see on the photo, or be out in tonight?'

'Of course, take your time.'

He sat down on an elegant couch and observed the 'nobs' at close quarters in one of the top hotels of the world. Mentally he had to pinch himself.

Upstairs, Fay slipped out of her jacket and dropped her skirt, kicking it away as she rushed to the wardrobe and took out the dress she had decided on. It had sleeves cut off just beneath the elbows, with a ribbon tie around her neck. She pulled her waist in with the attached thin belt, causing the short extra layer of material that fell just around her hips to flare out. Fay selected another pair of shoes with a matching bag, then sat at her dressing-table.

For the evening, she used a little more make-up and a richer lipstick. Satisfied, she tidied her hair, but didn't put on the little hat with a small feather — she wanted to be bareheaded for the photograph. The last thing she did was puff scent around her neck.

When she came tripping down the staircase he looked up and saw her straight away.

Fay chuckled with pleasure as he stood up and gasped, 'Oh my God, Fay, you're beautiful.'

Wincing, she chided him. 'Don't be silly, I'm just an ordinary country girl. Now come on, the photographer is waiting.' But she was pleased all the same.

They went to the desk and a young porter escorted them to a room on the ground floor. Inside a *chaise-longue* stood in front of a blank screen with a jardiniere to one side with an aspidistra in a brass bowl on top. The photographer was an elderly man with a wing collar, but his camera, mounted on a wooden tripod, was the latest from Germany. He fussed around, using a light meter and moving screens. Fay, seated on the *chaise* with Tom standing behind, whispered out of the side of her mouth, 'This is all a bit too Victorian for my liking.'

His hand on her shoulder gave a gentle squeeze. She placed hers over his, then turned back and said to the photographer, 'Can we have something less formal please. Both of us side by side would be nice — after all, this is the twentieth century.'

The man winced, but the photos that he later developed by the red light of the dark room, showed two young people, holding hands: two young people full of life, hope and love.

CHAPTER TEN

They did get in to the show, laughing as Arthur Askey bounded on shouting, 'Hello Playmates,' then singing along as George Formby, strumming his ukelele, went through a medley of songs old and new.

When they came out there was a light rain falling. They hopped on one of the droves of buses heading towards Marble Arch, crashing down on to the bench seat, laughing as they caught their breath.

The conductor came clattering down the stairs and stood with practised ease, legs apart, as the bus jerked through its gears.

'Where to, mate?'

Tom looked at her. 'Do you know the nearest stop for your hotel?'

'No, not really.'

The conductor turned his attention to her. 'Where you staying, miss?'

'Claridges.'

He grinned. 'Cor blimey, luv — only the

best for you.'

He told them to get off in Park Lane — he'd tell them when. They'd have to walk from there. He moved further on up the aisle, bouncing off seats to maintain his balance.

'Tom, I never thought, where are *you* staying tonight?'

Her voice was full of concern.

He shrugged. 'Sorry, but I can't afford to stay. I'll catch one of the workmen trains.'

Her face fell.

'Oh.' There was a silence for a second or two as they watched the surging crowds on the pavement. They had reached the bottom of the Edgware Road, before she said in a low voice, 'So I won't see you tomorrow then?'

'Afraid not.'

Tom was conscious that she was looking very miserable and felt rotten.

More silence followed then she said, 'I may be asked to play again in the morning, but afterwards I was looking forward to doing something together. We don't know when we'll be able to meet again, do we?'

He squeezed her hand, and said, 'We will — and very soon.'

The bus stopped outside a cinema on the corner with Oxford Street and people crowded on, filling the standing room in the aisle. Tom got up to let a woman sit down and stood over Fay as he hung on to a strap. She frowned up at him, one hand gripping his raincoat, as if to make sure he didn't leave her.

Tom felt depressed, but then again, he always knew he would be leaving her — hadn't realized though that she thought he was staying overnight.

The bus roared around Marble Arch and entered Park Lane.

The bell rang once and from somewhere near the front of the crowded bus the conductor's voice rang out. 'This stop for Claridges.'

As Fay struggled to stand and Tom made room for her, all eyes seemed to be on them. They were the only ones to get off. As the bus roared away, Fay slipped her hand through his and they began to walk.

'I've had a wonderful idea.'

He was relieved that she seemed to have perked up again. 'What's that?'

She stopped walking, forcing him to face her as she took a deep breath and said, eyes shining. 'Tom, don't think I'm being silly or anything like that, but why don't you come and stay with me?'

Startled, he began to protest.

'Fay — I couldn't . . .'

She interrupted him. 'It's a suite — so I'll have the bedroom, you can have the sofa.'

Her face beamed. 'It solves erything.'

Tom was taken aback. Frightened at the thought of them being together all night. If anyone found out . . .

Weakly, he stammered, 'But I haven't got a razor or anything — I'll look awful in the morning.'

Exasperated, she snapped, 'Don't be silly, married women see their husbands like that all the time.'

As soon as it came out she realized she'd said aloud what she had been day-dreaming about for days. The words hung in the air until he heard himself say, 'Will I be your husband one day, Fay?'

Blushing madly, she looked away. 'It's the man that proposes — remember?'

He didn't hesitate — shocking himself. 'Will you marry me, Fay?'

Although the breath seemed to have gone from her lungs and her heart first stopped then raced away she finally managed a matter-of-fact sounding, 'Of course.'

They both looked at each other in dazed amazement. They had only known each other for such a short time. Fay leant against him and he wrapped his arms around her. He could feel her trembling slightly so he tried to explain.

'I had no idea that was coming, I. . . .'

She suddenly came up on her toes and held her lips up to be kissed.

When they eventually parted, he gave a yell and picking her up in his arms, swung her around and around as she squealed with delight — so much so that two cloaked policewomen, walking on the other side of the road, paused and looked their way. He set her down again and they both waved to the constables before resuming their walk.

Tom suddenly became serious.

'Oh my God — your parents. They won't be happy will they?'

Fay, laughing, hugged him around the waist.

'No, probably not. But they'll get over it.'

But his gloom was not to be shaken off so quickly.

'Fay, I've got no money. I don't earn enough yet to support you, I can never keep you in the style you are used to.'

She squeezed his arm. 'Stop worrying. It's you I want and, in any case, we won't be marrying tomorrow, will we?'

Ruefully he sighed. 'I suppose not — though I would love to.'

She looked up searchingly. 'No doubts?'

'None at all.'

She persisted. 'You haven't known me very long. Are you really sure?'

'*Really* sure. And what about you?'

'Oh, I knew straight away.'

Tom tweaked her nose. 'Come on now, you were very haughty with me.'

She stuck the tip of her tongue out at him. 'It was fear. My mind and body were in turmoil at such a beautiful sight. I'd never seen anybody like you before.'

Playfully, he half-turned her and slapped her bottom. 'More respect, young lady, if you are going to be my wife.'

Fay giggled nervously at the thought then said, 'Fay Roxham has a nice ring, don't you think?'

'Very nice.'

They walked on again, before she broke the silence.

'What about your parents, Tom? They might not like me — it works both ways you know.'

'They'll love you, but. . . .' He frowned. 'We live in a terraced house, Fay, pretty basic, I. . . .'

She stopped dead and shook herself free. 'Now that's the last of that sort of talk, Tom, or I won't believe you really want to marry me. Stop putting yourself down.'

He pulled a face. 'I was just pointing out how different we. . . .'

Her eyes flashed. 'Are you going to marry me or not?'

Holding her firmly by the shoulders he said, 'Yes I am.'

She sighed. 'Good. Then no more talk about this or that. Right?'

Ruefully he nodded. 'Right.'

For a while they walked in silence, getting used to the extent of what had changed. It had been so sudden, but at the same time, so natural. That they would have got around to talking about it after months of tentative and disrupted dates seemed certain, but the speed and abruptness had overwhelmed them.

The main entrance to Claridges appeared whilst they were still deep in contemplation of their changed future.

Tom stopped in his tracks.

'How are we going to do this? I can't just walk in with you when you get your key. They'll throw me out and you as well, if you're not careful. Your parents would be shocked.'

Fay shook her head. 'Leave it to me. We're going in for a drink first. Let me take the lead — but look a little more cheerful would you?' She giggled, 'After all, you are with me.'

They started in.

Just level with the commissionaires, one of whom opened the door, she paused and said loudly, 'Really, you might be a bloody *lord* — but if you keep on like that you can get another room — husband or not.'

He felt the blood rushing into his face.

The door shut behind them. One commissionaire rolled his eyes.

'Oops,' he said to his mate quietly, 'Wouldn't put money on His Lordship getting his end away tonight, would you?'

They went to the bar, ordered a dry martini for Fay and a double gin and tonic for Tom, he'd asked her for something refreshing and good for his nerves after her little 'joke'.

He lifted his glass to hers and they clinked them together, eyes meeting over the rims.

'To us.'

'To us,' she responded.

Two more and an hour later he looked happily around. 'What happens now?'

She set her empty glass down and twirled the olive on a stick.

'You go up the staircase to the third floor, wait, then come down to the second. Take your time. When I get the key I'll go straight up — room 203 — and leave the door open.'

He'd never had a gin and tonic before, let alone three doubles but now he was glad of its fizzy stimulating effect. As he finished off the last one, he experienced a pleasant indifference to reality and the sense of loosening inhibitions glowed warmly in him.

She pulled the olive off the stick with her teeth and ate it. 'Right, I'm ready. Off you go.'

Tom smiled at her. 'Very well. I shall do as you say.'

He tried to be more serious but everything seemed altogether lighter. 'You sure you don't mind, my occupying your sofa?'

Fay gave him a warning look. 'No, now off you go, Tom, the staircase is over there.'

He hauled himself out of the leather chair and then picked up his raincoat. 'Goodnight then, Fay — sweet dreams.'

With that he gave a huge grin, winked and sauntered away.

Anxiously Fay looked at his retreating back. She hadn't realized that he was so unused to drinking. All the other young men she knew, especially Jeremy, could drink like fish — not always holding it mind you, but the amount Tom had had would have been nothing to them. She felt a frisson of excitement at the sight of his broad back and the thought that they would be so close that night.

Wasting no time she got her key from the desk.

'Goodnight, *Miss* Rossiter.'

Feeling guilty, she smiled fleetingly and headed for the metal gated lifts and their attendants.

When she stepped out on her floor it was to find Tom nonchalantly leaning against the wall waiting for her. Fortunately there was nobody around. Horrified, she rushed to her door.

'For god's sake, Tom.'

Her hand was shaking so much she dropped the key. He stooped down and picked it up, holding it like a trophy before opening the door for her all in one smooth movement. He stood back and held out his arm.

'After you, madam.'

Shaking her head she quickly walked in, pulling him roughly after her, closing the door and leaning back against it.

'Phew. Remind me never to let you have strong drink again, Tom Roxham.'

He grinned down at her. 'You really are beautiful my little wife-to-be.'

She prodded him with her finger, forcing him back until he fell over on to the sofa.

'You — stay there while I use the bath-room — then you can have the run of out here.'

He sat looking up at her, like a contrite schoolboy. She so desperately wanted to ruffle his hair, sit with him, kiss him, but the intimacy of being in the room together was overwhelming. She was afraid of what might happen, afraid of her own reaction. What they were already doing felt wicked enough.

When she came out of the bathroom he'd taken his jacket off. Those shoulders looked even more powerful, highlighted by his braces.

Feeling awkward she shuffled forward. 'It's all yours. Goodnight then, Tom.'

He sheepishly mumbled, 'Sorry if I was a bit reckless. Don't know what came over me.'

Suddenly Fay reached up and kissed him lightly on the lips. It felt like a hugely dar-ing thing to be doing in those surroundings.

She stepped back. 'Sleep tight.'

With that she made for her room.

He called after her. 'Fay, you did say you were going to marry me didn't you — it wasn't a dream?'

She paused with her bedroom door open. 'It was no dream. You proposed, I accepted.'

Tom smiled, that warm crinkling of skin around the eyes that she so loved. 'That's good.'

She nodded, slowly closed the door and leant back against it, her heart thumping.

Later, as she undressed, she was conscious that on the other side of the door was a man she physically desired — and who desired her. Tom only had to open that door, and she would be at his mercy.

And the most alarming thing was, she was half hoping he would.

Quickly she lifted her arms and let her silk nightdress drop over her naked body before scambling hurriedly into the bed. She turned out the light and pulled the sheet up to her chin. In the darkness she focused on the door handle that glinted in the light that came through a chink in the curtains.

If it turned she didn't know what she would do, how she would react, so muddled were her feelings. But one thing was certain, she would be disappointed in him. She loved him for the complete feeling of security, trust and respect that she felt held in when in his presence. But there was a rashness in her body, as well as her mind.

After half an hour of staring at the handle, the light under the edge of the door went out. He must be about to go to sleep.

She waited another ten minutes, but there was no creak of floorboards, no tapping on her door, no muffled calling of her name. She had been right in her trust of him.

Fay turned over, the silk of her nightdress pulled at her hip and in a flash the genie of her physical madness was released. She was out of the bed and opening the door before she knew what she was doing. His startled figure started to rear up but she pushed him back, cupping his face with both hands. The kiss was fierce, lip bruising. When she broke away she grabbed his hand forcing it under the top of her nightdress, taking it to her breast that was hanging down as she leant over him. It was like an electric shock when his calloused hand made contact. She guided his fingers to her nipple which was so hard it was hurting.

For a few seconds she let his hand, skin rough against her softness, caress the throbbing tip, her breathing more and more laboured.

Through the silk material of her nightdress she was suddenly aware of the effect she was having on him and, scared and excited all at the same time, she pulled his hand free, kissed him again — on the forehead, and fled back to her room. Over her shoulder she called, 'Tom, I love you.'

She closed the door, got into bed and pulled the sheets quickly up over her head.

She lay there trembling until, eventually, exhausted, she went to sleep.

Tom was on his back looking up in the dark at the unseen ceiling, waiting until his blood cooled, not daring to move.

She came to very slowly, eyeing the room without any real sense of change. It was only when she moved, and found her legs entwined in a knot of sheets and blankets that she realized that something was wrong.

Her lips were dry. When she ran her tongue over them they were tender and slightly swollen.

Sitting upright one of her breasts felt sore.

And then it all came back, and with it a tremendous feeling of humiliation. What had he thought of her? She'd behaved like an alley cat.

Fay got out of bed and pulled on her dressing-gown, tempted to dress immediately.

Timidly she turned the handle and eased the door open, peering round to see him.

The sofa was empty. She crept into the room, one hand holding the top of her robe tightly around her neck.

'Tom?'

There was no reply. She advanced further into the room. It was empty, and the bathroom door was open.

He'd gone.

Devastated she cried, 'Tom' again, in despair. He'd left her. He must have been disgusted at her behaviour. She slumped down on the empty sofa and felt the tears welling up in her eyes.

What *had* she done? She just sat there, devastated.

A tap came on the door, and a maid's voice called, 'Room Service.'

Fay stumbled to the door and opened it to find a maid holding a silver tray with teapot, cup and rack of toast. But she only had eyes for the rose lying across the middle. The girl came in and set the tray down on the table. 'Sir Tom says he is waiting for you in the breakfast-room, but that there is no need to hurry, he has coffee and the morning papers.'

Fay's jaw dropped.

'Will there be anything else, madam?'

'No. No thank you.'

The girl turned to go.

'Oh — yes, there is.'

The girl paused, waited expectantly.

'Could you take a message to *Sir Tom,* say I'll be as quick as I can but, I haven't had my bath yet . . . oh, and thank him for being here for breakfast — tell him I thought. . . .'

'Yes, madam?'

'Nothing — just that.'

Fay sang in her bath, sang as she dressed, sang as she applied a little make-up and lipstick. Satisfied she skipped down the staircase and headed for the breakfast-room.

He was sitting at a window table for two, paper propped against his coffee pot, one elbow on the crisp white table cloth, reading intently. As she approached he looked up, grinned, and stood up. With outstretched hands he took both of hers and kissed her on her cheek.

'Good morning, Fay.'

Beaming she raised an eyebrow. 'Good morning, *Sir Tom,* you do rise early don't you?'

'Working people usually do.'

He held her chair whilst she sat down and couldn't resist another kiss into her sweet smelling hair.

She whispered to him. 'I thought I'd upset you when I couldn't find you. I don't know what came over me, last night.'

He leant forward, just inches from her face. 'You certainly did upset me, Fay.' When he saw her look of horror, he chuckled. 'If you'd stayed a second or two longer we would have had to get married *this* morning.'

She knew she was blushing, but grinned with relief. 'You're looking smart.'

'Thank you, I borrowed a shaver from the porters.' He grinned. 'If you can't beat 'em, join 'em.'

Fay shook her head in disbelief and indicated the hotel with a wave of her hand. 'You don't care any more about all this, do you?'

'Nope.' He became serious. 'Fay, how do you feel this morning — about us I mean?'

She anxiously searched his face. 'Are you changing your mind?'

Tom smiled weakly. 'No — you know I'm not. It's just —'

He hung his head, 'You haven't got a ring and I can't afford one.'

'Is that all?'

'Well, that's pretty basic. If we're engaged you should have a ring.'

It dawned on her then how upset he was. 'Listen, Tom, I lve you, you love me, we've decided we're going to get married. That's what being engaged means. The bloody ring can wait.'

The blasphemy coming from her sweet lips was a powerful jolt to his senses.

'Fay — I will get you one. I swear.'

Matter-of-factly — she nodded. 'I know and I will be proud to wear it.'

To their relief Fay was not required again that morning.

They went to the Tower, then the Bridge, standing in the middle looking at the Pool of London. It was crowded with merchant ships from all over the world. Lighters and barges lay alongside each other and derricks and cranes rose and fell on the wharves. They looked like giant birds feeding their young as they laboured to load and unload the goods going out to, or coming in from the Empire, on which the sun never set.

The breeze played with her hair. Several times she had to lift a strand from her eye.

'Tom, are you coming back on the same train as me?'

He was leaning on the parapet beside her. 'I thought you might not like that. . . .'

'Why not?'

He half turned, resting on one arm. 'It's a small world. You risk being seen with me. Tongues would wag. Are you ready for that?'

She pulled her coat lapels tighter around her against the cold breeze and slipped her arm into his, guiding him back towards the Tower.

'I suppose not.'

She immediately stopped walking.

'Sorry — that sounded awful. It's nothing to do with you, it's just that if there were any hint of impropriety it would be such a shock. Even if it were Jeremy.'

She knew that wasn't entirely true — her father would probably react to *that* news by getting out a bottle of the Pol Roger *and* his shotgun. But Jeremy would redeem himself; asking for her hand — in the old world style. Her parents, too, still had the manners of an earlier time; after all, they'd both been born in the nineteenth century.

She searched his face, but he didn't seem to have taken offence.

Fay resumed walking. 'Darling, we've all the time in the world. When we're ready we'll tell them together — and you can ask Father formally if you like.'

She giggled.

'After all, he's got to give me away. I become *your* chattel then, don't I?'

'Sure do.'

She hit him on the arm.

Tom knew he'd changed. It was like a miracle, but now he had all the self-possession and confidence that had been sadly lacking before. It was her, he instinctively knew that. With Fay he had left the boy in him behind.

As a man he was calm, almost detached. Things would happen — and that was that — or he'd know why.

'I'll come back home with you now if you want. Or I'll wait, since I'm not a good financial catch. But I'll make you happy, one way or another.'

He took her firmly by both shoulders. 'And if you ever do what you did last night again — you'll have to accept the consequences — and they won't be pretty.'

In the startled silence before they both started laughing, a great klaxon sounded from the direction of the docks.

They boarded the early evening express to Gloucester that stopped at Kemble. While she settled into their first-class carriage, he popped along to the front to see what was hauling them, realizing as he did so that small bits of boyhood remained. It was a Hall class. He chatted for a moment to the driver. Exactly on time they eased out from under the great canopy, and slid at a steadily increasing rate through the western suburbs of London, gliding smoothly through commuter stations, occasionally lurching over points, signal gantries whispering by.

With a bang of compressed air and the

hiss of steam, a train in the opposite direction was gone in seconds.

They held hands. There was nothing else to say. Just before Kemble, he lowered the blinds on the windows to the corridor and they sat kissing and just holding on to each other.

When the train began to pass down the length of the platform, he stood up and got down her case.

'Are you being met here?'

'No, I'm getting the connection to town. I'm being picked up from there. And you?'

He shrugged. 'Something will be going to Cheltenham.'

As they ground to a halt he swung her case on to the platform where a porter stood with his barrow.

'This lady is for the Cirencester connection.'

'Very good, sir. It's just across there, madam.'

He pointed to the branch line platform and pushed his barrow in that direction.

Tom faced her. 'We've left it a bit late, but when shall I see you again?'

'I'm free Saturday evening, but Sunday's out — it's always church and family.'

He groaned. 'I'm playing in a band on Saturday night. I need the extra money for the lessons, but I could cancel, though it would leave them in the lurch.'

She wouldn't hear of it. 'I'm free on the Monday all day. Is that any good?'

Tom desperately tried to think.

'I'm due a day in lieu of Christmas working, but whether I can have it then. . . .'

The guard's whistle blasted. Their time had run out. She gave him a hurried kiss.

'Telephone me on Friday — at exactly five o'clock. I'll be by the phone. Daddy won't be back from The House till later.'

A porter came along slamming doors and reached theirs. 'Sorry, sir.'

He jumped on, pulling at the leather strap to drop the window as he shut the door and leaned out.

'Do I know your number?'

She came nearer. 'Cirencester 103 — or ask the operator for Codrington Hall, it's on the letter I sent if you've still got it?'

The whistle blasted again and with a jerk they began to move. He patted his wallet pocket and called out, 'I've got it next to my heart.'

She stood on the platform waving and blowing kisses as he leaned out of the window doing the same. Slowly they pulled out until the tiny figure on the platform was lost in a cloud of steam.

When it dispersed they had gone around a curve and the station was no longer in view.

CHAPTER ELEVEN

His parents noticed a difference in their son almost straightaway. When he went to work on Wednesday, his mother turned to his father.

'Told you. He's suddenly stronger, seems to know his own mind.'

His father grunted, took the pipe from his mouth. ' 'Bout bloody time he grew up.'

His mother jabbed him in the ribs. 'Less of the swearing.'

His father grunted, then lapsed into a paroxysm of coughing. When he'd finished, he spat into a large, discoloured jug and said, 'There's a woman, bet your bottom dollar and that always means trouble.'

She shook her head. 'You always look on the black side.'

But she did agree with his assessment. She wondered what the girl was like. Would she be good to her boy and a friend to his mother?

The 'girl' was just sitting up in bed, sipping the tea the maid had brought, and thinking about her day — another one without him. There had been no word from any of the auditions she'd attended. The midweek hunt was out at twelve. Restless with pent up energy and frustration, she'd ordered Jenny ready for eleven.

She looked out of the window. There were raindrops trickling down the panes and the skies beyond were the colour of Welsh slate.

She would have a bath, get on her breeches, ride to hounds, then bathe again before dinner. That way another day would be over with.

Tom was striding down the platform at Birmingham New Street, hand firmly on the collar of a gentleman who had been running a playing-card scam. He glanced anxiously at his watch.

The smiling prisoner, with the clipped military moustache, exuded charm and confidence. Looking up at him from under the rim of his brown trilby, he said, 'If you're in a hurry we could do this some other day.'

Tom gave him a good-natured shake. 'Quiet, you.'

All the same, he didn't dislike the rogue. Anyone daft enough to play cards with a stranger on a train deserved all he got.

The man had to be taken to the nearest police station and charged — all time consuming. He wanted to be back in Cheltenham, off duty, and at Staverton airport with at least two hours of flying time left. He glanced up at the sky. The clouds were leaden. Maybe there would be no lesson today even if he did make it.

Sergeant Whelan, dressed in full uniform with medals because of a court appearance as a witness, was writing in his meticulous hand with a scratchy pen when Tom walked in.

'Ah, there ye are.'

'Sergeant?'

The pen was placed down carefully, the thick eyebrows meeting like two furry caterpillars. 'If you're expecting fulsome praise, forget it. . . .'

Tom was dismissive. 'I'm not, Sergeant. Just tell me I can go . . .'

The bluntness made Whelan's eye bulge. What in the mother of God had come over Roxham? From being a rather shy fellow, though handy when it came to the rough stuff, he'd turned overnight into a forceful somewhat insubordinate character. He'd seen a few of them on the Western Front. They were always over the top first. Not many of them had made it back, at least, not in one piece.

'Is it this flying business again?'

'It is, with the Civil Guard.'

Whelan sighed. 'Very well, ye'd best be on yer way — I can see you won't be any more use to me today.'

'Thank you, Sergeant.'

The undisguised relief in Tom Roxham's voice irritated him. 'You be in here tomorrow, Constable, at seven thirty sharp — ye hear?'

'Yes, Sergeant.'

Tom didn't wait for Whelan to change his mind, he was out of there and on his bike in a flash.

The Master had blown the Tally-Ho and they were now in full pursuit, over forty horses and riders at the gallop, jumping the Cotswold dry-stone walls and hedges, climbing the steep hills and splashing through the valley streams.

Another fence came up, the horses in front of her taking off, back legs kicking out, clods of Gloucestershire earth flying up into the air.

The white breeches of a man in pink came out of the saddle, then back with a thump.

She lined up with the fence, feeling the

body of her mount tensing. With a surge of power that never failed to thrill her, they took off like a rocket. For a second she seemed to be flying, free of gravity, high in the air, not a care in the world. The moment passed, and with a bone jarring crash she came back to earth. Jenny stumbled, checked, and found her feet again. The chase continued.

Behind her Jeremy had watched her petite figure rise out of the saddle, such a small slim shape to be in control of such a huge horse.

But that was Fay. She was in charge — always was. Well, he was the man to tame her, and it would have to be soon. The world was beginning to lose its way. Heaven knew where they would all be this time next year.

He lined up for the fence, knew it was wrong even before they left the ground.

The sky changed places with the earth several times, before he hit the ground flat on his back. The air came out of his mouth and his backside like a tornado. For several seconds nothing happened, he thought he was paralysed, couldn't breathe or move. Then nature took over and his lungs started to work. He rolled over, got to his knees. By the time he staggered to his feet she was

215

only a speck in the distance. The sound of thundering hoofs on the other side of the fence sent him running to get out of the way, whistling for his horse that was grazing in the long grass at the edge of the ditch.

When he'd got the reins, he put his foot in the stirrup, his steed, ears flicking nervously, turned to try and prevent him. Once up he dug his heels in and resumed the hunt.

The tumble had done something. As he watched her riding into the distance around the edge of a wood he realized there was a message there. If he didn't do it now she'd get away, so he'd propose to her this weekend. Speak to her father first, of course. Time to get the whole thing tidied up. With a flick of the whip and another dig of the heel he urged the horse into a gallop.

Unaware of the resolution being made half a mile or so behind her, Fay, now out in a large field found her thoughts returning to Tom. She looked up at the sky. The solid cover of earlier had given way to broken clouds and heavy showers, one of which was just coming in. She remembered Tom had said that Wednesday was when he sometimes managed a lesson. As the rain lashed down she wondered if he'd get airborne at all — whether he'd found the time or not.

■ ■ ■ ■

Tom walked out to the Tiger Moth with Trubshaw.

'Well lad, it's a bit gusty today. I'd better get her off the ground.'

The take-off was indeed wild. The machine continuing to wobble and lift and drop violently as they climbed away from the grass strip in the gusting wind.

At five thousand feet, Trubshaw's voice crackled in Tom's ears as he handed over control.

They went through the same series of exercises, turns and rolls, until Trubshaw said enough was enough, and that the weather was getting rougher.

They got safely back down again on terra firma, albeit with a bone jarring thump. Near the hangar a couple of mechanics ran out and held on to the wobbling wings as the gale started to lift them alarmingly.

Back in the office, Trubshaw put their helmets on the table and slumped into his office chair.

'You were different today and it wasn't the weather. You seemed to be more aggressive, too rough on the controls.'

'Oh.' Tom was dejected, though he had

been aware of not managing so well.

Trubshaw continued, 'You were more relaxed before with a lighter touch on the stick. Now you are starting to grip the joystick and jerk it roughly.'

Tom's glumness was patent, his shoulders slumped. Trubshaw tried to get to the bottom of it.

'It's almost as though you are a different man. Tom, are you worried about anything?'

'No, no, well, not flying.'

Trubshaw nodded. 'All right, not for me to ask further. My advice is to get whatever it is off your chest. We all have bad days, of course.'

He stood up. 'See you on Saturday then Tom. Nine o'clock sharp?'

He walked to the window. 'Forecasters say all this will have blown through by then. We should be able to get a couple of decent hours in at least. By Sunday you will be nearly up to seven hours dual, possibly nine if the weather holds.'

He didn't go any further — holding back on any mention of a solo for two reasons: the first was that today had been a setback and if he continued like that he certainly wouldn't be ready for another week at least. The second was that whatever it was Tom had on his mind just now, the situation

218

wouldn't be improved by the extra pressure of knowing that that milestone was imminent. Ignorance was bliss. Trainee pilots sometimes started getting bouts of depression and frustration just before the event if they knew it was near. Better by far to judge the moment, unstrap, get out, and send them off without preamble. Bit of a shock, but the lesser of the two evils.

As Tom cycled home, standing up on the pedals, with the effort required to make progress against the wind, he knew what was at the bottom of today's woes.

Fay. And what had happened.

All week he'd worried about telling his parents. God love them, they hadn't two pennies to rub together really and lived with his gandmother in a house that was not owned by her. The whole family relied on his meagre income to provide little extras, more coal than perhaps they would have used to keep warm if he wasn't there and luxuries like a wireless with wet batteries charged up at the shop without thinking twice about it and a ticket to the football for his father on Saturday, or to watch Gloucestershire play cricket at the Cheltenham Festival.

As it was, the money for the flying lessons weighed heavily on his conscience.

His mother met him in the scullery and helped him off with his waterproof cape, shaking it out by the door and propping it in a corner.

'How did it go, son?'

'Not good today, Mum.'

'I'm surprised you went up in this weather. I've been worrying all day, hoped you'd been cancelled.'

He changed the subject. 'What's for dinner tonight, I'm famished.'

'Your favourite dear, Irish stew with bread and butter pudding to follow.'

He gave her a big noisy kiss on the cheek.

'Just the job on a day like today and I don't mean the weather.'

He began to untie his shoes.

His mother looked anxious.

'Is anything the matter, dear?'

'No.' He paused. 'I've got something to tell you and Dad.'

Immediately, he wished he'd waited — the look of anxiety on her face meant that he couldn't put it off now.

'What is it dear — are you all right? Have you been to the doctor, is that it?'

'No, no, Mum, I'm perfectly fit — nothing like that. Nothing for you to worry about at all, really — it's happy news.'

His mother looked at him oddly, then

said, 'Tom, it's a girl, isn't it?'

'Yes.'

'We *knew* it.' She was triumphant.

His father appeared in the doorway, taking the pipe he wasn't supposed to smoke out of his mouth. 'She's pregnant — that it?'

Resignedly, Tom drew in a deep breath. 'No, Dad, nothing like that, we're engaged to be married — not straight away of course,' he added hurriedly, 'probably in a couple of years' time.'

His mother wiped her hands on her dutch apron and held up her arms to hug him. 'Oh, Tom, that's wonderful.'

They wrapped their arms about each other as his mother seemed to be both crying and laughing at the same time.

When they broke apart it was to find his father looking less than happy. 'Who is she?'

Tom swallowed. 'Her name's Fay — Fay Rossiter and she lives in Cirencester.'

His mother blinked in surprise. 'Cirencester? How in the world did you meet her?'

He lied. 'On duty, Mum, just bumped into each other.'

Snorting, his father said, 'So you were with her in London eh, I hope there was no hanky panky.'

'Dad!'

But he knew he'd gone crimson with the memory of his hand on her . . .

His mother and father exchanged glances.

His father sniffed. 'That's why now, is it? How long have you been keeping quiet about her?'

Again he lied. 'Oh several weeks. And I'm telling you now because I proposed and was accepted this weekend. It's taken me a couple of days to pluck up the courage to tell you, because I knew it was going to be an awful shock and I'm so sorry about that . . .' his voice tailed off.

It was his mother who broke the silence.

'Why haven't you brought her home, Tom, it's customary and it would have been nice?'

Tom hung his head. 'I know. I'm sorry, but it all happened so quickly. I didn't know I was going to propose — it just happened.'

His mother started to smile.

'When are we going to meet her? Is she nice, luv?'

'She's wonderful, Mum; you'll adore her, I promise.'

His father suppressed a tickle in his throat.

'Has all this flying nonsense just been a cover? Have you really been meeting her all along?'

'No, Dad, I love flying. She was the one who introduced me to it.'

With a grunt his father just managed to say sarcastically, 'You *love* everything all of a sudden,' then his coughing started. It was a bad one. Anxiously, his mother moved to his side.

'You all right, Dad?'

The episodes had been getting worse lately.

Nodding between the spasms his father staggered to the wide flat sink, resting with both hands gripping the side as he finally coughed up bloody phlegm and spat it into the white porcelain. He turned on a tap, used his hand to wash it away then took a sip from the column of water. He knew he was dying, just as surely as if it had been a bullet on the Somme. It was only a matter of time, but at least he'd had twenty years, unlike those who had stopped a lump of lead. He turned to face them again, tried a smile of reassurance.

'Now, where were we? Fay, is it? That's a nice name. What does she do, Tom?'

'She's a pianist — accompanies singers.'

'Oh.' His mother looked bewildered. 'Is that a proper job?'

'More to the point,' added his father. 'Does it pay well?'

Tom grinned. 'I believe so.'

'And her parents. Have you met them, are

they nice?' enquired his mother.

'No, not yet. Soon.'

His father, feeling conscious of his own unemployed state asked, 'What's her father do?'

There was no way Tom could tackle that just now — her father being a junior minister, and a Tory one to boot, let alone being in the Lords.

Even he found it extraordinary, but he was no longer overawed. He just didn't care anymore. But his parents would be uncomfortable — his father downright unbearable.

'Oh, quite well-to-do. Something in London.'

Scowling, his father said, 'Was he in the war?'

'I believe so; I think he was wounded.'

That seemed to satisfy his old man who turned to his mother and said, 'What's for dinner?'

But his mother wasn't listening.

'This calls for a celebration. There's that bottle of sweet wine in the cupboard, left over from Christmas, let's have a toast — to Tom and Fay.'

His father grumbled a bit, he was hungry, but he eventually went and got the bottle, mother providing the tumblers.

As she poured the wine she asked, 'What

are you doing for a ring, Tom?'

He picked up his glass. 'We're doing without one for now, Mum. We can't afford it.'

She winced. 'Oh, that's terrible, the poor girl.'

Frowning, Tom said, 'Oh no, Fay doesn't mind.'

His mother wasn't having it. 'All girls want a ring to show they're spoken for. She's just being nice, I like that.'

Her face suddenly lit up. 'Wait a minute.'

'What?'

'Your grandmother has some rings in her jewellery box. Came down the family — one's her mother's. When she hears the news she might want to give you a present. . . .'

He shook his head. 'I wouldn't dream of it. Anyway, where is Gran?'

'At a whist drive. No, I'm sure she'll be offended if you don't have one. And where else at the moment are you going to get the money? You leave it to me.'

'Mum — please!'

'Leave the lad alone.' His father had already downed his wine in one and was opening a bottle of Watney's London Pride.

'Where you going to live, son? This place is not big enough for another married couple, and then there's nippers to consider.'

Tom hadn't thought beyond his love and need and fascination with Fay. His father had just uttered things that had not even been on his horizon. Momentarily it brought him up with a start.

He shook his head. 'Dad, that's years away. We'll find somewhere.'

His mother held up her glass. 'Let's have a toast to you both.'

His father stopped pouring and raised his glass. 'To our lad, and his wife to be. . . .' He hesitated, so Tom prompted, 'Fay.'

'*Fay* — long life and happiness.'

They clinked their glasses.

It came in the post on Thursday.

There were two envelopes for her. The first was stiffer, with 'photographs, do not bend' along the back and front. Fortunately her father had already left for London, so only her mother saw it.

'What's that, Fay?'

Her daughter pretended to turn it over and see a trade sign on the back.

'Oh, it's returned photographs from *Horse and Rider*. I sent them the ones with me on Jenny; they didn't use them, said they would be returned under separate cover.' She pretended to discard it without interest. Fortunately there was the other one with which to distract her mother.

'Oh, look at this, it's from the agent to Sir Trevor Keynes.'

She borrowed her mother's opener, slitting the top of the letter neatly open before pulling out the single sheet of paper, reading it swiftly.

'Well?' Her mother was on the edge of her bureau chair.

Fay looked up.

'Sir Trevor wants me to accompany him for a concert next month, and then for a six month tour of Australia, New Zealand and the Far East.'

'Oh, Fay, that's marvellous.'

Her mother got up and came over. They hugged each other, then drew apart, her mother chattering excitedly.

'You'll need a whole new wardrobe for the tropics. Isn't this exciting? We'll have a whale of a time. Harrods, Harvey Nichols — all the little shops and the Burlington Arcade. . . .'

Her daughter didn't seem to be reacting as she had expected.

'Is everything all right, darling? You do want to go, don't you?'

In truth Fay didn't. It would mean not

seeing Tom for six whole months. As it was her mind and body already ached at a separation of days.

'I suppose so. It's just I've never been away for so long before.'

Her mother became businesslike.

'My dear girl, we never had any problem with your boarding at school. And six months — it will fly by. You'll be home for Christmas.'

Unable to say why she didn't want to go, Fay just smiled weakly.

'Yes, Mummy, of course. I suppose it's the shock. I didn't think they'd select me, there were so many vying for the job — people who probably need it far more than I.'

'Don't be silly, girl. You're very talented. I'm going to telephone your father's secretary — he'll want to know straight away when he gets in to the office.'

As she bustled away, Fay picked up the photograph envelope. In her bedroom she used one side or her sewing scissors to open the letter. Excitedly she got out the prints.

The very first one she looked at became her favourite. There in black and white, frozen for ever, they stood, hand in hand. Eventually she touched her lips to him and placed it between the leaves of her Bible.

■ ■ ■ ■

When he finally got his rota, Tom found he had got the Monday he had requested.

That cheered him up no end. Tomorrow he would get some flying in before the dance commitment in the evening. Now, it was nearly time to ring her. He was in a telephone box situated at the approach to Leckhampton Station.

He felt in his jacket pocket at the little box smuggled there. His mother had been right, Grannie had been over the moon with his news and had immediately gone to her room. They'd heard the tin trunk under her bed being pulled over the linoleum. When she came down the stairs it was with the little box, and inside the ring with its single stone diamond. It wasn't big but, to his un-practised eye, it was just beautiful. He hadn't known how to thank her. She had tears in her eyes, as she sighed, 'It was my mother's. I've kept it since she died. She would have been delighted for you to have it — keeping it in the family. Your girl, is she beautiful?'

'Yes Gran, very.'

She had patted his hand. 'Then that's settled, dear. I hope she likes it.'

Now he looked again at it, sparkling up at him from its black velvet bed. He knew that Fay would be used to bigger things, but it really was delicate Victorian workmanship, even if the diamond was small.

And he knew Fay would treasure it, whatever its size.

He snapped the lid shut and put it back in his pocket. The hands of his watch neared the appointed time. With his money ready he dialled the operator. When she told him the amount he shelled it into the slot and stood waiting with his finger on button 'A'.

'Trying to connect you.'

At Codrington Hall the telephone in the stone-flagged entrance lobby gave out its loud double ring. The butler, in a white jacket over his pinstripe trousers was overseeing the laying of the dinner table when he heard the telephone. He started for the hall, but Fay called out, 'It's all right, I'll take it.'

She picked up the receiver. 'Codrington Hall.'

Tom pushed the button. There was a crash as the coins fell into the metal box and a second of infuriating silence, as he said, 'Hello — hello' and then suddenly Fay's voice was saying, 'Codrington Hall — is that you, Tom?'

'Fay, darling, yes, it's me.'

Her voice carne warmly down the line. 'Tom, I really miss you.'

'And I've missed you too.'

'You still love me then?'

Unseen Tom pushed his trilby back off his forehead and did a parody of an American voice from the films. 'You bet, baby.'

She chuckled. 'You fool. So, when can we meet?'

'Monday — I'm free all day.'

She had to restrain herself from shouting out with glee.

'Oh darling, I'm so pleased. Where — what time?'

His voice came down the line. 'I'll come to Cirencester if it's easier — and Fay, I've got something for you.'

Fay leant away, trying to see whether her mother had moved from her position in the drawing-room.

'What is it?'

'No, I won't tell you, it's a surprise.'

Intrigued she teased. 'Are you sure I am going to like it?'

'I hope so.'

She remembered the photographs. 'Oh, and I've got something for you.'

It was his turn to be both puzzled and tease. 'And am I going to like it?'

'Oh, I think so.'

They chatted for a minute, she asking him whether he had flown that week? He told her about his poor showing when, all of a sudden, the pips started going.

'Hang on,' he shouted, struggling to get more coins in the slot. The infuriating moment of no communication happened again before he heard her saying, 'Tom, are you there?'

'Yes, look, where and at what time on Monday?'

She turned, checking again that her Mother wasn't in earshot.

'I'll come to Cheltenham — it's easier. That all right for you?'

'Of course. You'll be on the early train?'

'Yes and I'm sorry about not being free on Sunday.'

Fay glanced around nervously again to check she couldn't be overheard.

'Darling, I love you. I'm so miserable without you.'

'Me, too. You're in my mind all the time.'

The pips went again. Over them he hurriedly called out 'I love you', to which she replied, 'And I adore you.'

They kept repeating 'Love you — love you' until the pips stopped. At the last moment, he managed one final 'I love you Fay,' then line went dead.

He replaced the handset, pressed button 'B' in case there was any change from somebody else and then pushed open the heavy door. He stopped, felt in his trouser pocket, though he knew there were no more coins. Down the road was a little corner shop called, Lords. He'd buy something and with the change ring Mr Trubshaw to make sure he could maximize his flying time over the weekend.

Fay, left with a dead line, still held the receiver to her ear, saying in a much louder voice — 'All right, Jennifer, I'll see you on Monday.'

She paused, pretended to be listening, then said, still loudly, 'Cavendish House will be fine, till then, bye.'

She put the phone down, went back into the room. Her mother was sitting there reading a *Woman's Own,* and looked up.

'Who was that, dear?'

'Jennifer, I'm meeting her at Cavendish House on Monday.'

'Oh, you could do some shopping for your trip. Shall I come as well, darling?'

Even though she felt a surge of panic she managed to stop herself overreacting.

She screwed her face up. 'We won't have

time for that sort of thing. She wants me to meet her for coffee, and then go and see some New Zealand friends who have come back with her.'

'I see.'

Her mother turned a page. 'Extraordinary.'

'Pardon?'

'I met her mother at the Pearsons the other evening. She never said anything about Jennifer being back, let alone house guests.'

Fay suddenly found it difficult to breathe and managed only a weak, 'Really. Must have slipped her mind.' With that she made for the door. 'Just going down to the stable, I need to check on Jenny. Had a feeling she might have been going lame on the walk home on Wednesday.'

When she'd gone, her mother lowered her magazine, frowning. Fay was behaving rather oddly these days, and now, with the offer of a professional position and exciting travel prospects, she seemed less than enthusiastic.

It could only mean that the boy she had met at the party was more serious than they had thought.

When Mr Trubshaw lowered the receiver,

he wondered how the heck he was going to square it up with the wife. He'd just agreed to give Tom Roxham a whole morning and an hour in the afternoon on Saturday as well. He must be crazy. But he knew why really. He picked up the Air Ministry Directive that had landed on his desk that morning. It was stamped *urgent.* They wanted all flying schools to double their efforts to qualify as many pilots in the basics by midsummer. Tossing the letter down, he leant back in his chair and closed his eyes. Nearly every month now they were putting the pressure on them all. His friend over at Worcester had reported a visit by two airforce types who had given him a pep talk on the necessity for advertising the scheme and checking on his aircraft. They'd even gone as far as to say that they might have funds that could be used to help with equipment.

No government agency did that unless there was a very good reason. Now the morality of it all sometimes got to him. Tim Mayhew was right. Young lads, like Tom Roxham — did they really know what they were being trained for?

And he was helping them.

It made him increasingly uneasy.

■ ■ ■ ■

Fay's father strode into the hall, giving his hat, cane and brief-case to one of the maids, allowing the butler, Wilson, to help him off with his coat.

'A good day, sir?'

'Very good, thank you. Where are Lady Rossiter and Miss Fay?'

'In the drawing-room sir, I took the liberty of pouring you your usual sherry.'

Fay's father shook his head. 'Not tonight Wilson, a bottle of the Pol if you please, we have a celebration.'

'Indeed, sir?'

'Yes. Miss Fay is going to accompany Sir Trevor Keynes on a tour of Australia, New Zealand, Singapore.'

'That's excellent news sir, and a very proud moment for the family.'

It was genuinely meant.

'Thank you.'

Lord Rossiter opened the door and entered the drawing-room, holding out his arms. 'Fay, darling, congratulations.'

'Daddy.'

He wrapped his arms around her and gave her a bear hug.

'I've been thinking of you all day. Sorry I

couldn't be with you yesterday, but it was a very late meeting, so I had to stay at the club.'

Her mother came forward and joined them.

'I've been trying to cheer her up. She's not happy with the idea of being away for six months.'

Her father held her at arm's length and studied her face. 'Is this true, Fay?'

She shrugged.

'I don't know, Daddy — honest. It's a long time to be away from you all.'

'Nonsense, my dear.' Her father enthused on and on until Wilson entered with the Pol Roger in an ice bucket and proceeded to open the bottle with practised efficiency.

Her father handed the first two glasses to her mother and Fay, then took his own.

'To our daughter — every success in her chosen career.'

They clinked their glasses in turn.

'Now, tell me about the tour, Fay, when does it start, and where are all the places you visit? Don't forget we have relatives and good friends all over the world.'

She sipped her champagne, feeling the bubbles go up her nose.

'Not exactly sure of all the details yet, Daddy. Anyway, I'm to play for him at a concert before we go and there will have to be rehearsals of course.'

'Good, that will give me plenty of time to write to people, make sure you always have somebody to turn to if needs be.'

'You're not doing anything tomorrow evening are you, darling?' said her mother. 'We could all go out for a celebration dinner at the Royal.'

Relieved that she didn't have to make up an excuse, Fay said quickly, 'Nothing at all. That would be fun.'

'I'll get Wilson to make a reservation.'

Whilst her mother busied herself her father, one hand in his pocket, asked. 'Have you got the letter, Fay. Could I see it?'

'Yes, of course.'

She went to the mantelpiece where they had left it earlier and held it out.

Her father pulled his hand from his pocket, took it and started reading.

He looked up proudly. 'Hmm, it says, "your expansive and lyrical playing helps to balance his tendency to excitement and narrative". Is that true?'

Fay smiled and shrugged. 'He kept trying to get away from me. We were going a couple of beats faster at the end, but I kept dragging him back.'

He tapped the letter. 'Well, he's very

complimentary about your timing.'

Wilson appeared in the doorway. Lady Rossiter explained what was wanted. He turned to go, but her father suddenly said, 'Oh Wilson,' he glanced at his wife, 'we will need four reservations for dinner.'

'Very good, sir.'

Puzzled, Fay said, 'who is the surprise guest?'

Lord Rossiter looked a little sly. 'Jeremy called me at the House today. Wants to see me about something. I suggested he came late Saturday afternoon — so he might as well come with us to dinner — should be fun for you, Fay.'

She pretended to shrug as if she didn't mind either way. 'Fine.'

'Nice lad. He was out with the hunt wasn't he, on Wednesday?'

'Yes, Daddy.'

'He's got a good seat and he's a fine shot.'

Fay didn't feel she had to say anything. It was just infuriating that, whatever Jeremy wanted with her father, the latter should inflict him on them at supper. Hadn't he got the message yet that she wasn't that close to Jeremy?

In the morning Fay decided not to go out again with the Saturday hunt. Instead she took all three dogs for a walk, the two Welsh

Springers and her own Jack Russell, Alfie. She climbed up the steep hill in front of the house and stood looking over the valley. Smoke rose in straight columns from the chimneys of the Cotswold stone cottages. Crows wheeled and cawed above the trees near the church. It was so still that she could clearly hear the bleating of sheep a mile away.

She climbed over a style, Alfie squeezing underneath while the two Springers, barking excitedly, scrambled up on to the drystone wall; they jumped on to the wooden step crashing off into the undergrowth.

Fay was in a turmoil. A short while ago the news she had received yesterday would have sent her over the moon but, because of Tom, everything had changed.

She needed to talk to him, see what he thought. Six months apart — it would be unbearable.

CHAPTER TWELVE

They had done all the pre-flight checks and after the shout of 'contact' the engine burst into life. The chocks had been cleared and now he was lined up on the grass runway, looking at the back of Trubshaw's leather helmeted head, the latter's voice crackled in his earphones.

'Right — in your own time.'

Tom's hands went to his goggles, brought them down over his eyes. He gritted his teeth, determined to do better.

Keeping his eyes on the Ts and Ps he advanced the throttle, holding the quivering machine on the brakes as he did a last magneto check. When he judged the time was right, he released them and they started bowling down the runway. Very swiftly the tail plane lifted and he could see beyond Trubshaw's head at the grass rushing under the plane and the trees in the distance, and one in particular.

The nose of the Tiger varied only slightly from one side of it to the other — he was keeping a better line. Then all of a sudden it was academic as the vibration ceased and the machine took wing. They soared into the morning sky.

He found himself looking into the eyes of Trubshaw in the latter's rear view mirror. The head nodded as the crackling voice said, 'There you are — you're relaxing again. These things iron themselves out. Now, let's do some circuits and bumps.'

For the next hour Tom did take offs and landings until Trubshaw was satisfied, then they climbed higher and started on stalls and spins. When Trubshaw went off to lunch at home, he stayed in the office eating bread and dripping sandwiches, washed down with a cup of tea made in a small pot that detached into two parts, the lower half being the actual cup and saucer. The sugar was in a battered 1934 Jacob's Assorted biscuit tin, the tea straight out of an opened Typhoo packet. A smooth-voiced crooner was singing on the Vidor radio.

The song ended abruptly with a few rising chords from the saxes. It was Jack Payne and his BBC orchestra and singers.

That reminded him about that night, he was getting a lift in a new Austin Ruby.

On a small side-table were a stack of flying magazines. He rifled through *Popular Flying* and *New Air Weekly*. There was also a guide to the Airport of London at Croydon. He took one and propped his boots up on the edge of the desk and began reading. The next thing he remembered was being rudely awakened by Trubshaw who swept his feet off the desk as he said, 'Oy — when the cat's away. . . .'

'Sorry, I didn't hear you come in.'

His instructor grinned, 'You are in luck. The lady wife was in a good mood so, so am I. Now then, wake up and let's go flying.'

The sun was low in the sky when Tom brought her in to land for the last time, bumping just the once before the plane settled back on to the grass. He taxied in and cut the engine, feeling utterly exhausted. They went through the post flight checks, then he unstrapped and climbed out, going around the Tiger Moth for a last inspection.

Trubshaw stood watching him, then they walked back to the office together. He ran a hand through his hair as he chucked his helmet on to the magazines.

'That was a damn good day, Tom. Let's see, you're up to how many hours?'

Tom was filling in his log book and ran the nib of his fountain pen down the column.

'I make it eight and a half hours.'

Trubshaw found his briar pipe and was busy stuffing tobacco from Player's White label Navy Mixture into the bowl.

'You seem to be over that period of stiffness. Today you were smoother, co-ordinated, had a good feel for the controls.'

Tom was delighted. 'Thank you for finding the time. Please send my apologies to Mrs Trubshaw.'

With the tobacco packed down with his thumb, his instructor started to apply the flame from a Swan Vesta, sucking on the stem. The flame was drawn down into the glowing mixture. Clouds of smoke rose up. When he was satisfied that he was well alight, he took the pipe from his mouth, waved out the charred remains of the bent up match and flicked it into an ashtray.

Eyes screwed up, he looked back at Tom through the rising blue cloud.

'You'll need to start doing more ground work.' He nodded at the small shelf of books above the magazines.

'Take the end two. Keep them at home. I've got other copies. You will be examined on theory as well as practical tests for your licence.'

Tom's heart leapt. *His licence.*

'Thanks.' He went across and pulled them down, glancing at the first of the titles, *Principles of Airmanship.*

Leaning back in his chair Trubshaw breathed out smoke, savouring the taste. 'When can you come again?'

Hesitantly, Tom said, 'Well I'm free all day tomorrow, but of course I understand. . . .'

Trubshaw stopped him with a wave of the hand.

'After church for a couple of hours — say twelve o'clock? Got to be home by two or thereabouts — the rest of the family is coming for lunch.'

'Oh.' Tom was surprised. 'Yes — that would be great.'

'Sure you haven't had enough after today?'

'No — not at all.'

Trubshaw nodded, teeth clenched around the stem.

'See you tomorrow then — twelve o'clock sharp. Weather forecast is the same as today.'

Tom took his leave. He put on clips, got on his bike and cycled past Trubshaw's new Riley Four Door Saloon in British Racing Green. As he left the owner was thinking about his progress. It had been a very rewarding afternoon. He enjoyed another draw on his pipe. The decision would be his tomorrow, of course, but if today was anything to go by it could well happen.

Tom took the smaller round galvanized tub, not the full-length one, from the outside wall and into the scullery. He ladled hot water from the boiler into it and added some cold from the tap.

'Right, Mum, I'm getting undressed.'

He heard his mother's voice from somewhere upstairs and his Gran next door, saying, 'We've seen it all before, boy.'

Nevertheless he pushed the door nearly shut before he stripped off and stood in the tub. He used the bar of lifebuoy soap and a flannel to give himself a wash under his arms, around his body, and then one foot at a time. It took less than five minutes and he was out and towelling himself vigorously in the cold air. With his dressing-gown on, he baled out his water until he could pick up the tub and empty out the rest.

He quickly nipped outside and hung it back up. He'd missed bath night, not getting home until gone nine o'clock from his stint on the London to Fishguard express. He'd been briefed to sit in the same coach as three Irishmen bound for the ferry to Rosslare. He'd got on at Swindon and off at

Cardiff. They were suspected Irish Republican terrorists; Tom wasn't sure whether they were just being shadowed to make sure they were leaving or what. All Special Branch had asked for was a lot of manpower so that they could cover every possibility.

Upstairs he changed quickly into his dark trousers, white shirt and black tie. His dinner jacket had been taken by his gran who had pressed it for him.

He'd barely got it on and put his saxophone case on the table, sorting through his music when there was a knock at the door.

He kissed his mother and gran and with a cheery wave at his father he was gone.

The little Maroon Austin Ruby saloon went down to a crawl up the steep part of Cleave Hill. Tom asked his friend how much he'd paid — if he didn't mind his asking?

'A hundred and thirty-one pounds,' was the answer.

He shook his head in awe. 'How did you manage that?'

They reached the brow of the hill and the little car slowly began to pick up speed again.

'The Kathleen Mavoureen system.'

Puzzled, Tom said, 'What on earth is that?'

His friend, Paddy Redmarsh, cast a guilty smile at him.

'I borrowed the money. You put down a deposit and pay the rest off in monthly instalments over three years.'

He began to sing in his Irish tenor voice:

Ma-vour-een
Ma-vour-een
It may be for years
And it may be for ev-er . . .

Tom was aghast that anyone could think of buying something so expensive on credit. He shook his head in disbelief.

'Aren't you frightened you might not be able to make the payments?'

The Irishman laughed. 'Jeez, Tom, the whole damn world's going crazy. Everybody's having fun — I want some too, before it's too late.'

Shaking his head, Tom looked at the road ahead caught in the headlights of the car. The new cat's eyes reflected back at them. He didn't like swearing much, but it seemed natural to Paddy, part of the musical way he spoke. 'Where exactly is the venue tonight, Pad?'

'Some bloody place called Sudely Castle. It's an engagement party.'

Tom swallowed. Poor Fay, she would be

denied a lot because of his background.

Fay was at her dressing-table, fixing an earring. With a last touch of the powder puff on her neck and shoulders she stood up, smoothing the dress over her waist and hips. It fell to her shoes with their cuban heels and straps with pearl buttons over the arch of her foot.

She picked up the evening bag she had selected and checked that she had her cigarettes.

Fay had heard the door chime earlier and the voice of Wilson as he had let Jeremy in, then her father's, before the study door had closed.

What on earth did he want? The best she could come up with was a shooting arrangement on the estate, or some other form of business. A sudden idea struck her. Jeremy might be considering going into politics — her father could help a lot there.

She closed the bedroom door behind her and tripped down the wide curving staircase.

Her mother wasn't there, so she opened her bag, and fished out the silver cigarette case and pearl handled lighter. The spark from the flint didn't ignite the petrol fumes until the third go. She applied the flame to the end of her Marcovitch Black & White. When it was alight she snapped the cover back over the flame and put everything back in her bag.

She was holding her right elbow with her cupped left hand against her waist, cigarette between her first and second fingers, the smoke trailing lazily up in the high ceilinged room. Her father's study door opened and he emerged, already dressed in his dinner jacket, laughing, with one hand clapping the shoulder of a similarly attired Jeremy.

'Well, my boy, I'm doubly glad you are joining us tonight and look, here's the talented girl herself and doesn't she look beautiful?'

Frowning, Fay turned, as Jeremy agreed, his eyes intently on her.

'Indeed she does, sir — you must be very proud.'

Indignantly, Fay waved the cigarette from side to side.

'What's all this? Here's the girl herself. What have you two been talking about?'

Lord Rossiter made for the decanters and gestured with the cut glass to Jeremy.

'A little snifter to settle our talk.'

'Yes, thank you, sir.'

Her father poured out two generous measures of the single malt, replacing the glass stopper.

'And you Fay. Would you like a sherry?'

'Yes please, Father.'

He dispensed her drink from another bell-bottomed decanter and handed out the glasses to them both.

'Cheers.'

They both responded and took sips.

'Mm — very good, sir.'

Her father nodded. 'It's the nectar of the gods. You can keep champagne and brandy. A single malt is the most superb drink — always have one in my flask on the shoot.'

Fay tapped some ash into an ornate silver tray made in the shape of a scallop.

'Really, Father, I've heard the same thing said by you about Port.'

Just then her mother appeared and, taking in their drinks, said, 'What's all this?'

Fay put the cigarette to her dark red lips, screwing up one eye as the smoke drifted up. 'They won't tell me, Mother, perhaps you can find out?'

Her mother looked at them both, directing her remark to her husband. 'You do look a little smug, darling. Anyway I'll have a sherry please since you all seem to have started without me.'

The talk turned to the political scene at Whitehall, and Fay, taking a last draw on her cigarette before stubbing it out, thought, 'Ah ha, that's what it was all about.'

Just then Simpson, the chauffeur appeared in the doorway.

'Excuse me, sir, will the Lagonda be all right tonight? The Bentley's got a flat tyre and it will take at least twenty minutes to change.'

'Of course, Simpson.' Lord Rossiter looked at his watch.

'As it is we're a bit late. Ready in five minutes.'

'Very good, sir.'

Outside they all got into the car. Fay in the back seat was squeezed between her mother and Jeremy, who was very conscious of her lightly clad thigh pressed hard against his own. So was Fay of his. It was going to be a long evening.

The dining-room of the Royal was packed. As they followed the Head Waiter to their table, heads turned and some nodded. Her father was something of a figure in the district. He stopped by a table to have a word with the occupants, leaving the others to continue to their table.

When he rejoined them they were already being handed the leather-bound menus.

'Would you like the sommelier to bring the wine list now, sir?'

'Yes, of course, but we'll have a bottle of your best vintage champagne to start with — we are having a little celebration.'

'Very good, sir.'

The man bustled away.

Lord Rossiter beamed around at them all.

'I must say, this is marvellous, having you with us, Jeremy, as we celebrate Fay's start to her career — at least, until she gets married.'

'Married,' hung in the air.

Fay smiled, knowing that she would be seeing her fiancé on Monday, and lied.

'I may never get married, Father. Haven't thought about it much.'

Her father winced. It wasn't exactly what he wanted to hear just at that moment.

The sommelier arrived to present the chosen bottle of champagne for Lord Rossiter's approval, his chain clanking against the glass.

'That's the one. Capital.'

They chattered lightly about nothing of consequence until four glasses of finely bubbling wine were placed before them. Lord Rossiter picked his up first and looked straight at his wife.

'Let's have a toast, to Fay and Jeremy — their future.'

Her mother repeated the toast.

Fay smiled weakly, a little irritated at the coupling, but at least it wasn't something more embarrassing — you never knew with daddy.

The meal was excellent, her father insisted on an excellent port with the stilton cheese, despite all the wine she had consumed, so she was quite tipsy by the time they were back in the car, squeezed up against Jeremy yet again. The latter laid his hand across the back of the seat as they drove home.

Somewhere along the way it must have happened. She wasn't even aware of it, until they were in the drive and her father turned around and said, 'Good to see you young people getting close.'

It was only then that she realized that Jeremy had a hand around her shoulder.

She sat bolt upright, unfortunately giving the impression that she was embarrassed by being caught out.

When they pulled up at the entrance and Simpson opened the door for her mother, she slid rapidly across the ribbed leather after her and got out, pulling her fur wrap tightly around her shoulders as she did so.

But Jeremy was faster. Already beside her, as her father said, 'You'll come in for a nightcap, old chap?'

Jeremy turned to look at Fay, as if seeking

her approval, but she was already on her way to the opened front door. Inside a maid took her wrap. She yawned extravagantly.

'I'm very tired, I'm going to bed.'

She kissed her mother on her cheek, then stood on tiptoe to give her father a peck as he stooped for her, saying, 'Oh, are you sure? I thought you and Jeremy would show up us old things and spend half the night talking?'

She smiled as sweetly as she could, debated swiftly in her mind how to say goodbye and finally held out her hand.

'Goodnight, Jeremy, thank for being with us, I enjoyed your company very much.'

With that she made for the staircase.

'Goodnight, Fay. See you soon.'

She called out over her shoulder, 'Yes, of course, look forward to it.'

She wished she hadn't added that bit, trying to be polite. As she climbed the stairs she heard her father saying, 'You must come to lunch tomorrow — after matins.'

She winced. What was the matter with her father? As if she didn't know.

Later, tucked up in bed, she looked at the photograph of herself and Tom.

Eventually she kissed his image, slid it under her pillow and turned out the light.

She went to sleep with the alcohol in her

blood fueling thoughts about his strong arms around her lightly clad body, her breathing only slowing as she finally drifted off.

He enjoyed a bit of a lie-in, getting up finally at ten to nine to be greeted by the delicious smell of fried bacon.

His gran was at the range, tea towel over her shoulder, dutch apron on.

'Morning Tom. Ready for your breakfast?'

It was a Sunday tradition in the household: bacon cut by the big, red, hand-driven slicing machine from the corner shop; eggs from a neighbour; a little bit of black pudding from the sawdust-floored butcher together with a couple of slices of fried bread.

'Yes please, Gran, I'm famished.'

She set the plate down in front of him. He tucked in immediately, a book out on the table beside him.

'What's that you're reading?' she asked.

His Father, the *News of the World* open, reading all the court cases of the week looked up as he said, '*Theory of Flight,* Gran.'

His father snorted. 'Why the hell are you filling your head with that rubbish and wasting good money?'

Tom had felt the resentment before and

said resignedly, 'It's the future, Dad and in any case, I want to.'

With another snort his father returned to his reading. He'd just come to a particularly salacious part where the private detectives had caught the Honourable Teddy Houghton in bed with a well-known lady. She had, in reality, been hired to lie in a revealing nightdress with him, without any other service being provided, in order that he might be 'caught' *in delicto flagrante.* That way the divorce could go through.

Tom scoffed the lot and added a chunky slice of white bread with lashings of home-made blackberry jam. All washed down with a mug of stewed tea. He closed the book and stood up.

'Right, I'm off. Put my dinner in the oven, Gran. I'll be in a little late.'

His father didn't look up, just said, 'First a funny-shaped football, now this flying — you're getting above yourself, Tom. Mark my words, no good will come of it.'

Tom paused in the doorway behind his father, winked and grinned across at his gran as he said, 'See you at *luncheon,* Grandmother.'

Half an hour later he was on the grass strip again, the nose of the Tiger with the tree, noting that there was a ten degree cross wind that hadn't been there yesterday.

Trubshaw's voice crackled in his ear. 'Right, let's see if you've forgotten how to do it.'

He hadn't.

As they climbed away Trubshaw mentally ticked off the first of the points he had set in his head before he let Tom go it alone.

He made him do a few circuits and bumps then climb to 10,000 ft, before doing stalls and recovery, followed by forced landing procedures.

'Right, take us down and enter the circuit, land and taxi in.'

Tom frowned, it was a bit early, but he didn't say anything, perhaps Trubshaw's wife had been getting at him.

He did a text book landing and taxied to the hangar. Trubshaw's voice came over the R/T. 'Bring her round into the wind and keep the engine running.'

Puzzled, Tom did as he was told then, to his astonishment, Trubshaw undid his straps, levered himself out of the cockpit, leaned back in and did the straps up again. He then jumped off the wing and came back to stand beside Tom.

He leaned closer and shouted above the idling engine. 'Right off you go, try a circuit of your own, and for God's sake don't bend the machine — it's more valuable than you are.'

He looked at Tom, po-faced for a second or two, then burst into a grin.

Tom sat there still numb, until Trubshaw suddenly yelled, 'What are you waiting for? If you don't go soon I'll change my bloody mind.'

With that he stepped well back and waved Tom away.

He taxied out, feeling weird looking at the emptiness of Trubshaw's seat. He lined up with his favourite tree, went through his checks, then with a sinking stomach he opened the throttle and held the stick forward, managing to keep in line with his tree. The tail came up and in no time at all he was airborne, the wind whistling in the quivering bracing wires. Trubshaw's absence was frightening.

Later, he could hardly recall the circuit. He just remembered turning on the final leg, then lining up for the approach, adjusting for the crosswind, selecting flaps, and then bleeding off the speed.

The boundary hedge went by underneath him then he panicked as the ground came rushing up at him. He heard himself yellling, 'Check her, check her,' as he pulled the stick back. There was an almighty thump, the plane leapt back into the air, then came down again with a smaller thud, followed by another tiny one that ran into the continuous shuddering of landlocked motion. He was down safely and nothing had been broken.

As he taxied back to the waiting figure by the hangar it really began to dawn on him that he had actually soloed. He'd flown on his *own*.

As he switched off the engine and deafening silence descended, Trubshaw held out his hand. 'Well done.'

Tom shook it.

As he cycled home he kept saying to himself, 'I'm a pilot,' even once calling it out as he passed a bunch of bewildered schoolboys on their way to Sunday school.

He was so thrilled that he thought of telephoning Fay, even going so far as dismounting and counting his change. He had enough. But then he realized it might cause her a lot of embarrassment and, reluctantly he got back on his bike.

Fay was embarrassed enough already. They'd been to church, sitting in the pews reserved at the front and had listened to a sermon on the evils of the flesh and the way the very fibre of society was being weakened by divorce.

Now, out in the cold but sunny day, she was standing around as her father and mother talked to the vicar, congratulating him on his sermon. She was embarrassed by the fact that the rest of the congregation was backed up inside, waiting dutifully until they moved on. Her father was like that though, very old school. When they finally came towards her she was reading a tombstone.

They drove home to find Jeremy's car in the drive. Cheerfully, her father said, 'Ah good. Nice to have that young man with us again. It's a solid family and he's an interesting chap.'

Fay did not respond. The dogs rushed out to greet them.

'I'll take them down to the stables.'

Her mother frowned. 'Don't be long — luncheon in half an hour.'

Jeremy was in the conservatory reading the papers.

'Good morning,' boomed her father, 'or I suppose it's afternoon now, though I don't feel that that's right until I've eaten.'

Jeremy, dressed in sports jacket and cavalry twills, grinned. 'I agree, sir. Good afternoon, Lady Rossiter — Fay.'

She smiled, but couldn't help saying,

'You'll be living here soon, Jeremy.'

It was a mistake Fay realized, as soon as she had said it. Her father gave a hearty chuckle, and glanced at his wife as he said, 'Well now, that's understandable, isn't it, my dear? You're always welcome, Jeremy, always welcome.'

Fay winced. How long would this blatant matchmaking go on?

'I won't be long, Mother.'

As she made for the rear entrance, her father said, 'Jeremy, why don't you go with her?'

The dogs raced around on the short grass as they walked towards the stables.

Jeremy said nothing for a while, just threw the ball for the Springers who competed in a flurry of leaping bodies, hanging tongues and the occasional snap.

At last, he said, 'Fay, I wanted to ask you something — away from your parents.'

'Yes, Jeremy.'

She expected it was going to be a plea to accompany him to some sort of shindig — probably a weekend house party, with all that that implied.

He threw the ball again and the dogs raced away.

'I wondered if we could get things sort of on a more permanent basis — an *under-*

standing if you like?'

Hurriedly he went on, 'Not straight away, of course, but I would like you to consider becoming my wife.'

Fay was stunned, found herself floundering hopelessly.

'Jeremy, I'm really flattered — but honestly, I'm not ready for that sort of commitment just yet. I'm so excited about this trip and the job and everything I've just not thought about anything like that.'

Her mind was racing. There was no way that she could say she was already engaged.

He frowned. 'I'm not expecting you to immediately drop everything, Fay, not at the moment anyway. Please do whatever you need to do, but when you come back we could, perhaps, make a formal announcement — even maybe a spring wedding?'

Such detail suddenly alarmed her. She had to do something decisive, stop it before it got out of hand.

Fay stopped and faced him. 'Jeremy, it's very nice of you, and I do value your friendship very highly, but I've never considered you as anything but a very good friend, one of the crowd.' She took a deep breath, 'And I've told you a lie — there is somebody else.'

His jaw dropped. It occurred to Fay that

he had never seriously considered such a possibility.

When he finally spoke he said hoarsely, 'Who is it?'

She was evasive. 'Nobody you know.'

Roughly, he grabbed her arm. 'That can't be possible.'

There was a harder edge to his voice.

Her chin came up. 'Well, it is true — it's no one from around here.'

His eyes bore into her. 'Your parents certainly don't know about this.'

Getting angrier, Fay pulled her arm free. 'How do you know that?'

'Because I asked permission from your father to pop the question today — that's why.'

She swallowed, irritated by the noise it made. 'Father never listens to me — always thinks he knows better.'

She whistled for the dogs. 'I'm sorry, Jeremy, but that's the way it is.'

He stood rock still, fists clenched as the Springers came bounding up.

'So you are saying there is no possibility. . . .'

She shook her head. 'No — none. I'd be misleading you, Jeremy. I'm in love with somebody else.'

He just stood there for a second or two,

then without another word spun on his heel and walked rapidly towards the house.

She wondered whether to follow him, but as the dogs fussed around she picked up the discarded ball and flung it away from the house.

She needed time to think and to cool down. What sort of reaction was she going to get? Her mother and father would be shocked, although she had hinted of somebody she had met at the fictitious party in Cheltenham. Hadn't her father taken it onboard when Jeremy was asking for her hand? She shook her head resignedly. Daft thing to ask — she knew her father when he got the bit between his teeth. He'd wanted Jeremy all along.

Eventually she arrived back at the door to be confronted by a very dark looking father. 'Fay, are you mad, turning down Jeremy?'

She looked around, seeing only her mother. 'Where is he?'

'Gone.'

'Gone?'

Exasperated her father said, 'Yes. He couldn't face being where he wasn't wanted.'

She tried to lighten the atmosphere. 'Oh, that's silly. He's a very good friend, I wouldn't dream of hurting him, but really, asking me to marry him — it's ridiculous.'

Lord Rossiter was suddenly icy calm. 'And just why is asking for your hand in marriage so ridiculous?'

She looked to her mother for help. 'Well, I've never led him to believe that there was anything special between us, he was just one of the crowd.'

'Rubbish. Last night we could see with our own eyes how close you were. He was full of the way you two did everything together. It was a sort of an understanding you both had.'

Fay started to get angry. 'That's not true, Daddy.' She appealed to her mother. 'You know I've been interested in another boy.'

Her mother frowned. 'This would-be pilot — what's his name?'

Blushing, she nodded. 'Yes and it's Tom, Mother. Tom Roxham.'

Her Father sneered. 'It's just a schoolgirl crush, Fay — get over it.'

'No — of course it's not.'

Lord Rossiter shook his head. 'I must say that I'm deeply disappointed in you.'

She protested, 'But Daddy, all I've done is turn down Jeremy. I'm not in love with him — it's as simple as that.'

'And you are with this other fellow?'

'Yes.'

There, she had said it.

'Well, in that case perhaps he would be good enough to present himself to us. Or is it unrequited love?'

She felt on the verge of tears. 'No — we're *engaged*.'

There was a deathly silence.

'Engaged?' Her mother was incredulous.

'Yes, Mummy. I'm sorry I haven't told you — it only happened last weekend.'

Lord Rossiter shook his head in disbelief. 'You saw him when you were in London?'

'Yes.'

His face was like a thundercloud. 'I presume nothing untoward happened between you?'

She cried out, '*Father* — of course not.'

But she knew her face had gone brick red — hoped they would interpret it as embarrassment. If they ever found out. . . .

'And you didn't tell us?'

'No. I mean I was getting round to telling you.'

'When?'

She shifted uncomfortably. 'Soon — I promise.'

'What have you got to hide, Fay, what is it about this man?'

She didn't have time to answer her father before —

'If you're engaged, where is your ring?' It was her mother, who was nodding accusingly at her hand.

Instinctively Fay covered her left one with her right, hiding the naked finger.

'We haven't had time to choose one yet.'

Her father snapped, 'Well?'

'Well what?'

She was beginning to get over the shock of what had happened, almost relieved. It was something she had dreaded.

'Why are you being so reticent about telling us about him? Or for that matter, why hasn't he presented himself like a gentleman — come to see us as a matter of courtesy? Has he something to hide?'

Fay shook her head. 'No of course not. It's all happened so quickly — that's all.'

'I see.'

Her father paced the floor. 'I don't like this, Fay. Do his parents know?'

She faltered. 'Frankly, I've no idea.'

'Who are they? What does his father do?'

'He doesn't do anything — he was gassed in the war.'

For once Lord Rossiter looked sympathetic. 'I'm sorry to hear that. So where do they live? Is it really Marlborough?'

'No. In Cheltenham.'

'And this boy — has he got prospects?'

It was coming to what she knew — *feared* — would be the most dreadful, shaming part for them to accept.

Fay defiantly brought her chin up. 'He's hard-working, bright, intelligent —'

But her father cut her off with a wave of his hand and barked, 'That's not what I asked. Just what does he do — *exactly?*'

She swallowed. 'He's an acting Detective Constable with the Great Western Railway Police.'

They were both visibly shocked. It tore her apart to see her parents hurt so much.

It was her mother who spoke first, her voice trembling and hushed. 'You intend to marry *beneath* you?'

Fay winced. 'Oh Mother, don't be so silly.'

In contrast to his harsh voice before, her father whispered icily, 'Enough of that Fay. Don't insult your mother when what you propose to do will humiliate us both.'

Suddenly Fay felt the tears coming. 'I'm sorry, Mother — I didn't mean to hurt — you are both so very dear to me. It's just well, we're made for each other — just like you and Father.'

But Lady Rossiter remained indignant. 'You can't share the same interests, the same friends, you come from wildly different backgrounds. It will never last, and you *must* know that.'

Her father joined in. 'He's probably after your money — nothing but a fortune hunter.'

She shook her head in despair. 'Daddy, how can you say something like that when you've never met him?'

'And whose fault is that, young lady?'

She hung her head. 'Mine really. I knew this would happen, I just wanted to put it off as long as possible, do it properly.'

'So why now?'

She looked up. 'Have you forgotten? Because of all this nonsense about Jeremy. And if there was ever a fortune hunter. . . .'

'Fay!' Her father bellowed at her. She knew she'd gone too far, even though she felt it to be true.

'Sorry. I'm upset, not thinking.'

'You're right there for once, you've lost your head, my girl. You must be ill or something.'

There was a brief respite, when only the sound of the dogs barking somewhere in the house broke the silence.

Suddenly, Lord Rossiter commanded, 'I want to see this boy — first thing tomorrow.'

Anxiously her mother asked, 'Is that wise?'

He continued staring at Fay. 'Yes. If he comes here after you tell him how we feel about him, then I shall at least be able to admire his courage — or gall.'

Worried, she prevaricated. 'I don't know if he is free — he has to work you know.'

But her mother's eyes flashed. 'You told me you were meeting Jennifer on Monday. It's not true is it — you're meeting him?'

Fay knew her face gave her away. Reluctantly, she nodded, her mother's lip curling. 'Then bring him here. Let's see this man who seems to have swept you off your feet.'

The contempt in her tone was only thinly disguised.

Fay turned back to her father.

'I forgot. You have met him *already,* at the station. When I came back from Cheltenham you tried to tip him, but he gave the money back — don't you remember?'

When it dawned on him whom she mean, he breathed, 'My God — *that* impertinent fellow.'

He wasn't being impertinent, Daddy, he was being honest.'

Her father shook his head in disgust. 'The least you can do is present him to us tomorrow. Tell Simpson to drive you to Cheltenham in the morning and bring him back.'

'But Daddy, haven't you got to go to the House?'

'Nothing that can't wait. This is more

important.'

'Very well, may I use the telephone? I shall need to send a telegram.'

He nodded.

When she was gone he turned to his wife, shaking his head. 'This is a nightmare. I would never had believed Fay could behave like this.'

Her mother agreed.

Fay didn't know what to say, but finally managed to dictate to the telegraph operator:

Meet you at your home same time tomorrow — but with car. Stop. Parents wish to meet you. Stop.

Love Fay. Stop.

It was read back to her.

'Thank you.'

It was with some trepidation that she lowered the telephone. Tom and his parents would get a terrible shock receiving a telegram but she didn't want Tom to be unprepared. Forewarned was forearmed. She felt ghastly. It had all happened so unexpectedly.

But one thing was a relief, *their* being together was now out in the open.

They'd had their usual Sunday main meal — a bit of roast mutton together with home-grown mashed-potatoes and carrots. Following this, they had tinned peaches topped with condensed milk.

Now Tom was cleaning all their shoes in the scullery, newspaper spread under the last on which he was steadying the shoes as he vigorously buffed the toe-caps.

His father was asleep on the couch and his mother and gran were chatting in front of the grate with cups of tea, when there was a loud knock on the door.

The women looked puzzled.

'Who on earth can that be?'

His mother got up and hurried down the linoleum floored passage. When she opened the door the sight of the telegram boy made her hand instinctively fly to her throat.

The boy asked if Tom Roxham was at home. Somewhat relieved she turned and called, 'Tom, there's a telegram for you.'

He wiped his hands on a cloth as he joined her at the door.

'Sign here please, sir.'

Doing as he was asked, Tom gave the pencil back and tore open the envelope. It took a second or two for the message, printed out on the ticker tape stuck to the sheet beneath, to sink in.

'Any reply, sir?'

He shook his head, fumbling in his pocket until he found a penny. 'There you are.'

'Thank you, sir.'

He stayed at the door, watching the boy give a running push to his bike and jumping on all in one go.

When he shut the door and turned back into the house he was confronted by his worried-looking mother and gran, and a father who was now sitting up.

'What was it, Son?' His mother's voice was full of anxiety.

Tom knew he couldn't delay the matter any more — especially with Fay coming tomorrow.

'It's all right, Mum, it's just from Fay — trying to get hold of me urgently.'

Nonplussed they waited. He took a deep breath.

'She's coming here tomorrow in a car. Her parents want to meet me.'

His father grunted. 'A car — fine. You said they were rich, so is there something else you haven't told us?'

Tom nodded. 'Yes, her father is Lord Rossiter, he's in the government.' Lamely he added, 'I suppose technically that makes Fay, the Hon. Does it?'

'God Almighty' exploded his Father, 'you're going out with bloody gentry.'

His mother looked flustered. 'Oh dear Tom, oh dear.' She couldn't say anything else.

Gran shook her head. 'No good will come of it, boy. They'll look down their noses at you and she won't fit in around here, I can tell you. You're daft.'

His poor mother tried to come to his defence. 'We've never met the girl, Mum.'

'Got nothing to do with it,' growled his father, who sagged back on the couch. 'She can be as nice as pie, she just won't fit in. And I daresay this summons by the high and mighty is because they bloody well don't approve of you, my lad. Bet your bottom dollar they're going to tell you what you can do.' He gave a humourless chuckle that ended up in a coughing fit. 'Better take the bus fare, you'll be bloody walking home.'

His mother started crying.

Tom, feeling awful, wrapped his arms around her. 'Don't mind what he says, Mum. I know you'll like Fay — she's a girl in a million.'

'With a million,' cackled his father in between spasms of coughing and getting his breath back. 'When the allure has worn off, it won't last.'

Tom spoke only to his mother, knowing that his father was a lost cause. 'We're made for each other, Mum — you'll see.'

His gran didn't help. 'Love match or not, I don't know what she'll make of this place.' She waved her hand around.

His father had the last word. 'She'll be used to it — must have visited the estate workers cottages at Christmas to give out the master's largess.'

CHAPTER THIRTEEN

Simpson brought the car around to the front of the house. She'd asked him to use the Lagonda not the great big Bentley.

As she sat in the back and watched the countryside go by, she thought of what the day would bring, of what lay ahead.

Firstly of course, she was going to meet his parents. How would they take to her? That made her nervous, as if she wasn't tense enough already.

Then there was this awful, authoritarian summons by her parents. How had Tom taken that?

Her tummy felt as if something was adrift inside. She'd hardly eaten at breakfast and the atmosphere could have been cut with a knife.

Father had followed her to the door, looking at this watch. 'We're not ogres, Fay. He's invited to luncheon.'

No doubt they would watch his table

manners keenly.

They reached the outskirts of Cheltenham. Simpson, who'd looked at the address, had said that the best way to go was via the Air Balloon public house and then down Leckhampton Hill, past the Devil's Chimney and the house where there had been a famous murder several years earlier.

'It's around here somewhere, miss.'

They'd entered a long tree-lined road. Passing the entrance to Leckhampton Station she suddenly noticed the street names to her right were similar. 'Down one of these, Simpson, please.'

He turned the Lagonda. The area was no longer made up of large Edwardian houses, but of terraces of red brick.

'There, miss, just coming up to it.'

They turned into a road where there were houses on both sides. Each house had a front garden only a couple of feet wide separating it from the pavement.

'There it is.'

They drew to a halt before number 12.

'Don't get out — please.'

'Very good, miss.'

Fay opened the door herself and stepped down. Nervously she smoothed her coat and opened the gate. She had only taken one step before the door opened and Tom stood there. She wanted to run into his arms, but they both felt restrained. Neither spoke for a moment. Her heart sank, he looked so glum.

'I'm sorry about this, Tom.'

He shook his head. 'Don't be, it had to happen. By the way, I've got something to tell you — but later. First come and meet my mother and father.'

She made a face. 'Oh God, Tom — what do they think about me?'

He just smiled and led her down the linoleum covered passage into the living-room. There before her was a man she instantly realized was Tom's father because of the same blue eyes and once dark hair that was now streaked with grey. The woman beside him still retained something of the looks that had captivated his father but years of hard work had produced lines in her face and her hair was listless and dull.

Fay held out her hand. 'Mrs Roxham, how do you do.'

His mother as overcome with shyness, even though the girl her son said he wanted to marry was really beauful. Fay's wide smile and open, honest face made his mother like her instantly.

She took the hand and only half suppressed a little curtsy which ended up as a tiny bob.

'Pleased to meet you.'

Fay turned to find Mrs Roxham's husband was staring at her with a piercing look that warned her this was where the trouble was going to come from. Mentally she registered the fact that her father also looked like being the main obstacle on her side.

He took a second to survey her before he finally spoke, 'So, *this* is the girl who has cast such a spell over our son, eh?'

Fay kept smiling. 'And he over me, don't forget, Mr Roxham.'

His father moved nearer and delivered a barbed compliment. 'I can see that you have a lively wit, Miss Rossiter, as well as good looks.'

Fay chuckled. 'Thank you for the compliment, but I'm not sure about the lively wit — or the good looks.'

An older woman, still dressed in clothes fashionable in the twenties came forward. 'I'm his gran, miss, also pleased to meet you.'

Fay shook her hand, reminded in a way of her own, now dead grandmother, with her long hair piled into a bun on the back of her head.

His father said, 'It's a rum do, our lad and you — you must know that.'

Nervously, Tom decided to intervene before she could reply. 'Well Fay, that's the family — except for the dog.'

But she wasn't to be distracted. Her eyes flashed in that way he had become accustomed to when she rose to a challenge.

'Rum do or not, Mr Roxham, Tom and I are getting married; isn't that so Tom?'

He looked at his father, and said it with a quiet determination, 'Yes we are, Dad — she's going to be my wife — your daughter-in-law.'

His mother broke the awkward lull. 'Would you like a cup of coffee, my dear?'

Relieved, Fay beamed. 'I'd love one, Mrs Roxham.'

His mother grinned sheepishly. 'I've had the kettle on and off all morning waiting for you. It won't take a second.'

His gran pulled a chair out from under the table. 'Sit yourself down, lass.'

'Thank you.'

Fay settled in the chair as Tom whispered in her ear, 'It's Camp coffee — you won't like it.'

She smiled up at him and patted the hand that he was resting on her shoulder. 'Oh yes I will.'

Mr Roxham noticed the little intimacy. Although she seemed a pleasant enough girl, and he had to give it to Tom, a real good looker, her clipped, educated accent riled him.

'Have you got a chauffeur out there?'

She nodded. 'Yes, Mr Simpson. Why?'

His father made for the door. 'I'll go and see if he wants something.' He winked knowingly at her. 'Got to look after the workers.'

Tom shot him a black look as he passed. Gran was helping with the coffee, so he whispered, 'You're marvellous — thanks for coming in. You could have stayed outside, just picked me up.'

She was indignant. 'I *could not,* Tom Roxham. If you make an honest woman of me I'll be Mrs Roxham — don't forget — this will be my family as well.'

He couldn't help it. He leaned down and lightly kissed her on her forehead. 'I love you.'

His mother, just bringing steaming cups on a tray through the doorway, caught him, and then looked at Fay as she nuzzled her head against his arms. She paused for a second, before coming further.

'There we are.'

She set the cups down, Gran following with sugar and a jug of milk.

Fay took the sugar and popped two lumps

in and added milk. Stirring her cup she said, 'All this has happened very suddenly. It must have come as a great shock to you both. Are you happy, Mrs Roxhan — we honestly don't want you upset, do we Tom?'

His mother smiled. 'My dear, now that I've met you I can see why Tom wants to marry you — he's a very lucky man if you'll have him.'

His father came back in, pointedly saying, 'Jack would like a glass of water, if that's all right, *Miss Fay.*'

Tom had never seen anything like it before. His mother suddenly shot up, went into the kitchen, came back with a glass of water which she thrust, slopping, into his hand.

'If you are going to behave like a silly old grouch, why don't you jolly well sit out there with Jack — I'm talking to my daughter-in-law to be.'

In the amazed silence, Fay said, 'You can invite *Jack* in if you like — I don't mind, but I suspect he'll be a bit uncomfortable.'

His father looked at the two of them in amazement, then left without another word.

Fay turned to Tom's mother. 'I do hope I haven't upset Mr Roxham.'

'Don't worry about him, my dear, now tell me about your parents.'

'Ah.' She shot an uneasy glance at Tom. 'Well, they're waiting to meet Tom. We're having lunch together.'

'Are we?' He raised an eyebrow.

She nodded. 'We are.' She didn't add, 'I'm afraid' but she guessed he knew it wasn't going to be easy.

Gran suddenly nudged him and said, 'Tom, what about the' — she nodded — 'the you *know.*'

He knew what she was on about. He had meant it for a private moment, but he owed it to his Gran that he had the ring in the first place.

He looked at the three women in his life. 'Very well.'

From his pocket he took out the little box. Immediately Fay's eyes lit up in startled surprise as she realized what it was.

She looked from him to the smiling Roxham women and back again.

He flipped open the lid. The ring with its perfect little stone glinted in the morning sunshine.

'Oh, Tom, it's beautiful.'

He took it out and held it up into the light.

'Where did you get it?'

He nodded at Gran. 'My grandmother gave it to me — it was her mother's.'

Fay turned to her. 'Are you sure? It's so

284

beautiful — it must hold a lot of memories for you.'

His gran put a hand on Fay's arm. 'My mother would be thrilled to know it was being worn by Tom's wife.'

Fay nodded with gratitude. 'I will do so with pride, and think of her for the rest of my life.'

'Come along, Tom — don't keep Fay waiting.' His mother had found her voice.

He started to reach for her hand, but his father, who had come back in, said sarcastically, 'What, not going down on your knees, lad? Where she comes from the women expect that sort of thing.'

Tom hesitated but it was Fay who said, 'I won't have you doing any such thing, Tom Roxham.'

With that she pushed her chair back and stood up before him, flashing a glance at his father before looking Tom in the eye. 'Well?'

He held the ring. 'Will you marry me Fay?'

'You know I will.'

With that he slipped it on to her finger.

She held up her hand, turning and looking at it for a few seconds, then fell into his arms. 'It's wonderful.'

Their tender hug widened to include the women in a joyful welter of cheek kissing, congratulations and thank yous.

His father sniffed. 'All very touching, but the hard reality is that you are not used to our way of life, nor is our young lad here, yours. He's going to stick out like a sore thumb among your lot and you're far too posh for the likes of us.'

His Mother exploded with horror. '*Father,* what a terrible thing to say.'

But her husband wasn't going to be put off. 'Your troubles are only just beginning, lass.'

Fay rounded on him, eyes blazing. 'And let me tell you, Mr Roxham, that I don't really care a damn. You are as bad as my father. A plague on both your houses.'

He shrugged. 'You may not care now, but what about when you are living in a house like this and with no car?' He waved his arms around. 'And you've got to do your own washing and ironing. It won't be such fun then, will it?'

Fay squared up to him. 'You don't think I can do anything, do you? Well let me tell you, at boarding-school we had to take care of ourselves and we learned domestic science and needlework. I've always looked after my horses until very recently, getting up at six o'clock to muck out.'

His father shook his head again. 'You're going to have to live on Tom's wage. I bet it's a lot less than your allowance.'

'My allowance!' She nearly spat the words out. 'You really do have me down as a poor little rich girl, don't you?'

She put her head on one side, hands on hips. 'You're right I won't be having *my allowance* when I marry, we will just have to make do. Though I intend to work when I can.'

Tom blinked. 'As an accompanist?'

She shot him a challenging look. 'Yes.'

Unthinking, his mother, desperately trying to steer away from the confrontation said, 'That's interesting. Do you go with people to things?'

Humiliated, Tom groaned, 'Oh Mum, Fay plays the piano while people sing — you know.'

Mortified, his mother mumbled, 'Of course. Sorry.'

Fay put her hand reassuringly on her arm. 'Don't be.' Fay chuckled. 'It sounds like that though, doesn't it?'

Fay turned back to his father. 'Well then, Mr Roxham, what's next?'

His father, sorry for his wife, who was not stupid and had blundered in her desperation to stop him, tried to contain himself. 'What about babies?'

Fay's right eyebrow went up. 'What about them?'

He shuffled his feet. 'Think you're up to looking after them on your own — no nannies — all those nappies and bottles?'

Fay grinned. The devil in her knew she was going to shock him, but she was quite pleased to, in truth.

'Well first the nappies — I'll get my father-in-law to help with all that manure — he seems to be good at it. And as for the bottles, I shall be using my breasts.'

Tom went bright red.

His mother and grandmother nearly fell off their chairs, hooting with laughter. His father looked shocked, eyes wide, then a slow grin suffused his face. 'I don't know how your parents are taking it, gal, but you are one formidable young lady.'

With that he held out his hand. 'Good luck to you both.'

No hug, no kiss on the cheek, but Tom knew that — for his father — that was warmth indeed.

They stayed for another half an hour, chatting about nothing, though Tom's father did ask about her father. He ended up shaking his head in incredulity, and muttering, 'My old man would never have believed it — in fact, I didn't either this morning, but now I've met you, Fay, and can see what a single-minded young lady you are, I don't think our boy stood a chance. He was a goner as soon as you decided he was the one for you.'

All the women groaned, but Tom was serious. 'That's all right by me.'

His father finished with, 'You'll need to keep a tight hand on her lad. She'll walk all over you otherwise.'

But it was said without the rancour of the start of the meeting.

Fay smiled up at Tom. 'Oh, he has his moments. He threatened to put me over his knee once!'

'Tom!' His mother sounded shocked.

Tom's face turned crimson yet again as he managed, 'That wasn't meant in earnest, Fay. I'd never lay a finger on you.'

She giggled. 'I know that silly. But it was rather exciting.'

When they finally left, they all followed them out into the street. The car was surrounded by youngsters, with Simpson keeping a wary eye on them. A couple of neighbours watched from their doorways across the street and a little group of women near the corner shop could be seen whispering to each other as they got into the car.

Simpson jumped behind the wheel and

started the engine. They lowered the windows and blew kisses, as he eased in the clutch and they moved slowly away.

All three were still standing at the gate waving when they turned the corner.

As they drove away in the back of the Lagonda, Tom said, 'You were wonderful, Fay.'

She lolled against him, looking at her ring. 'I think your parents are lovely, especially your Mum. And your father was growing on me — he's an interesting man — been through a lot.'

Her face clouded at the memory of the coughing fit as they were leaving. 'His chest is pretty bad, isn't it?'

Gloomily he nodded. 'Getting worse over the last few months.'

They sat, shoulders touching but not talking, conscious of Simpson's presence, but after five minutes she drew in her breath and said, 'Now we've got to face my people. Look, Tom, it may be hard to believe when you meet them today because they've had a hell of a shock, but they're good people really.'

'Of course they are — you're their daughter.'

She smiled her thanks, but then looked serious again. 'Daddy's very worried about

290

you — thinks you're after my money.'

When he made to protest she stopped him. 'I know — but they don't know you, don't forget. I've had a wonderful childhood, I love them dearly. Be patient — please.'

Tom took her hand, gave it a squeeze. 'Don't worry, I'm sure it will turn out all right.'

Fay smiled weakly — then suddenly her face lit up. 'Oh — you said you wanted to tell me something?'

He hadn't forgotten — how could he? — he'd just been waiting for the right moment.

They were going up Leckhampton Hill. He glanced at Simpson in the mirror. 'Can you stop by the view point over there?'

Simpson looked at Fay for her approval. She nodded.

The Lagonda drew into the edge of the road at a wide spot. He pulled her towards his door, helped her get to her feet, to stand on the grassy bank. The view was of the Severn Valley, with Cheltenham to the right and Gloucester to the left with the little hill of Churchdown straight ahead. Puzzled, she looked at the view.

'What is it?'

He stood beside her, smelling the freshness of her hair, arm around her shoulder as he pointed with the other.

'See that bit of green there, to the right, with the hangars?'

She was ahead of him. 'It's Staverton aerodrome — oh . . .' She turned around, eyes alight with excitement. 'What's happened?'

He couldn't contain it any longer. 'I've soloed.'

Fay's mouth flew open, her arms went around his neck as she screamed, 'Tom, that's brilliant.' He clasped her waist and lifted her off the ground as she continued to squeal with pleasure. Simpson coughed and discreetly looked away as she reached up and pulled his face down to hers and gave him a big kiss.

'You must be good, Tom.'

As he started to protest she butted in. 'Tell me about it.'

He did his best. In the end she sighed. 'Oh God, I do envy you so.'

He felt for her, held her tightly as they continued to look at the view, Tom's attention caught by the far-away white plume of steam and smoke from an express heading south.

Reluctantly she released him and gave him a tap on the shoulder. 'Come on, we'd better go.'

They got back into the car, sitting in the

corners, a space between them.

Fay opened her handbag for the photos. 'And I've got something for you.'

Tom looked down at the glossy black and white prints of them both, standing side by side, caught forever at the very beginning of their life together.

'Oh, Fay. Can I keep one?'

She nodded. Seeing them had brought a lump to his throat. He leant over and gave her a kiss on the cheek, unconcerned whether Simpson saw him or not. He took out his wallet and put the photo in and put it back into the jacket pocket over his heart, tapping it with his hand as she watched.

The car cleared the Cotswold escarpment and neared Cirencester. When they finally passed through the village of Bagendon she reached for his hand and squeezed it.

'Here we go.'

They swept through the gates and up the drive, Fay watching him closely as the house came into view in all its glory.

Their eyes met. Tom grinned. 'Nice little place.'

There was nobody in the doorway, not even Wilson. It seemed ominous.

Fay jumped out and met Tom as he came around the back of the car.

'Now remember, I love you, so whatever

my parents do or say, keep that fixed firmly in your head.'

He smiled. 'I will.'

He looked up at the façade of the house and felt very daunted.

They entered the stone-floored hall, Fay leading the way. There was nobody around. Frowning, she made for the drawing-room doors which were closed. She opened the left-hand one and walked in. Her parents were standing close together by the fireplace, looking very serious. The atmosphere was decidedly chilly.

'Daddy, Mummy, this is Tom.'

He had followed her in. For a second or two they faced each other in silence before Tom took a step further forward and held out his hand.

'Sir.'

Lord Rossiter paused for a second that frightened Fay to death, before he grudgingly took the hand and shook it — just the once, letting go quickly.

Her mother held back, didn't offer her hand as her husband said rather sarcastically, 'So — *you* are Tom Roxham.'

'Yes, sir.'

'And where did you meet my daughter?'

Tom shuffled his feet. 'Well, *the* very first time we saw each other was at a dance in

Cheltenham.'

Her mother spoke for the first time. 'You were in the orchestra, I believe?' She managed to make it sound as if he had been cleaning the drains.

'Yes.'

Fay stepped forward and said proudly, 'Look, Mummy.'

She held out her hand with the ring.

Lady Rossiter gave it a cursory glance. 'Very nice.'

The way she said it was dismissive, making Fay burn with anger — and embarrassment for Tom.

Her father only looked at it passingly, and grunted, 'What exactly did Fay say you did for a living?'

She noticed that he hadn't yet called Tom by his Christian name and was irritated by the fact. 'I'm a Police Constable with the Great Western Railway, sir — acting as a detective.'

'Hmmm.'

There was no disguising the disapproval in his voice. 'Can you honestly expect to keep my daughter in the manner to which she is accustomed on your salary?'

'Daddy.' She could stand it no longer. 'What is this, an interrogation?'

Her mother joined in. 'Fay, we have been

so worried.' She turned to Tom, saying, 'Can you understand that?'

'Yes — Mrs — sorry — Lady Rossiter. I am well aware that I'm not from the same background, but all I can do is reassure you that my love for Fay is genuine.'

'And mine for you,' butted in Fay.

'That's all very well.' Her father struggled with himself visibly for a second before saying, '*Tom,* but the cold reality is that Fay is used to all sorts of things — a decent home, horses, the best hotels. Can you give her that sort of life?'

'Oh really, this is too much.' Fay was getting angry. 'We've hardly been in the house a minute.'

Seeing her anger her mother placed a restraining hand on her husband's arm. 'Would you like a drink before lunch?' she asked Tom.

He looked at Fay, who said quickly, 'A sherry would be nice, wouldn't it?'

He turned back to her mother. 'Yes, that's very kind — thank you.'

Wilson had appeared from nowhere and now proceeded to pour three glasses which he served to them on a silver tray.

'Sir?'

Her father shook his head, held up a tumbler of whisky. 'I've already started.'

Awkwardly, Tom took his glass and waited until Lady Rossiter sipped hers before he did the same.

A sort of uneasy truce descended.

'Shall I serve luncheon soon, madam?'

Lady Rossiter nodded. 'Ten minutes.' She looked at them all. 'I think we're nearly ready.'

While they drank the sherry he was conscious of them watching his every move as they made small talk.

Fay put her arm through his at one point, emphasizing that they were together.

When they sat down, it was in the dining-room to her surprise — one of the most formal rooms. Her father sat at the head of the table, her mother at the other end and Fay and Tom opposite one another in the middle. They were unable to see each other easily because of a very large and elaborate silver candelabra. Fay fumed. They often ate quite informally in the Orangery at lunchtimes. This had all been set up to intimidate Tom.

Wilson held the serving dish whilst her mother and then Fay helped themselves to slices of cold beef, potatoes and beetroot. When it was Tom's turn he did the same — unfortunately dropping one of the slices half off the plate. He quickly put it in place using his fingers. Fay noticed the looks exchanged between her parents.

But any hopes that they may have had about his misuse of the knife and fork, especially how to hold it were quickly dispelled. His gran had been in service and had supervised young Tom's table manners from a very early age. So he wasn't phased by the use of his table napkin, or which items of cutlery to use for what.

Red wine was poured into his glass. After his 'tasting' fiasco on their first date, Fay had told him more about wine so when Lord Rossiter said 'I hope you like the Bordeaux,' he swirled it in his glass, took a sniff and a sip and said, 'Yes, very good, sir.'

By the end of the meal, Fay was bursting with pride — and relief.

Wilson presented the humidor, which Tom declined. Lord Rossiter selected one, rolling it between finger and thumb, then cut the end.

Lady Rossiter pushed back her chair as Wilson hurried to help and threw her napkin on to the table.

'Come along, Fay, let's leave them to talk.'

Fay put her napkin on the table and stood up. She knew what her parents were doing — separating them deliberately. She shot her father a hard look. 'Don't be long, will you?'

When they'd gone, clouds of blue smoke rose around Lord Rossiter as he sucked the cigar into a glowing, fiery end before waving the match in the air until the flame extinguished.

'Shall we take a stroll on the terrace — need a bit of fresh air?'

Obediently, Tom followed him through a french window held open by Wilson. Outside Lord Rossiter took a few steps to the stone balustrade and looked out over the parkland, taking in exaggerated lungfuls of air before sticking the cigar back into his mouth.

'Ah, that's better.'

'Beautiful house and grounds you have, sir.'

Lord Rossiter nodded slowly in agreement. 'And you, Tom — tell me about where you live and your parents.'

He did, making no fabrications to improve his standing.

'I live in a terraced house rented to my grandmother, with my parents. Father is unemployed — gassed in the war at Passchendaele.'

Just for once Fay's father betrayed a trace of softness. He shook his head. 'Thank God

I missed anything like that. Bad enough getting blown up, but *that*.' He shook his head again.

'Give my best wishes to your father. What unit was he with?'

Tom told him. 'The County Regiment, sir.'

'Well now, they were close to my sector of the front — but I dare say I had my Blighty one before him.'

They walked in silence for a moment or two until Lord Rossiter stopped and faced him. 'You are a very agreeable young man. It's nothing personal. Nonetheless you must know we are bitterly opposed to this marriage, Tom — it's not going to take place.'

This time there was no coldness in the way he said 'Tom'.

The latter's heart fell to his boots.

This conversational friendly manner seemed so frighteningly absolute — more of a done fact than an expression of their feelings.

Bleakly he dug his heels in.

'Yes, it is.'

Lord Rossiter twitched his lower jaw. 'You hardly know each other.'

That was something Tom was prepared for. It was true but. . . .

'I know and Fay knows it, sir, but the fact

is we are meant for each other, something happened to us both when we first met.'

'Stop talking like a character in one of those American films — life is far harsher than fiction. Look, Tom, now I've met you I can see you're a decent enough type, but you should know that Fay is a very strong-willed girl and the more she thinks she wants to marry you, the more she will convince herself — whether it's true or not.'

Tom persisted. 'But it is true, sir. We love each other.'

Lord Rossiter didn't reply immediately, resuming his stroll. After a while he said, 'You do know, I presume, that she has just had a marvellous offer to pursue a musical career?'

'Yes, of course.'

Her father paused. 'It involves an overseas tour of six months.'

'So I gather.'

'We do hope that she intends going through with it. You haven't tried to talk her out of it I hope? Her mother and I would be most upset after all the years of hard work?'

'No, of course not. To be honest it hasn't been on our minds at all.'

Lord Rossiter took a pull on his cigar, then said challengingly, 'The two of you are not entertaining the thought of any hasty action, I hope?'

'Hasty?' Tom wasn't sure what he was getting at.

'Yes — like eloping?'

His mouth dropped open. 'Good Lord, no.'

A faint smile flittered briefly across Lord Rossiter's face. 'That is a relief. I did not confide my fears to Fay's mother, she is under enough strain as it is.'

Tom shook his head. 'We're engaged, sir. That's all. There are no plans for the wedding — we haven't even talked about it.'

Her father walked on. 'Good, I applaud your correctness, Tom.'

To the latter, it seemed to be going quite well again, then like a dagger thrust from behind a cloak, Lord Rossiter said, 'Of course, we shall now automatically exclude Fay from our wills — you will get not a penny from any union with this family.'

After the shock, in which Lord Rossiter carried on strolling as if nothing had happened, Tom felt his anger rising. But he recalled Fay's plea to remember that whatever the provocation, she loved him and to keep calm.

But he couldn't help saying sarcastically,

'Nor you from entering into the Roxhams — sir.'

Lord Rossiter was not amused. Bleakly he answered, 'You may joke, young man, but I am deadly serious. You will gain nothing financially from this venture.'

Despite everything, Tom began to lose his composure.

'I thought we were coming to an understanding, sir. I love your daughter — she loves me. What you have just inferred is not only insulting to me, but, far worse, you can't think much of Fay to say something like that.'

The older man grunted. 'I wouldn't be carrying out the obligation of being her father if I didn't protect her, at least until she becomes the concern of another man — her husband.'

Tom bit back the desire to say it sounded as though he was talking about Fay as if she was property or something. Instead, he managed, 'Fine, sir, but I'm not concerned at all with your family's wealth, you can be assured of that, nor is Fay.'

'Really? Have you asked her?'

'No.'

'Then perhaps you should.'

Tom was getting exasperated by the whole trend of the conversation. 'I have no need.

Is that "it" sir. Is that your main concern?'

'Of course not, Tom.'

Lord Rossiter grinned in such a friendly way that what followed was unnerving. 'You are completely unsuitable; with neither the education, background, prospects — need I go on? Tom, for all our sakes, think again about this madness. It can't be right, can it?'

Tom shook his head. 'I'm sorry you think that.' This time he deliberately stopped himself from adding 'sir'. 'Fay and I so wanted your blessing. It will make her very sad.'

'Perhaps it will make her see sense.'

Tom had had enough. He was sure that Lord Rossiter had been a good father to Fay — and was, in his way, doing what he thought best for her, but he was being very direct and somewhat rude.

He felt his patience running out and struggled to control himself. 'I think we have nothing further to say to each other, have we? We're engaged. I'm sorry you cannot accept that.'

Lord Rossiter raised an eyebrow, waited until he'd drawn thoughtfully on his cigar before replying.

'Tell you what, Tom, you help us persuade Fay to go on her tour, demonstrate this is no five minute wonder, and I will do nothing in the meantime to come between you — how about that?'

'And afterwards?'

Fay's father's lips compressed into a thin line. 'We will cross that bridge when it comes.'

After seconds of silence, Tom said, 'I wouldn't dream of standing in Fay's way — if she wants to go, there will be no opposition from me.'

Lord Rossiter nodded. 'Good.'

Fay had followed her Mother into the drawing-room and straightaway challenged her. 'Well, now that you've met him, what do you think?'

Her mother frowned. 'Oh really dear — if you mean do I think he's good-looking, in a rough sort of way, yes, but he's — well, working-class. You really can't be serious?'

Fay took a cigarette from the box on the table.

'Never so sure about anything before in my life, Mother.'

She lit up as Lady Rossiter protestd, 'But he is totally beneath you socially — you'll be a laughing stock.'

Fay took the cigarette from her lips.

'You're ashamed, aren't you, Mother?

That's what's really hurting you!'

Lady Rossiter sat down in a wing chair. 'Fay — please, *please,* let this madness pass. It's as though you are ill or something. You've only just met, how can you carry on as if you really *know* him?'

Through the thin curl of smoke going up from her cigarette, Fay said, 'I knew straightaway.'

Her mother made a clicking noise of disapproval.

She continued, 'So, you would throw away everything — and I mean everything, your career, your position in society, your family, for a life of poverty with a man you know nothing about.'

Fay took her time answering, as though she was seriously considering the question, then said brightly, 'Yes.'

Lady Rossiter just shook her head in despair. 'He will not get a penny from this family — you do realize that, don't you, Fay?'

Her daughter's eyes widened with disbelief. 'My God. I can't believe you said that.'

'Why not?'

Fay threw her arms wide.

'You've *met* him, Mother. Need I say more? He is so obviously not a cad.'

'Hmmm. And what about your career?

Have you thought about that?'

For the first time Fay's eyes clouded. Seeing her success, Lady Rossiter added quickly, 'All those years studying, you finally start to get somewhere, and then a complete stranger comes along and spoils it all.'

'Not necessarily, Mother.'

Lady Rossiter sniffed. 'Are you telling me he's not going to try to stop you?'

'No — of course not.'

But in reality they had not discussed it and, more to the point, she suddenly realized that she had been pushing it to the back of her mind.

Lady Rossiter continued, 'You don't know much about men, do you, Fay? Once they are in charge they become very selfish. He'll want you around *him* — taking care of *him,* you wait and see.'

Fay restrained herself from saying that whilst her mother might feel that way about her father, she had no such feeling like that for Tom — they were equals.

She remained silent, taking another pull on her cigarette, then resting her hand on her cheek, elbow on the arm of the chair as the smoke curled away above her head. But her mother wasn't going to take a rest from it.

'When would you expect to marry this man?'

Fay was getting tired of her mother's disinclination to use his name. 'Do you mean Tom?'

Grimacing, Lady Rossiter snorted, 'Of course — unless you are engaged to more than one man.'

Exasperated, Fay snapped, 'Oh Mother, don't be ridiculous.'

'Well — when?'

'We haven't thought about that yet.'

Her mother sighed. 'I really can't take this seriously, Fay. If it ever comes about, have you thought about the arrangements — how your side of the church would be packed with family, friends — some including people from the Government — and then his people?' She was incredulous. 'It would be a nightmare. And we would be expected to pay for this . . . this spectacle.'

Fay, instead of feeling crushed, chuckled.

'Could be fun. His mother is a lovely person and it could be very lively between his father and Daddy.'

Lady Rossiter was clearly not amused. 'Oh really, Fay, be serious. His family are not even middle-class. They would have no idea how to behave — how to dress. And can you imagine the reception and the speeches. . . .' She shuddered.

Fay stood up. 'All right, Mother, I can see that there might be problems. Maybe we should just get hitched in a register office.'

Her mother was horrified. 'You can't be serious?'

Fay took a last pull on her cigarette and tossed it into the fire. After she had breathed out the smoke she said, 'Perfectly. Since you and Daddy are so set against the whole thing, I wouldn't dream of asking you to pay for it.'

Her mother was still speechless when the men returned and entered the drawing-room. Lord Rossiter, with his hand on Tom's shoulder, guided him into the room.

'Well, that's all settled then.'

He signalled Wilson. 'Let's have a bottle of the '35 Pol, please, we need to toast the happy couple.'

It was almost too much for Fay's mother. 'But. . . .'

Her husband waved his hand to stop her. 'Tom and Fay's engagement is a *fait accompli,* my dear, and I agree, it did catch us off balance. But now that I know Tom has Fay's best interests at heart, and won't do anything to jeopardize her career, then I think it only right that we give them our blessing.'

When it looked as if Lady Rossiter was

going to explode, he silenced her with a hard look behind their backs.

The cork was expertly released by Wilson, and the glass bowls filled with the bubbling wine from the Champagne region. Lord Rossiter raised his glass.

'To the happy couple — Tom and Fay.'

They all touched their glasses, Fay moving next to Tom and holding his hand. Her mother looked bleak and bewildered, her smile thin and forced.

Lord and Lady Rossiter stood on the steps of Codrington Hall and waved as Fay and Tom were driven away.

Out of earshot and still waving, she said. 'What on earth are you doing, giving them our blessing — are you out of your mind?'

Lord Rossiter took her by the elbow and guided her back indoors.

'My dear, you know Fay, and she is besotted by this fellow. If we forbid her, she'll do something silly. As it is, this *Tom* has promised me he won't get in the way of her career — and that means almost six months abroad.'

His wife began to see the light. 'You think the novelty will have worn off by then?'

'That's the general idea.'

She looked doubtful. 'Absence could make the heart grow fonder? It did with me when you were away at the front.'

He smiled down at his wife. 'But we had known each other for some time before — not like this flash in the pan.'

Lady Rossiter didn't answer. Although he was right that they had known each other for some time, she had fallen in love with him the moment they had met. It worried her that her daughter might prove to be a chip off the old block.

Her husband gave a grunt. 'And meanwhile I'll have a word with old Abercrombie — he's on the Great Western Railway Board, used to be my fag at school; see if we can't put a few obstacles in the way of young Roxham's plans.'

Lady Rossiter looked relieved. 'That's a good idea, but be careful, any suspicion that we have had anything to do with it and it could misfire badly.'

But Lord Rossiter was rubbing his jaw, not listening, mind suddenly far away. He looked very tired and unhappy. She prompted.

'What is it?'

He came out of his reverie. 'I was just thinking where we might all be in six months in these troubled times.' He shrugged, looked at his wife sorrowfully. 'Every dark cloud they say has a silver lining. In our case that might also upset their wedding plans.'

Inside the car Fay cuddled up to Tom and asked, 'What happened with you and Daddy?'

He had his arm around her. 'Nothing — but he made it pretty plain that I wouldn't have been his first choice for a son-in-law.'

Fay wasn't satisfied. 'But he came in agreeing to our engagement.'

Tom gave her a squeeze. 'Well, what's wrong with that?'

'Nothing — but you must have said something.'

'All he asked was that I wouldn't get in the way of your career. I said I had no such intention. I'm very proud of you — over-awed in fact.'

She sat bolt upright. 'So *that's* it!'

'What?'

'They think that when I go on this tour I'll forget all about you, that we'll just drift apart. They must be counting on it.'

He pulled her back to him, whispering in her ear. 'That's not going to happen is it? It will be agony though.'

She turned his face and kissed him fiercely. 'No, it will not — especially if I don't go.'

Tom kissed her just as fiercely back. 'You

will go. I'm looking forward to being married to the world famous pianist — Fay *Roxham*.'

She playfully punched him and said, 'I'll keep my maiden name professionally, thank you very much.'

Then in a rush of euphoria that it was all over, she flung her arms about him and just hugged and hugged him. It was if a great weight had just lifted from her shoulders. There were no more secrets, no more lies.

But as they drove through the Cotswolds, with an AA man on his motor bike and sidecar saluting them as they passed, Fay experienced a growing sense of unease. As they started the descent into Cheltenham, with Simpson double de-clutching to engage a lower gear to slow them down, she finally understood why. Her parents wouldn't give up *that* easily. If things didn't seem to be working out as they expected, they would also bring pressure to bear in some other manner as well — probably were planning that *already.* They would *never* give up.

From her position nestled against his chest she looked up at him, at his face. For the few seconds before he sensed that he was being studied and looked down at her and smiled, she saw for the first time — at least consciously — the firmness of his jaw and mouth and the sharpness of his look as he gazed out of the window at something in the distance — like a hunter. It was only a fleeting glimpse of this man she now felt was part of her, but it was exciting. There was more to know, more to look forward to. But one thing remained the same: nothing would separate them now, even when they were physically apart.

And to that end she began there and then to plan ahead, to think in terms of the actual wedding.

CHAPTER FOURTEEN

In the following weeks the weather steadily improved.

One sunny day Tom, flying solo, found himself utterly relaxed, looking down through his goggles at the rolling brown and green fields of the Cotswolds, and the tiny moving white dots that were its flocks of sheep.

The slipstream battering his head, the whistling rigging wires and the steady roar of the engine had now become second nature to him. He banked away to the right, looked down again, saw a couple of little cars moving along a road, like beetles scurrying along well trodden paths. Over Gloucester way there was a blue-grey haze from the factories. Tom felt so incredibly free. He looked up — at the darkening blue that marked the end of the earth's atmosphere. Beyond was space.

Not for the first time he felt *something.*

He didn't go into it with anybody — except Fay. He'd told her once that he felt he wasn't alone up there. She hadn't laughed at him, in fact she'd said nothing, just squeezed his hand.

Trubshaw began to teach him air navigation, more aerobatics and sideslipping, a little instrument flying, emergency procedures — dual and solo — all the time stretching his ability.

Life was busy for both of them. They managed to meet on average once a week, usually in Cheltenham, squeezed between his work rota, flying lessons and her increasing involvement with Sir Trevor Keynes.

On several occasions Tom accompanied her to concerts in London and Cheltenham Town Hall, and under her guidance, began to take an interest in classical music. The first time he was really moved was at a performance of Elgar's Cello Concerto, when something in the music seemed to be talking to his English soul.

For her part, Fay sometimes accompanied him to the airfield, if it was a nice day, sitting on a chair beside the hangar, reading when he wasn't in sight and sometimes being taken for a joy ride by one of the other aircraft owners. Afterwards they would go into Cheltenham, sometimes to the cinema, or a tea dance, or just strolling around happy to be together.

For Fay things at home had been good — too good really. They very occasionally asked after Tom, but in many ways it was as if the whole engagement had never happened. She'd even been clothes shopping for her trip with her mother in London, with luncheon thrown in by daddy at The House.

This treatment more than anything strengthened her conviction that there was only one answer to their predicament. It would by-pass her scheming mother and father and ease the problem for Tom's parents.

And the moment to tell him what had been in her mind since that drive after the first meeting came as they were sitting outside, in the Montpellier Gardens, on an unexpectedly warm afternoon watching people playing on the public tennis courts.

'Tom.' She reached out and took his hand.

Bemused by her tone, he looked around at her. 'Yes.'

'It won't be that long till I go off on this tour.'

Crestfallen he nodded. 'I know.'

When she didn't immediately say anything else he prompted, 'Fay, what is it?'

She looked down into her lap, took a deep breath. 'Tom, I don't want to hurt your parents — in fact, they could attend, but I don't want my parents to know anything about it.'

'About what?'

'I think we ought to marry in a register office as soon as possible, but keep it a secret.'

Stunned, he just kept looking at her, even when a young man in white flannels and holding a wooden tennis racquet called out, 'Could you toss the ball back, please?'

Tom came out of his daze, stood up and got the ball, throwing it back with a flick of the wrist, oblivious to the 'Thanks.'

She watched him with bated breath as he came back and sat down beside her, still saying nothing.

'Well?'

Tom finally looked directly at her. 'How soon can we do it?'

She smiled. 'I've got the forms; all you've got to do is sign up and set the date.'

He shook his head in wonderment. 'What am I getting myself into?'

Fay giggled. 'Matrimony, my love.'

But secretly he was churning with excitement. He had assumed some distant time, a year or more. There was so much to work out, where to live, what he could afford, and so on. And the meeting of the families — if hers came at all — and guests . . . the problems had been on his mind for weeks.

'So what do we do for my best man, and your bridesmaid?'

She shrugged. 'We'll rope witnesses in on the day — can't use friends, word would get back.'

Tom knew she was spirited, but he was continually being amazed by her.

He tried to act as the Devil's Advocate even though the idea was rapidly gaining credence in his mind.

'When we've done it — what then? Should we have a honeymoon? They'll get suspicious if we disappear — and I would have to get time off from work.'

For a second Fay thought about it, blushing, before saying, 'We should have a few days together, don't you think, Tom? But if it's impossible, then so be it. The important thing is we will be man and wife — *married,* and there is nothing anyone can do about it.'

He tried another tack. 'But will that be enough for you? Don't you want it to be in a church, married by a vicar?'

Wistfully, Fay nodded. 'Ideally, but there is nothing to stop us having a church wedding later, is there?'

So it was decided. He used his fountain pen to sign the forms she had pulled from her handbag. When he finished she put them back, did up the button that closed it, then stood up.

'I need a cup of tea.'

Grinning, he got up, looked around, then gave her a quick kiss on the lips.

Just as he did so a tennis ball hit him on the back of the head. He pretended his legs had buckled under him.

Laughing, she playfully slapped his arm. 'You fool.'

They were both so happy as they walked into town to the cinema.

The bombshell dropped next day.

As usual, he presented himself to Sergeant Whelan exactly on time. The latter inspected his acting detective constable and seemed to find everything in order by the softness of the grunt he made. He then said, 'I hope your replacement over the next few months won't be another would-be pilot.'

Tom was shocked. 'Replacement? I don't understand, Sergeant.'

The moustache was given a perfunctory sweep by the back of the right finger, then the same hand picked up a sheet of paper.

'You're being sent on secondment to the

London North Eastern Police, we're taking one from them.'

Feeling slightly sick at the thought of what it would do to them he protested.

'But why? I've never heard of that happening before, Sergeant.'

'For what it's worth, Roxham, neither have I.'

He passed the letter over to Tom who saw it was from their Headquarters in Paddington.

'Seems they want an undercover officer whose face won't be known in the area. Can't be too careful; apparently it's something serious.'

'I can't go.'

Suddenly Whelan's face became rigid, his voice that dangerous softness Tom knew presaged a serious reprimand.

' "Can't" Roxham? I'm afraid it's an order, and we don't disobey orders do we, *Constable?*'

Tom took a deep breath. 'Then I'll resign.'

Whelan exploded. 'Don't be a silly fool; it's only for a few months and if you do well it will increase your chances of promotion — it's a golden opportunity.'

'I don't care.'

Sergeant Whelan's black eyebrows nearly joined in the middle of his forehead. He had trouble restraining himself.

'So, you'd rather be out of a job with no references than be away from home for a few months? Very clever. And what about those flying lessons you've been going on about — won't be able to pay for them with your dole money, will you? If you get it.'

'Is it this girl I've heard about? If she's worth it she'll be waiting for you when you come back.'

Tom was still stunned, and the realization that the flying, which was coming on in leaps and bounds would be affected, added to the turmoil in his head.

'Where am I to be stationed, Sergeant — King's Cross?'

At least, in London he could continue to see Fay.

'Read the orders, laddie. No, it's Peterborough. Bed and breakfast accommodation has been arranged for you next to the station.'

Staggered, Tom asked, 'When — when am I supposed to go?'

Sergeant Whelan's face lightened. 'You report first thing on the day after tomorrow — your ticket from here to Peterborough is in the booking hall.'

Looking shattered Tom turned to go.

Whelan called after him. 'And laddie, my

Bridget waited for a damn sight longer than a few months.'

Tom nodded. 'Yes, Sergeant.'

He rang from his usual box near Leckhampton Station. When she came to the telephone Fay sounded concerned. It wasn't their usual time.

'Darling, what is it?'

When he explained the line was silent for a few seconds. Anxiously he prompted. 'Fay?'

Her voice was strained. 'This isn't normal, you say?'

'No — I don't think so.'

'It's my father's doing.'

He frowned out of the window at a passing Wolsley car. 'That's impossible.'

He couldn't see her vigorously shaking her head. 'Oh no it's not; you have no idea of the strings he can pull. Look, Tom, this can play into our hands.'

Puzzled and feeling rotten he questioned, 'How?'

'You know that matter we were discussing yesterday?'

'Yes.'

'Well, think about it. We do the deed either where you'll be, or London, or wherever it is — no one will be any the wiser. You can even have a few days off. Sir Trevor lives in

Norfolk. I can use that as an excuse to be over that way.'

Tom slowly began to see what she was driving at. Her voice came again. 'When do you go?'

'Tomorrow.'

'Oh, that is quick. Which route are you taking?'

He shrugged to himself. 'Up to London, then mainline to Peterborough.'

She seemed to make up her mind. 'I'll go up for the day — we can share a train and have some time together.'

That bucked him up, that and her general cheeriness. He told her which train he would be on, stopping at Kemble.

She promised to be there.

His voice dropped. 'See you tomorrow then, sweetheart.'

She managed a rather breathy 'Goodbye, darling' and put the phone down looking thoughtful.

Tom stepped out of the box and unexpectedly found himself with a day off. As he turned his bike for home, he wondered if Mr Trubshaw could fit him in today. Then it hit him like a brick. He'd been so concerned about himself and Fay that he'd never thought about the flying. What would happen now? Had it all been in vain?

Without further thought he turned the bike for Staverton.

Mr Trubshaw was in his office listening to the wireless when he knocked and put his head around the door.

'Have you got a minute?'

The instructor turned off the wireless and sat up. 'Tom, what brings you here on a week day morning?'

He told him. 'So you see, I won't be able to come for sometime by the look of it.'

Trubshaw steepled his hands. 'Hmm, that's not good Tom — you need to keep up the training.'

Miserably he agreed. 'I know, but what can I do?'

Trubshaw stopped steepling his hands and opened a drawer of his battered desk. 'There is one possibility. Where did you say you were being posted to?'

'Peterborough.'

Trubshaw produced a booklet and began flicking through it. 'Here we are — East Midlands.'

He studied it for a minute as Tom sank despondently into a chair. 'Right.'

With his finger on an entry he picked up his telephone and dialled the operator.

Tom listened as he said, 'I want to make a trunk call please, to' — he looked more closely at the page — 'Peterborough 253. Thank you.'

He put his hand over the mouthpiece.

'I'm ringing the nearest club to where you're going, to see whether we can get you transferred. The trouble is, they might be full up.' He looked at him warningly.

'Everybody is busy with these government contracts, it's good business.'

Tom waited in a state of apprehension.

His mother had been working overtime; cleaning and pressing shirts, socks, underwear — everything he needed. She was a bit emotional, it was his first time away from home. The family suitcase had a leather belt tied around the middle in case the catches popped open under the strain.

'You will write now, Tom, won't you?'

'Of course, Mother and I'll be home soon enough.'

She had a clothes brush and did the shoulders of his jacket before he tossed his raincoat over one of them and put his trilby on his head.

'Right, I've got to go, Mum, or I'll miss the train.'

As she gave him a kiss, she fussed and worried around him.

'Don't do anything silly now, Tom —

promise?'

He picked up the case and winked at his father who shook his free hand.

'I won't, Mum, I promise.'

The suitcase weighed a ton and felt as if it was pulling his arm out of its socket by the time he got to the bus stop. What on earth had she put in there? He hoisted it on to the platform and put it under the staircase as the bus pulled away. Stumbling, he fell on to a bench seat and looked out of the back window, at the receding streets of his childhood. He had a sense of leaving something behind — forever.

Fay was waiting as the train appeared in the distance in a blue haze of heat, finally rumbling past her, coupling wheels clanking, metal shrieking on metal as the brakes were applied.

She saw his head sticking out of a window long before the train ground to a halt. Waving furiously she ran up the platform towards him.

He opened the door and stepped down on to the platform — straight into her arms. They held on to each other tightly before they got on the train and sat side by side.

They lapsed into silence for several minutes. The carriage was full, he'd had to save her seat several times from people walking up and down the corridor and sliding back the door.

The man opposite was deep inside his *Daily Telegraph,* the headline, something about Europe, his bowler hat, umbrella and mackintosh on the rack above him. Two women were reading books, one, he noticed was by Daphne Du Maurier. A small boy in school cap, short trousers with knee-length grey socks and a dark blue gaberdine raincoat was reading a *Wizard* comic, with the *Hotspur* waiting on his lap.

She whispered to him. 'Have you got your new address?'

He'd already written it out. He took it from his wallet and passed it to her.

'There is a phone number as well, although I don't know how the landlady feels about that.'

She nodded. 'Write and let me know when you are going to be free and we can meet in London. Didn't you say you could travel on the trains for free?' She knew his budget was tight.

'Yes. I'm getting an LNER warrant card, or at least a temporary one.'

As the train rumbled and lurched over the points and reached the fast track she suddenly remembered, 'Oh Tom — what about the flying?'

'It looks as though that will be all right. Mr Trubshaw has found a flying club that will take me, although I suspect I might have to pay a little more. I've got my log book with me.'

'Oh, thank God.'

After another pause she whispered, even more quietly this time, 'There is a register offce in Peterborough. Can you get things started?'

He found her hand. 'Yes. I've no idea when I can get off, but if it's a problem they can fire me the way I'm feeling.'

Fay looked worried. 'Don't do anything too rash, darling, I'd hate to get you into trouble.'

He looked at her fresh face against the upholstery of the seat, her beret with its pom-pom raked down one side, hair flowing out in an unplanned riot of curls and at the red lipstick adorning her small mouth. A rush of madness came over him that took him completely unawares. Even as he was saying it, whispering into her ear, he could hardly believe it.

'There's nothing I can think of better than getting you into trouble.'

Nature had been tormenting him with desires he'd never known before.

Startled, Fay turned her head so that she

329

could look directly into his eyes and saw that they were not twinkling with fun. He had a look that she'd never seen before. Ever since that night in her room at Claridges when she had had such a heat on her that she had taken his hand to her breast, Fay had tried to keep her mind off such things. But she had had difficulty some nights, lying there thinking of him, unable to sleep. She ran the tip of her tongue suggestively along her top lip and whispered back, 'You'll have to wait until I'm your wife.'

He just looked steadily back at her, holding hands as the buttercup-filled meadows of Wiltshire flashed past.

At Paddington they went on the Circle line to King's Cross. The inside of the station was, for Tom, disappointing, lacking the grandeur of the Great Western Terminus. But he was taken by the sight of a dark blue stream-lined engine with the name, 'Kestrel' that had just drawn in. Sir Nigel Gresley had designed them. It radiated power and speed. One of its number, 'Mallard', had broken the world steam record of 125 mph over a part of the track he was about to go on. When it sounded its whistle, it was an excitingly low, klaxon-like sound, not a high-pitched shriek.

'Here you are.'

Fay, completely oblivious of his interest in the engines, pointed out the departure board. 'Hang on, I'll get a platform ticket.'

While she scurried away, he rested the heavy case on the ground, watching the throngs of people coming off the train. A lot of sailors with their kitbags over their shoulders were clomping down the platforms.

When she came back he took up the weight of the case. Walking down the length of the train he enjoyed looking at the natural teak coaches with their cut back ends and white roofs.

'Here we are.'

He boarded and entered the first compartment, flinging his coat on a seat next to the sliding door by the corridor, with his hat on top. He had to use a lot of muscle to swing the suitcase up on to the luggage rack.

Back on the platform they didn't care about the crowds surging past, they just hung on to each other. He talked into her hair.

'You going to go straight back?'

She shook her head. 'No, I'll pop in to see Sir Trevor's secretary — I've told them I'm up in town. They've got some sheet music to give me, and more details of the itinerary. It all fitted in rather well.'

They continued talking about nothing in particular, conscious that time was running out. People started to find it difficult to find seats.

'You'd better get on.'

He looked around, then back to her. 'I'd rather stand all the way than leave you a second earlier than I have to.'

She chuckled. 'Oh yes? No, you get on, I'd rather know you had a seat for the next couple of hours. Come here' — she reached up and pulled his head down. For a kiss in public it was rather daring, in fact Tom Roxham distinctly heard someone say, 'Oh really!'

When she released him, she said, 'I can't wait to be married — now go, and don't forget to write.'

She pushed him on to the train and motioned him along the corridor, then pointed to his seat, blowing him kisses. She had meant to walk away, but found she couldn't. They stayed like that until eventually whistles blew, doors slammed. The coaches began to move. In the distance she could hear the locomotive labouring to get the great weight moving.

She walked alongside for several yards but the train seemed to accelerate quite quickly.

She blew a last kiss and halted, the carriages passing with the regular double beat of the bogies on the track junctions, until the last coach went past with a hiss of steam.

As she stood and watched the receding train, she realized there was quite a downward slope out of the station which explained the quickness of its departure and then a rise into a tunnel. The red light of his train seemed to hang in the dark for a long time before it disappeared.

The green light of the semaphore signal at the end of the platform turned to red.

She turned and walked back feeling empty.

The digs turned out to be very good, a house in a street near the station run by a Welsh lady called Mrs Chick.

The breakfast he sat down to after a restless night on a brass bed that creaked with every move, was vast — eggs, bacon, a lump of black pudding and slices of fried bread. Tea was poured from the biggest pot he'd seen. Mrs Chick bustled around as other paying guests came down and sat around the one big table in the dining-room, introducing themselves. Most were travelling salesmen.

In her sing-song voice Mrs Chick told him about a footpath between the houses that would get him to the station quickly.

After a last visit to the lavatory he went back to his room and inspected himself in the full-length cracked mirror in the middle of his oak wardrobe. All seemed to be in order.

As he walked down the footpath between the back gardens of terraced houses, he could hear the railway long before he saw it. The squeal of steel and the crash of buffers accompanied by the labouring 'chuffs' of engines denoted a large marshalling yard.

As he approached the mainline, the thunderous roar of each train travelling at high speed lasted only a few seconds. It was followed by a wash of drifting smoke which made him tingle with anticipation.

The station was bigger and busier than Cheltenham, which seemed sedate in comparison. The police office there was large, with an inspector as well as a sergeant and several constables.

He was shown into the inspector's office and stood to attention before a man who couldn't have been more different from Sergeant Whelan if he'd tried. Frowning as he examined the documents Tom had brought, the man finally looked up at him. He had a thin face and baleful eyes.

'Well, Roxham, what are we to make of all

this, do you think?'

Blinking, Tom said, 'Sir?'

The inspector tapped the sheaf of papers with the back of his hand. 'You — being transferred to us? What did you do to upset our country cousins so much?'

Tom objected strongly to the country cousins' bit.

'Isn't it about needing new faces for important undercover work, sir? That's what I was told.'

The man sneered. 'We're a big force, Roxham, why would we need to get you when there are people as far away as Aberdeen and Norwich who could do any job we wanted?'

It was at that moment that Tom knew for sure that what Fay had said was true. Her father had engineered this to drive them further apart.

Any lingering doubts about their elopement vanished. As soon as he had some time off he would go to the register office — even *before* the flying school.

By the end of the week he had done both and sent a brown envelope to her containing all the forms she needed to fill in. He already had his birth certificate with him.

He borrowed Mrs Chick's son-in-law's bike to get to the airfield. Like the station it was busier than Staverton and had a tarmac strip. In the clubhouse, with its walls adorned with a wooden propeller and black and white photographs, he found the man he wanted at the bar, talking with a lively group of young men.

'Mr Dickinson?'

The chiselled features and jutting jaw of the man were completed by pale-grey eyes that seemed to bore into him.

'Yes?'

'My name is Tom Roxham — I believe Mr Trubshaw at Staverton Aero Club has been in contact with you about me?'

'Ah, so you're the laddie I've been waiting for eh? What will you have to drink?'

Although nothing was further from his mind, Tom instinctively realized that to get on with Dickinson he'd better not refuse.

'I'll have a pint of the Adnam's, if that's all right.'

'Of course it is.'

The barman had already heard and was manning the handle, mug at an angle as the gold coloured liquid gurgled out of the spout.

Dickinson waved his hand at the four other men. 'These are current members of our elementary Civilian Reserve Flying Training School — CRFTS for short.

They all greeted him in turn with a hand-shake, saying their names as they did so.

Tom turned back to Dickinson as his beer was put on the counter. The latter handed it to him.

He took it, said 'cheers' as he raised it to his lips, and was greeted with a reciprocal chorus. When he'd had a few swallows, he lowered his glass and nodded at the talking group.

'Am I joining them?' he asked.

Dickinson shook his head. 'These are all men who've taken the King's shilling. Once they're finished they either go back to their jobs to await the call, or straight to the air force for their uniforms and square bashing, then on to intermediate and advanced training.'

Seeing the look of disappointment on his face, Dickinson explained. 'It's the Volunteer Reserve, laddie; they've actually signed up for the air force who've put them on to these courses. It's expanding rapidly since Herr Hitler tore up the Non-Aggression pact.'

Feeling somewhat out of it, Tom said, 'I want to fly, Mr Dickinson, but I've got a job to hold down.'

A look passed between a couple of the men and Dickinson said, 'Well, let's hope that's the way it stays — for all our sakes.'

But there was no mistaking the lack of belief in his voice.

Next evening, Tom flew a familiarization sortie, with Dickinson in the front seat. When they got back, the latter climbed out and said, 'All right. Now do a circuit and try not to break our toys.'

Did they always say the same thing?

Off he went. When he taxied back Dickinson was nowhere in sight. He found him in his office — a little shed on its own, between two vast new hangars. He was signing something which he then rubber stamped. Without looking up he said, 'Congratulations, you're officially on our Civil Guard course now, Roxham.'

And from then on everything went at a faster pace. Because of a lack of work for him to do he increasingly found himself spending more time at the airfield than he ever did in his digs.

He met Fay in London twice in the following three weeks and a date was set for the wedding — 22 May.

They were in a small restaurant off the Haymarket, with the pre-West End show crowd wearing ties and dinner jackets all around them. There was talk of Flannagan and Allen and the Crazy Gang.

She was looking even lovelier to Tom, who

had missed her badly.

'So.' She took a sip of red wine, seeming to roll it around in her mouth before swallowing. With hooded eyes, she looked over the rim of the glass at him.

'That's the day fixed then — and the *night?* You *can* get the next day off as well, I presume?' She raised one eyebrow, eyes bright and challenging.

Tom finally found his voice. 'You try and stop me.'

Afterwards, they walked hand in hand to the bright lights in Piccadilly Circus, watching the Schweppes Fountain for a while before she said, 'Come back to my hotel for a nightcap?'

'Of course.'

They sat in the American Bar at the Savoy.

'Where are you staying tonight?'

He pulled a face. 'I'm not. I'm getting the 1.30.'

'Oh Tom! You could bunk on the sofa in my room like last time.'

He looked back at her levelly. 'No I could *not.*'

There was no denying what he meant.

She just nodded. With a little shiver she knew he was right.

It wasn't that she thought her virginity important any more — after all they were going to marry — but it was all about self respect.

A week before the wedding Dickinson told him to come to his office after he'd finished his post-flight checks. Tom wondered what he'd done wrong. He bumped into him coming out of the door.

'Come and have a pint.'

When they were seated on their bar stools with their glasses, the foam sliding down the sides, Tom asked, 'What's this all about?'

'How passionate are you about your job?'

Frowning, Tom took a sip. 'To tell you the truth, at the moment I've got other things on my mind — why?'

'Dicky' Dickinson offered his Navy Cut cigarettes. Tom took one as the instructor continued, 'Trubshaw was right — you do have a talent and I think it's being wasted at the moment. The CRFTS course will finish in a month's time. You would do better if you were on the next one.'

Tom held the end of his cigarette in the flame of Dickinson's lighter, then leant back blowing smoke out.

'Apply? But you said they were people who had been put on the course by the RAF?'

'That's right. You either get your employers to agree to a two-month absence and then return to them, or you could be accepted by the RAF — continue to train as pilot at one of their Advanced Flying Training Schools.'

Perplexed, Tom asked, 'You mean — join the RAF permanently?'

Dickinson nodded. 'The way things are going you might not have much choice in a year or two — unless you are in a reserved occupation — are you?'

Bewildered, still trying to come to terms with what Dickinson was proposing, he lamely shook his head.

'I have no idea and what do you mean — no choice?'

Dickinson rolled his eyes in disbelief. 'Dear God, Roxham, I don't have you down as a dunce. I'm talking about the gathering storm — Hitler, Germany all that rot.'

Tom shrugged. 'Don't read the papers much except for the cricket and rugby. Besides, I'm getting married next weekend.'

That did make Dickinson's jaw drop.

He took a large draught of beer, setting the glass down on the bar and wiping his lips with the back of his hands before saying, 'Ye Gods, you're a close bastard, I'll give you that.'

Tom wasn't shocked by the language —

he'd heard far worse aloft. He smiled, added by way of explanation, 'We're running away — nobody is to know so I'd appreciate. . . .'

'Of course, of course.'

There was a pause until Dickinson said, 'What does your fiancée think about all this — your flying, I mean?'

'She was the one who actually got me into it. Without meeting her I probably would never have done it. Funny that, isn't it? I'm in the railway police because I wanted to be near my boyhood passion — railway engines. Aeroplanes were for toffs, really. I've never heard of a working-class boy as an aviation hero in the Great War.'

Dickinson inclined his head. 'True. Well, you're a trainee pilot now and, I don't usually say these things, but with great potential. What I want to know is, have you really thought through what you are going to do? I've told you what I think, go away and talk it over with the boss' — he gave a cynical chuckle — 'I mean the wife. See what she thinks. There is no guarantee, of course — you'd have to go for an interview and so on, but I still have a few strings I can pull and the time is right. In the end it comes down to, do you want to stay in the police, or have a career in the air force?'

Numbly, Tom looked into his drink.

'Strings?'

Dickinson grinned ruefully. 'I don't use them much, except to get a good table in a restaurant, but I could call myself "Squadron Leader" — I had twenty years in the service.'

Tom was amazed. 'You don't look old enough.'

Dickinson laughed and clapped him on the back.

'Thank you. When I joined up in 1917 I lied about my age.' He stubbed his cigarette out. 'Let me know as soon as you can what your decision is. Then I'll set the wheels in motion if you decide Yes. How long are you on honeymoon for?'

The very word made Tom Roxham dizzy. 'Only a couple of days. It's all we could manage.'

Dickinson patted his shoulder as he left.

'Let me know by the end of next week, would you? Time is running out.'

Tom promised he would.

Left alone, he wondered what she would say. He thought of this Saturday. They were going to meet at the register office at twelve o'clock. She didn't want him to see her before then — bad luck apparently. She was going to stay overnight in a hotel and then, as a surprise, had booked them three nights at a hotel, she wouldn't tell him where. It was her treat because she knew he had had to fork out for the wedding ring.

Tom had had no trouble getting the time off. It was as if they really didn't care for his presence there at all. It was only three nights because Fay was having trouble concealing the real reason for her absence.

So, his life would change irrevocably from Saturday onwards, whatever else happened. But Dickinson's proposal had left him troubled. It was as if he had no control over events anymore, he was like a child's paper boat in a bubbling stream.

Fay went out for a ride on the Wednesday morning and was hacking along one of the lanes when she was suddenly conscious of another horse and rider on the other side of the hedge, making for the same gateway as she was. They arrived at the same time. It was Jeremy. He reigned in, looked stonily at her for a second, before raising his whip to touch his cap.

'Morning to you.'

'Hello, Jeremy.'

There was an awkward silence for a moment or two as they walked on, then Fay said, 'I didn't mean to hurt you Jeremy — this has all just happened — I can't explain it, I know my parents think I'm mad. I suppose in a way it is a madness. But what about you — what have you been doing?'

He sniffed. 'Been busy.'

He told her about some parties he'd been to and a theatre trip arranged by Lord and Lady Forster that had been great fun. All the usual crowd had gone — hadn't she been invited?

As it was she hadn't, but she shook off the implied slight. It was a relief hearing about her old friends again.

Fay had been aware of the isolation from her usual crowd of friends and to be talking to Jeremy meant that things might slowly be getting back to normal.

He asked, 'What are you doing before you go?'

'Doing? Nothing really.'

'You ought to have a party, celebrate your success.'

'Success? But I haven't done anything yet.'

'Oh come on, Fay, you know what I mean and in any case just to wish you bon voyage.'

She pulled Jenny to a halt. 'Jeremy, any party would have to include Tom. You do realize that?'

He stopped slightly ahead of her, so she couldn't look him directly in the face, but saw that he had stiffened. 'So, you are still seeing him?'

She frowned. 'What do you mean — *still?*'

His horse was restless and in order to line up beside her again he had to turn in a circle to do so. 'I thought perhaps you might have had second thoughts by now.'

Stung, she was hardly able to resist saying that she was getting married that Saturday. 'No, Jeremy, I haven't.'

His face darkened. 'But your parents said you'd been busy and that he wasn't around any more.'

The penny dropped then. It hadn't been a coincidence; Jeremy had bumped into her because her parents had set this up.

'I have been busy, but we've written a lot to each other.' She was not going to reveal the extent of their meetings.

His face remained bleak. 'I see. In that case forget it. I don't think I could face seeing him.'

Gently she said, 'I'm sorry you think that way, Jeremy — I think you'd like him a lot if you got to know each other better.'

Jeremy snorted. 'Be serious, woman. Why would I want to do that? I could have taken your rejection better if the chap was — well, you know — he's not even *trade,* is he?'

At that moment any sympathy Fay might have had for him was utterly destroyed. She didn't trust herself to say anything civilized, just flashed him a look that said it all and dug her heels into her mount.

Jenny whinnied as she leapt forward, but Fay goaded her into a gallop. She was furious with her parents, but out of sight of Jeremy she slowed Jenny back to a walk.

Her first inclination had been to steam into the house, pack and leave earlier to the hotel in Peterborough. But in the peace of the countryside, common sense prevailed. She paused and looked down on the valley below, conscious of being in the last few days of her girlhood. Come Saturday she would become a married woman.

She could not suppress a little tremble. Would it hurt? Would she be all right for him? One thing was for sure. Nothing would ever be the same again, not her mind — nor her body.

Saturday dawned bright but cloudy, with a promise of clear skies later. Tom packed his case and sat down to a hearty breakfast. Mrs Chick fussed around him, then went off to change. She and her husband had been thrilled to be asked to be the witnesses.

For the next couple of hours Tom thought he would go mad. He went for a walk, into the city, found himself standing in the cathedral, looking at the stained glass windows. He walked back again, went into the North Station and sat down as the distinctive klaxon of an A4 streamliner gave only a second's warning before it roared through, going so fast he couldn't catch the name. Not for the first time he wondered where he would be that night. She had made all the arrangements and had taken great delight in keeping it a secret. He only knew they were going by train.

On his platform a big locomotive drew in with a down express for York. He stood up and went to take a closer look at 'Flying Fox' in its apple green livery.

The large pacific locomotives of the London North Eastern certainly had a glamour about them, and a look of brute force.

Checking his watch he made back to his digs. Mrs Chick was in a dark-blue linen suit, with big buttons and a hat with feathers everywhere. Mr Chick was in a pinstripe suit with a shiny bottom to his trousers and elbows. Looking anxiously at her watch she said 'Tom, where have you been? I was beginning to get worried.'

He smiled. 'Sorry Mrs C — I'm just so pent up — I was trying to walk it off.'

She produced a carnation for a buttonhole and began to fix it to the lapel of his suit. In her sing-song voice she continued, 'We don't want you late — that's Fay's prerogative. I'm thrilled to bits to be going to meet her in the flesh.'

She'd only seen the photograph Tom had shown her when in a desperate and inspired moment he'd asked her and her husband to be their witnesses. He'd had to explain that it was because they wanted to keep it a secret because of family problems and, thus reassured, Mrs Chick had been overwhelmed at the thought.

She began brushing his suit shoulders as Mr Chick dragged the net curtain aside and called out, 'Taxi's here.'

It was only a short ride to the register office. He'd just finished paying the cabbie when another pulled in.

She was sitting alone in the back seat. He opened the door and held out his hand.

Fay was dressed in an ivory-coloured two-piece suit with mother-of-pearl buttons. On her head a small feathered hat with a matching net, behind which her eyes gleamed with anticipation.

He drew her out gently. 'Darling, you look wonderful.'

It just didn't seem enough. She was so mouth-wateringly, achingly desirable.

'Thank you. And you're looking very handsome too.'

When she was standing beside him, he said, 'I'll pay the taxi.'

She held his arm. 'No — he's going to wait for us. I've booked him for the rest of the day.'

The Chicks were waiting in the foyer as he steered her proudly towards them.

'This is Fay.'

'Oh, Tom, she is more beautiful than in your photograph. I'm pleased to meet you, my dear — and at such a wonderful time for you both.'

Fay nodded. 'And I'm delighted at last to meet you, Mrs Chick — and your husband. I've heard so much about you from Tom here.'

They shook hands. Mr Chick was clearly impressed with the vision of the young bride before him, but Mrs Chick butted in before he could get a word in edgeways.

'Are you sure you want *us* at this most momentous occasion and not your parents?'

Fay put her gloved hand through her arm. 'Quite sure. I can't thank you enough for doing this for us. Come on, let's get it over with.'

She winked at Mrs Chick as the latter looked askance. 'Need to make an honest man of him, poor lamb, he's lost without a woman.'

Mrs Chick roared with laughter. 'Aren't they all, my dear, aren't they all?'

It was a simple ceremony, but the very simplicity seemed to add a greater meaning, a greater solemnity to the vow-taking than all the ceremonies Fay had seen in grand churches.

As she faced Tom and said, 'I do', she felt as if they were at the centre of the universe. It was a moment so quiet, so devoid of any other sensation that it was as if a spiritual force was reading the marriage lines, not the man in the dark coat and pin stripe trousers. And as Tom faced her and took her to be his wedded wife, he experienced a strange sense of timelessness, as if the moment when he slipped the ring on her finger had happened before, would happen again, that he was eternally bound to her in a way that had no meaning in wealth, sickness, health — or even death.

Afterwards, out on the steps, the Chicks threw rice. The men shook hands, as the women kissed cheeks, then everyone piled into the Rover 14. It only took five minutes to take them to a restaurant where they had a reserved table overlooking a garden. It was a jolly afternoon, with champagne, lamb chops and spotted dick.

Whilst they ate, Fay and Tom could hardly

take their eyes off each other. Mrs Chick elbowed her husband and grinned broadly. 'Remember when we were like that, Fred?'

Her husband rolled his eyes.

They dropped the Chicks back at their home and said goodbye.

'I'll be back on the Thursday morning then,' Tom shouted from the car as they drove away.

At the station he cocked his head at her and enquired, 'Right, are you going to tell me where we are going?'

She chuckled. 'The seaside. I've always loved the sea. A little place called Sheringham, on the North Norfolk coast.'

His eyebrows shot up. He'd thought it was going to be London or York perhaps.

'Why there?'

'I have very happy childhood memories of being taken there with cousins when we stayed in Norwich — you'll like it.'

He put his arm around her tiny waist. 'If you're there, I'll like it all right.'

She gave him an admonishing look. 'Come on then, or we'll miss our train.'

In their compartment they sat opposite, just smiling at each other. Whether it was the rice that had somehow found its way on to the seats and floor, or their demeanour, but several people paused at the sliding door, then carried on down the corridor. When they finally got under way, he stood up and with his fountain pen wrote, 'Just Married' on a piece of paper and stuck it on to one of the blinds, pulling all three down.

'Tom!'

But she was half-hearted.

He pulled her to her feet, held her face firmly with both hands and kissed her with all the pent-up excitement he'd had since he'd first seen her in the car that morning.

When he finally let go, she gulped for air. 'My God Tom. . . .' It had been so hard and fierce and bruising, but she had been aroused and wanted him to do it again.

He did so, only more gently this time. Eyes closed, her hands played with the back of his head and then she gave his hair a tug.

She said, 'Stop — someone might come in.'

Breathless himself, he let her go. Frightened of what he wanted to do; the taste of her powder and her scent was driving him mad.

He slumped down in the seat opposite. 'Sorry, I'm behaving rather badly.'

'No, you're not, but patience, darling. Only a couple of hours and we'll be alone.'

She looked away, out at the smoke and

steam drifting gently away across the fields. If truth be told, now that it was imminent, she was more anxious than ever about the coming night. Surely it couldn't hurt *that* much — after all women seemed to survive it all right?

More worrying still — would she be any good? Maybe she was frigid?

By the time their train trundled through the Norfolk countryside, it was early evening, and the sun was beginning to lower in the sky.

They steamed into a little station called Weybourne. Fay stretched her arms.

'Next stop us.'

Tom stood up. 'I'll get the cases.'

She watched him reach up, broad back flexing as he swung his down, followed by her rather smarter one and a hat box.

Lifting the arm rests he put them on to the seats.

With a whistle, the unseen locomotive drew them out under the latticed iron footbridge, and began to draw the four coach train the short run to Sheringham.

'There — there's the sea.'

Fay was bouncing up and down on her seat like a little girl, but Tom was more taken by the rolling hills and pine woods.

'I thought Norfolk was supposed to be flat.'

Passing a golf course with the coastline beyond they started to brake for Sheringham. Out in the corridor he marshalled the luggage near the end door. When they drew in and squealed to a halt, he leapt out on to the platform and heaved them down on to the flagstones. A porter and his barrow came up. 'Let me, sir.'

Fay stepped down beside him and pushing her arm through his, reprimanded, 'Come on, darling, let the man do his job.'

Confused, he looked at her, then realized she was a little embarrassed by his handling the luggage. He grinned, muttered in her ear, 'Why, you little snob, I can see that I will need to bring you down a step or two.'

Out of the corner of her mouth, she breathed out, 'I'll have to take you in hand.'

She hadn't meant it to be saucy — had she?

She coloured up and hung on to his strong, muscled arm.

Outside were two taxis. The driver of the first one held open the forward facing rear door. Fay got in, sweeping her legs and skirt out of the way as the driver slammed the door shut. Tom got into the leather smelling

355

interior from the other side and sat beside her.

Tom was surprised by the shortness of the journey — just a matter of two streets. Suddenly they turned on to an esplanade with the sea on their right as they stopped in front of a very large, red brick hotel with a central dome and side turrets. Coming out down the steps was a small laughing crowd, the men, some in white tie and tails, others in black tie and dinner jackets, the women in evening dresses. They set off across the gardens to the sea front.

A commissionaire came to the car and opened Fay's door as the taxi driver got out and went to the rear to help a young lad with a hotel luggage trolley.

'Welcome to the Grand, madam, sir.'

Tom paid off the taxi and looked up at the façade.

'Phew, it's rather big compared with the rest of the town.'

At the reception desk he was greetd by a black-coated man with a silk tie. 'Good evening, sir. Have you a reservation?'

They looked at each other. 'Yes — Mr and Mrs Roxham.'

Out of sight, Fay's hand had found his and squeezed.

CHAPTER FIFTEEN

In the morning Fay watched him shave, fascinated by the paths of exposed bluish skin left by the safety razor in the white fields of snow that was the lather.

She sat cross-legged on the bed, her pink tipped breasts exposed but with the sheet tangled around her waist and legs. Fay felt sore, bruised, and very very happy.

In the mirror his eyes met hers. All that had happened between them in the night was contained in the look that passed between them. Shyly she glanced away, down at her lap. When she raised them again he was busy rinsing the soap off the razor with water in the basin. Fay let her eyes run down his body, from his wide shoulders to his narrow hips and tight little buttocks and on down his muscled hairy legs. It was all hers now. From the moment she had lain on the double bed and called out that she was ready, nervously arranging the new

357

pure-silk nightdress around her, to the time when she finally fell asleep, naked, curled up with Tom behind her, his breath on the top of her head, rough hands cupping her breasts, one leg possessively over her, she had become his flesh, and he — hers.

He finished shaving and pressing a towel to his face, turned around. She was still taken aback by the sight of the passive male genitalia so casually displayed. And then she realized with a start that *it* was taking an interest in her — again.

As he came nearer, throwing the towel aside, she sank back on to the pillow, hands splayed out defensively before her and clowned, 'No — No —'

He leapt on her as she screamed and giggled, then all went quiet until she took him into herself for the fourth time in their married life, and Fay Roxham found her voice again as she used all the strength of her arms and legs wrapped around him to hold on to his thrusting body.

It was like riding Jenny to hounds — only better.

After a breakfast of smoked kippers they strolled hand in hand along the front till they reached the lifeboat station, then turned back as the sparkling waves fell at regular, lazy intervals on to the pebbles and drew noisily back through the bouncing, dragging stones.

Up in the town he bought a *Daily Sketch* and they found a little teashop attached to a bakery, and ordered coffee.

Tom read the headline which stated that Germany and Italy had signed a formal alliance, something that was being called a 'Pact of Steel'. He began to realize that what Dickie Dickinson had been talking about was probably becoming reality. In the pit of his stomach he felt a heaviness, a sickening feeling that somehow there would be an intrusion into their lives that he had not properly realized before.

He lowered the paper.

'Darling, I want to ask your advice.'

She looked up from her magazine, sensing the seriousness in his tone. He showed her the headline then told her about his talk with Dickinson.

'So you see, — should I leave the police if they won't allow me two months off, and try for the air force straightaway?'

Dismayed, just like he had been, with this invasion into their new found happiness, she was pleased with the time to think, provided by the interruption when the waitress returned with their coffee.

When she'd gone Fay reached for his hand

on the table and covered it with her own.

'Darling, the decision must be yours. Is it as inevitable as your man seems to think?'

Tom shrugged. 'Who knows? The point is, would you mind if I lost my job, and ended up in the Royal Air Force, or on the dole?'

She shook her head. 'You do what feels right. But Tom —' She looked imploringly at him. 'Whatever you do, take care, won't you?'

For the next two days and nights, he tried to push it from his mind as they walked and talked, ate, drank and made love and slept in each other's arms.

On the last afternoon, when the weather had turned even warmer, they walked out of Sheringham on the coast path, up Skelding Hill to the lookout point. There, he sat with his back to the steep grassy slope with Fay leaning against him and looked down along the coastline of cliffs and beaches leading into the distance as far away as Blakeney Point. A mile inland was a windmill, with behind it the pine covered hills that rose to a sky filled with the twitter of skylarks. To complete his heaven a burst of white smoke in the far distance heralded a train coming from Holt.

He chewed a stalk of grass and watched as two men in plus-fours drove off from the golf course just below them.

'Fay — thank you for this.' He swept his arm around. 'It's so beautiful, so. . . .'

She rolled on to her tummy and looked up at him.

'So England? Like an illustration from a child's story book?'

Smiling, he nodded. 'Yes.'

He looked intently at her. 'Tomorrow, you're sure — ?'

She cut him off. 'Yes. Come to the station — but that's *it*.'

She was going to Norwich then on to London. He was due back at work, but had tried to persuade her to let him come with her for the extra few hours together, but she wouldn't hear of it.

A week later she was sailing from Southampton on the Union Castle Mail ship the RMMV *Warwick Castle* to Cape Town, which would take fourteen days. After two concerts there they would continue on to Australia and New Zealand, with the Orient Steam Ship Company.

'All right.' He saw that she was adamant. 'But only if you let me come to Southampton to see you off.'

'Of course.'

'What about your parents?'

She sighed and held out her hand, showing the new wedding rings on her third finger, left hand.

'Father might not notice, but Mother will. Besides, I'm now most definitely your wife — I shall tell them so.'

She leant over him and gave him a very gentle kiss on the lips. 'Mark you, my passport is still Miss Rossiter, I've had no chance to change it yet.'

He stroked her hair, teasing a strand back over her ear. 'You sure you don't want me there when you tell them, after all, you are my wife?'

She grinned. 'I'll be all right. Whether they come to see me off is another matter. All I want is for you to be there.'

They lapsed into silence, except for the soft whisper of the grass and the skylarks above them and the gentle far off lap of the waves.

Next morning they were up earlier than they had been the previous few days. To Tom it all seemed to happen so quickly. Their luggage was collected from their room after breakfast, and the taxi was waiting for them at 8.30.

As they drove the short distance through the streets watching the shopkeepers open up, some putting boxes of fruit and vegetables on display on the pavement, others cleaning their windows and pulling out the white canvas awnings with hooked poles, they said nothing.

Tom paid off the taxi and followed the porter through the small, wooden-floored booking-hall, giving his ticket to the collector who punched it.

'You're platform two, sir — another half an hour.'

Her train was already in, the coaches right in front of them. The porter found her a seat and put her suitcase on the rack, then rejoined them on the platform for his tip.

Fay turned to Tom. 'Darling, I'll see you in Southampton.'

'I'm not looking forward to your leaving.'

'Neither am I. But this is important, Tom, and I'll soon be home.'

He nodded. 'By the way I'm going to do it Fay — try for the RAF. If it comes off it will help fill the void whilst you are away. In any case, I'm not happy with policing on the railway anymore — not for life anyway.'

'Good for you.'

The guard looked at his watch, but still kept talking to the station-master.

Tom said, 'You'd better get on.'

She nodded. They moved closer, held each other, said nothing.

When the guard's piercing whistle came it

made them break apart. She kissed him quickly on the lips then boarded the train. He closed the door behind her as she pulled the strap and lowered the window and put her head out.

'Take care, Mr Roxham.'

'I will. And you too, *Mrs Roxham.*'

The carriages began to move slowly. She stayed at the window as the train drew away, over the level crossing with the white gates that stopped the traffic going down into the town.

He stayed where he was until he could no longer see her. Picking up his case he walked slowly over the footbridge, feeling utterly desolate.

Dickinson looked at him through a haze of cigarette smoke.

'Good, I'll see what I can do, you will have to go for an interview — it will all depend on that.'

Tom nodded. 'Will that be for the volunteer reserve or the regular air force?'

Dickinson flicked some ash off his jacket. 'If you've made your mind up to chuck your job, come what may, I'd go straight for the service. You've got a better chance than the reserve; they'll know you're serious, and besides, the reserves can be a bit snooty, a bit cliquey.'

Fay walked into the house and found her parents in the drawing-room. They were looking gloomy. Her heart quickened. Had they somehow found out about them?

'What is it? Is everything all right?'

Her mother, who had a hand on her husband's arm as he sat in his chair, said, 'Yes. Your father's just concerned about the way the international scene is developing, that's all. He's worried about another war.'

He waved his free hand. 'Don't let it concern you, darling — you go and enjoy your tour. It's probably me being silly, you know how upset I can get about these things.'

She felt genuine concern. Her father had never really got over the effects of the Great War and was sometimes a little emotional.

'Oh, Daddy.'

Unthinking, she pulled her gloves off and put her hand gently against his cheek. 'Don't worry. I'm sure Mr Chamberlain will do something again.'

Her father sniffed. 'I fear not, I don't think there is anything more he can do.'

All of a sudden, out of the corner of her eye Fay sensed her mother had frozen. As the realization dawned, she knew what it was.

She drew herself upright, held out the hand so they could see the single, gold band properly. 'Yes, Tom and I were married.'

The effect on them both was devastating — and different.

Her father's shoulders slumped; he looked old and defeated, but her mother's eyes flared with anger.

'You silly, ungrateful little hussy — do you know what you've done? You've ruined your life, the reputation of this family, and for what? A common little man who is only after you for your money.'

Her mother's vitriol took Fay completely unawares, as she continued, 'I hope God forgives you for this, Fay, because I *won't*.'

Fay pleaded, 'Mother, we wanted to spare both families —'

'Tosh. You did it because the wretch wanted to get into your knickers before you went off on tour, that's the real reason.'

Startled by her mother's crudeness, Fay struggled to keep calm. 'Don't be vulgar, Mother. You met Tom — you must know he's not like that. I know you tried to separate us by having him moved.'

Contemptuously, her mother almost spat the words out. 'Where were you married then, without your family present? Some back street church in a cheap area of London?'

'Actually, it was in a register office — we thought —'

She got no further.

'So, you've been to bed with this man and you're *not* even married in the eyes of God. How low can you get? You're nothing but a whore —'

Fay slapped her mother's cheek.

The effect was startling.

Her father roared, *'Fay!'* and then there was absolute silence.

She felt drained, wretched.

It was some time before she said in a low voice, 'Mother — I'm so sorry, I. . . .'

Without another word Lady Rossiter turned and left the room. Fay felt the tears coming.

Her father surprised her by saying, 'I'm sorry it's come to this, Fay. You should never have done that, but I don't need to tell you. I'll speak to your mother later and, if you are capable of saying sorry again, I'm sure it will be all right.'

He seemed to have shrunk into his chair, his voice thinner, as though he had become older. Shaking his head slowly from side to side he mumbled, 'What's happening to us

Fay? I can't help worrying about everything.'

She dropped to her knees before him, resting her arms on his knees as she looked up at him. 'Daddy, I'm really very happy. Tom's a good man and he's as concerned as you about the international situation. He's even trying to join the Royal Air Force — does that sound like a gold digger to you?'

Her father looked down at her, blinking. 'Is he?'

Fay was bursting to talk about Tom. She explained about Dickinson, and the advice he was giving Tom about getting into the service.

Lord Rossiter grunted. 'Is that what he wants — is that what *you* want — after all, he is your husband now?'

She searched his face, but there was no trace of malice, or irony.

'Well, Daddy, he's passionate about flying and so am I. If a war is looming he'll have to go sometime, won't he, and if not I'll just be an air force wife — with my own career.'

Her father looked at her sadly. 'Darling, you do understand he won't get a commission?'

She stiffened, then realized he was only concerned for her. 'Yes, Daddy, but I don't care.'

Resignedly he nodded. He knew that any

resistance to his daughter and Tom's union was now pointless.

'You say he's got to go for an interview first?'

Fay tried to remember what Tom had said. 'Something about him needing to be accepted by an air board, then going to a civilian flying school full time. If he gets through that, he'll be taken on by the service for further training.'

There was a pause, until, looking guilty, Lord Rossiter said, 'I have intervened — unfairly — once before, but would you like me to make sure his application is, at least, not lost in the bureaucracy?'

Fay rubbed his knees and smiled affectionately up at him. 'Thank you, Daddy — I know he would appreciate it.'

Lord Rossiter laid a hand gently on her head. 'Give me the details then, but I can't do anything about the actual interview — *that* he'll have to pass on his own merit.'

Fay said, 'Of course.'

The remaining days were hectic as she visited relatives and friends. Her large travelling trunk that opened into drawers on one side and a hanging space on the other, was carefully loaded on to a Union Castle lorry under the supervision of Wilson.

Her mother was conspicuous by her absence most of the time, though she had begrudgingly accepted another heartfelt apology from a tearful Fay.

On the last night, as they sat in the drawing-room Fay finally plucked up courage to ask, 'Will you come to Southampton to see me off?'

Her mother paused, on the point of bringing a glass of sherry to her lips, and said quietly, 'Is your husband going to be there?'

Fay nodded.

'In that case I think it would be better if we said goodbye here.'

And that was that. On the morning of her departure Simpson, with further cases aboard, brought the Rolls around to the front door. They all stood in the hall.

Her father handed her several letters and a packet.

'That last one is for Aunt Blanche in Singapore. She knows she's not seeing you until you're on the way back. There's no rush — it's just a few photographs and a couple of mementoes that belonged to my brother. She left them here when she was last visiting us.'

Fay knew that Uncle Robert had died in the Great War and his widow, Aunt Blanche, had married again, only to become a widow for a second time when her planter husband had died of malaria. There had been no children from either union.

She reached up and kissed his cheek, tasting a trace of shaving soap.

He whispered, 'I've had a word. His application will be highlighted.'

She gave him a hug and whispered back, 'Thank you.'

Fay faced her mother. Lady Rossiter spoke first.

'Have a good journey and my fondest regards to all those on the list I gave you.'

She leant forward to be kissed on the cheek, but there was no great warmth.

Lord Rossiter watched as his wife and daughter went through the motions of saying farewell, and felt a great sadness. He had a feeling that this family feud between the two women in his life was set to last for a very long time — if not for ever.

Fay reached the terminal at two o'clock. In the great crush of people and the confusion she looked around. There was no sign of him. Her luggage was delivered to the receiving officer whose men took it away.

'Well Miss Fay, if that's all I can do for you?' Simpson was obviously eager to get away.

'Yes, that's fine, thank you.'

She held out her hand, he hastily removed his driving glove and shook it, as he also touched the peak of his cap with his other hand.

'All the best, miss.'

When he'd gone, she checked her tickets again and watched as the throng milling around the white picket fence that marked the start of the embarkation point, began to dwindle, the crowd spreading down the quayside to stand, looking up at the great white wall that was the side of the ship — the RMMV *Warwick Castle*. People were already lining the rails of several levels of decking, and the odd streamer floated down. Near her a woman in a fox-fur tried to call up to someone, as a ceremonial military band started playing light music. Just as Fay began to worry that he had been held up, or something worse, she saw a figure running at full tilt from the train station entrance. It was *him.*

Shouting 'Tom,' she ran towards him. When he reached her he lifted her up in the air and whirled her around and around, her legs bent, before lightly setting her back on the ground, still keeping his arms around her.

'Oh Tom, I thought something had happened to you.'

He shook his head as he tried to get his breath back. 'Derailment somewhere held us up — so sorry.'

She put her hands behind his head, brought his face down and kissed him, long and passionately, uncaring whether or not it was seemly. When she let him go, she murmured, 'You made it — that's all that matters.'

With their arms wrapped around each other they walked slowly to the embarkation desk, stopping short of it.

'Oh God, I'm going to miss you.'

He felt his throat constricting.

Tears started to stream down her face.

'Tom, I'm not going. I can't leave you.'

He drew her tightly into him, held on, one hand gently stroking her hair.

It took some time before he could manage it.

'Darling, you *must.* It will soon pass, then we can be back together. I'll never let you get away from me again. That's a promise.'

He felt her nod, then whisper, 'Have you got a handkerchief?'

He found his and gave it to her. She gave a large blow.

'Sorry. Oh, Tom, I'm so miserable.'

He tried again.

'Fay, if I get accepted by the RAF, I'll be very busy over the next few months — I wouldn't be able to get away. It's perfect, we get both our careers going, then we'll never be parted for longer than a couple of weeks. What do you say?'

'Right.'

She seemed to find an inner strength. She straightened up as voices carried from the ship.

'All ashore who are going ashore.'

One of the officers on duty at the desk called across to them, 'The gate is closing. Final call for all passengers travelling on the RMMV *Warwick Castle* to Cape Town.'

They looked long and searchingly at each other, then he cupped her face in his hands and gave her a gentle, loving kiss.

'Goodbye, darling. I'll write to you every week.'

Fay nodded. 'You've got all the addresses — keep them safe and I'll do the same, I promise.'

Hoarsely, he managed, 'I love you.'

She smiled weakly. 'But I love you more.'

The officer called out again. 'Gate now closing.'

She turned and ran.

From a few yards he watched as they processed her ticket. Another officer took her by the arm and rushed her to the canvas enclosed gang plank. She turned, pulling her arm free and blew a kiss, which he returned, then she was gently ushered out of sight.

He stayed on the quayside, pushing through the crowds, looking up at the rows of faces and waving arms. The streamers now formed a mass of paper lines joining the ship to the shore. The band, in red jackets with white blancoed belts and white pith helmets was going through a selection of sea shanties, ending with 'Rule Britannia'.

The gangway was swung aside. Tugs started hooting in the Solent. The *Warwick's* deep siren on its funnel blew long and hard. Hawsers were released, splashing into the water. Imperceptibly at first, and then, agonizingly slowly the white hull started to pull away, the gap of water inching wider.

Straining, he could see no sign of Fay — it was impossible.

The band paused and it was at that point that, incredibly he heard, 'Tom, Tom, over here.'

He had no idea where to look, except the voice seemed lower down — then he saw her at a porthole.

He waved furiously and yelled back, 'Fay, I love you.'

It was the last she heard of his voice, as the band struck up, 'Now is the Hour'.

They kept waving as the liner pulled steadily away, until Fay became just a tiny dot. He kept his eyes relentlessly on her, knowing that if he looked away he might never be able to identify her again amongst all the others.

In deeper water the *Warwick*'s propellers began to stir the Solent into a white leaping foam. Her siren blasted out, the tugs stood off and she began to move forward under her own power. In no time at all, the *Warwick Castle*'s hull was foreshortening as she turned for the open sea. Tom had lost Fay by then, and as the dark cloud of diesel exhaust from the ship's funnel wafted over the quay, it started emptying of people, until only he was left, and a couple of dock workers. He watched as the ship slowly receded, became first a dark blob, then lost in its own haze.

He still stayed as the paper streamers blew aimlessly about his feet. He couldn't have moved even if he had wanted to: he seemed to have gone into shock.

It was some time before he realized that the *Warwick Castle* was nowhere in sight, and that the tears that had streamed silently

down his face had dried in the freshening
wind.

CHAPTER SIXTEEN

For both of them, the following months changed their lives for ever. At about the time Fay nervously walked on stage in Cape Town, to polite applause, and then seated herself at the piano, followed by the warm reception for Sir Trevor Keynes, Tom, with bated breath, was holding a letter marked 'Air Ministry'. When he opened it, he read that, in reply to his communication and application form he was required to attend a selection board for the next E&RFTS course. This selection process could, if he was successful, lead to entry into the General Duties Branch of the Royal Air Force.

By the time she was at sea again on the RMS *Chitral,* heading for Australia, he was waiting nervously in his only suit, freshly pressed by Mrs Chick, at Adastral House in the Kingsway. The first question was fired at him before he'd hardly sat down. It came from the central panel member of three serious looking men in Savile Row suits, 'Why do you want to join the Royal Air Force?' Until the last question, he had no time to think anything through. In the sudden silence, after fifteen minutes of intensive questioning the chairman's fountain pen scratched as he signed something, then blotted it and handed a blue slip to Tom.

'Take this to the commissionaire, he will tell you what to do.'

He thanked them, then managed, to his mortification, to trip over his chair as he got up to leave. He closed the door behind and let out a gasp. It did not appear to comfort the young men sitting in a line of chairs to his right, each waiting his turn.

In the lobby, the commissionaire took his slip and then referred to another book.

'Can you go straight to the medical board now, sir?'

Tom looked at him blankly. 'Medical? I didn't know I was going to have a medical?'

The commissionaire grinned and tapped the blue chitty.

'You've passed, sir, that's why.'

Five days later a letter arrived telling him he had been assigned to No. 7 Elementary and Reserve Flying Training School at Desford, Leicestershire, for *ab initio* training, and to attend not later than noon on the day assigned.

From the stern of the ship, Fay watched as the great red ball of the sun slipped through, gathering purple clouds into the warm tropical ocean.

Under that sun Tom would still be having his day. She wondered what he was doing right then. Was he flying?

Fay leaned on the wooden handrail. He must have heard by now whether he had been accepted? The last letter she had received in South Africa had told her he was going for an interview. She pushed some hair, that had been ruffled by a warm sea breeze, out of her eye, and wondered if her father had indeed helped to expedite matters. She had, so far, only received two letters from her parents, both in her father's beautiful Victorian script, telling her about happenings at home. Jeremy it seems had applied to the army and was waiting to go to Sandhurst. A lot of her other male friends were also applying for the forces. Some were even talking of going to Cranwell — the Royal Air Force College. It troubled her to think that one of them could end up being Tom's superior officer.

In Melbourne, where they would dock in a

few day's time, they were scheduled to stay for nearly two months. She would surely find several letters waiting for her, sent via the Air Mail service run by the Imperial Airways flying boats.

The little, warm breeze played around her exposed shoulders; she drew the stole that matched her evening dress a little higher. She was about to attend a pre-dinner cocktail party at the invitation of the captain and his officers. Fay walked across the deck to the double doors that led into the first class saloon. These were guarded by two ratings who saluted her and opened the doors. Inside was an elegant scene of ladies in the latest evening dresses, some even with the occasional white fur wrap around their shouldes despite the heat. There was a dazzling array of jewels around necks and pinned to breasts. Most of the men were in black dinner jackets, but several had on creamy white tropical ones; none of these were a match for the tropical uniforms, though, worn by some of the dashing young officers, their brass buttons gleaming in the overhead light.

But Fay could only think of her husband. Would Tom be wearing the blue of the Royal Air Force by the time she got back?

■ ■ ■ ■

Tom passed out of the *ab initio* without a serious hitch and was accepted into the RAF as an acting sergeant pilot, and posted to RAF Cardington in Bedfordshire for basic training.

As Fay reached Brisbane, enjoying the lovely warm weather, he was issued with his course serge uniform, and in the pouring rain, taught to march, arms swinging up to the level of the waist, an NCO shouting at him and all the other new arrivals every waking moment. There followed two weeks of square bashing, arms drill, lectures and a visit to the doctors for inoculations.

Then came the news of where they were going for their intermediate and advanced flight training — Little Rissington in the Cotswolds, so close to Cirencester and Cheltenham.

He was now flying the North American Harvard, and the pressure was suddenly enormous. The heavy monoplane with retracting undercarriage had a fearsome reputation for being very unforgiving. Towards the end of the month he had soloed and was doing aerobatics. The news from the outside world had an awful inevitability about it. Germany and the USSR signed a non-aggression pact and later Hitler guaranteed the neutrality of Belgium, Luxembourg and Denmark. But for Tom, working at night on his books, and all day, everyday, walking out to the line of aircraft, flying from dawn to dusk, there was no time to pay much attention to anything — except to write to Fay.

He finished the latest letter just before lights out. In the dark he turned on his side, found her photograph, and kissed her goodnight as he had done every night since they had parted.

Fay got back to her hotel bedroom after the performance, showered, and put on her robe. After attending to her hair she sat at her dressing-table and started to pen her latest letter to him. Tomorrow they were off to Auckland, the furthest point of the tour. Three weeks there, and they would start the return journey. After that, despite stops for recording and radio dates in Australia, and a short stay in Singapore, every day would bring her nearer to him.

When she'd finished the letter and had sealed it down, Fay took up the photograph she had propped up against the mirror and gazed longingly at Tom.

In bed, after kissing him she put the photograph under her pillow.

On 1 September flying went on as usual despite the momentous news at reveille that German troops had crossed into Poland at 04.45 hours, and by 09.00 England and France had issued an ultimatum for their withdrawal.

Walking out to the aircraft his instructor said, 'All civil flying has been banned, and when we get back the aircraft are to be dispersed around the perimeter.'

But Tom was lost in his own thoughts. How would all this affect Fay? Was she safer where she was?

Two days later, they were all around a wireless in an ante room as the Prime Minister, in a defeated voice, ended his announcement with the words, 'and consequently, this country is at war with Germany.'

■ ■ ■ ■

PART TWO

■ ■ ■ ■

CHAPTER ONE

By the beginning of May 1940 Fay was still in Singapore, staying with Aunt Blanche on the Cavanagh Road. Worried sick, she had no idea what was happening to Tom, his letters had ceased after she had left Adelaide.

All thoughts of getting home quickly had perished in a welter of confusion and other personal matters — to wit the health and well-being of her aunt.

A lot of passenger sailings into the European war zone had been cancelled. Already U-boats had been active, sinking the aircraft carrier *Courageous* and the battleship *Royal Oak.* To say nothing of the SS *Artheria* which was attacked, with the loss of 112 lives and a Dutch Liner, the *Simon Bolivar,* victim, in November, to a magnetic mine.

She had thought of throwing in her lot with groups talking of going via Africa and across to France, but it always came back to

Aunt Blanche.

It had come as a bit of a shock to Fay, and would no doubt be an even greater one to her father and mother to find that Blanche was now what might be called a frail, ill, distressed gentlewoman. Although the bungalow was large it was rather dilapidated and she only had one cook-houseboy.

It transpired that her second husband had been a big gambler and, on his death, she had had to pay off all his debts. Slowly, Fay had enticed her to come out of a semi-reclusive life, and was going to meet her later for lunch.

At the moment she was reading all the newspapers she could get, courtesy of the Raffles Hotel as she sat drinking a coffee in the main hall.

The frustrating thing was, all the news from home was — that *nothing* now seemed to be happening. It was already being called The Phoney War.

She wondered where and what Tom was doing? At least he couldn't be in the fighting — there wasn't any. Some said there never would be, that Herr Hitler wanted no more than an accommodation with Great Britain.

After she tossed the last paper down, it was immediately seized on by a gentleman in a white suit and a panama hat. She finished her coffee and ordered a taxi. It pulled swiftly in by the steps as a uniformed Sikh commissionaire in his turban opened the door for her to get in.

'Cricket Club, please.'

She was going to treat her Aunt to lunch. It was the social centre of the colony, and though she had met some very nice people, there were many 'tuans' whom, frankly, she found offensive.

The way they treated their servants and the general Chinese population at large was awful, and she detected that many of them were not as top drawer at home as they led people to believe.

Aunty Blanche was already there, a slim frail figure dressed in an immaculate, but somewhat faded linen dress, watching the tennis on the padang from the veranda. If it wasn't for the predominance of Chinese faces above the white coats and brass buttons of the Club's uniform — 'the boys', you could have been forgiven for thinking you were in Surrey she thought, or anywhere in the Home Counties.

'Darling'. Her aunt stretched up her withered arms as Fay leant down and kissed her on both cheeks, then sat at the table beside her.

'I've taken the liberty of ordering two Slings for us.'

There was no doubt in Fay's mind that her presence was having a beneficial effect on the old lady.

Half a million pregnant women and thousands of children had been evacuated from London and other cities by hundreds of extra trains. Two million men had been called up for military service; there was rationing of butter, sugar and bacon, and wrought-iron railings everywhere were being cut down for scrap metal for the war effort, before Sergeant Pilot Thomas Roxham was allowed to put the coveted wings on his uniformed chest. Now, after four weeks of firing live ammunition at a coastal camp with target tugs, he had been posted directly to a front line squadron.

He was driven in past the guardhouse, manned by RAF Regiment personnel with .303 rifles over their shoulders, tin hats on, gas mask packs on their chests. He arrived in a three tonner with four other sergeants and their kitbags.

He looked across the field. The sleek outlines of his new steeds were dotted around, some were inside the hangars being worked on, some under camouflage netting, others on the strip, engines running.

Hurricanes: he'd got fighters.

For Tom life was great except for one huge, awful thing — he had temporarily lost touch with Fay. Ordinary cables didn't seem to be getting through. He knew she should be in Singapore, but he'd had no definite news for weeks on end. At first it had been difficult to concentrate — in fact he'd nearly flunked it, but an interview with the senior instructor had helped him see the way ahead.

They jumped out of the lorry, heaved their kitbags on to their great-coat-clad shoulders, and made for the adjutant's office.

A wingless pilot officer went past. Tom, as the nearest of the group, should have put up a salute on their behalf, but his mind was elsewhere, considering whether to contact her parents or not.

'Sergeant.'

He came out of his thoughts to find a very angry, very red face pushing up into his. For the next minute, he was berated, and threatened with CO's parade before being dismissed. The others were waiting for him.

An Australian shook his head. 'You took that calmly. I'd have decked the bugger.'

He shrugged. 'Had my mind on other things.'

The CO was a blunt speaking Irishman

from Dublin, scion of an old Anglo-Irish family, the type who had led the likes of Sergeant Whelan in the trenches of Flanders Fields.

'I'll be frank, Roxham, if things weren't so urgent I'd never accept anybody into this squadron straight from training camp. I can't afford to have you breaking one of my precious aircraft — understand? Now — get out, see the Duty Officer, and go and fly a Hurricane — *and bring it back in one piece.*'

He did a dual check flight in the 'Master' and seemed to get everything right.

Now he was walking out to the Hurricane he had been assigned, for his first ever solo flight. His heart hadn't beaten so fast since that first ever solo in the Tiger Moth.

The ground crew helped him up on the wing, put on his parachute, and strapped him into the small cockpit. A cockney corporal asked 'All right, Sergeant?'

He nodded and went slowly through the pre-flight checks. When he was completely satisfied he waved to the waiting ground crew and pressed the starter button. With a terrific cough, a stab of flame from the exhaust, and a billow of smoke, the engine roared into life. The tremendous power was immediately apparent. Tom Roxham secured his oxygen mask, licked his lips. This was what he had spent nearly a year working for, a period during which he could have been dropped, 'bowler hatted' at any point, or finally, sent to multi engines.

But now, all he had to do was fly this beauty and get it back down in one piece, and he would be a fighter pilot. Tom hoped Hayes, Trubshaw and Dickie Dickinson were going to be proud of him.

And *Fay.*

She received a cable from her father, via the Governor's Office. It told her that she would be better off where she was, that Tom was safe — he'd checked through the Air Ministry but that he wasn't allowed to say anything more than that. Initially delighted and relieved that he was all right, her elation gradually gave way to frustration. Her parents more than likely hadn't told Tom she was safe, and she seemed unable to contact him, in fact, didn't even know where he was.

She pondered on that as she got on with her work. She was helping the Red Cross, toiling under the ceiling fans on suffocatingly hot days — the temperature always seemed to hover around the nineties. Ever since the declaration, Singapore had beenn a hive of activity, though strangely remote from the war. Rubber, tin and other strategic materials were urgently needed, and the docks were working day and night to fulfil orders from home, and the USA. Although there was no sense of urgency affecting themselves directly, everybody was keen to show 'Home' that they were doing their bit. Consequently Fay was one of many volunteer nurses rolling bandages and filling medical boxes, whilst others were organizing themselves into air raid wardens, auxiliary firemen, defence volunteers, and queueing to give blood to the bank.

It was all done in earnest, but with a sense of unreality — the war was too far away. Admittedly the battleships *The Prince of Wales* and *The Repulse* had arrived at the naval dockyard, but people just took it as an essential safeguard to the supply lines. Life went on as usual, but even more hectically.

She'd got used to the smell of the place, the drains, spices, fish, and the swamp land on which the place was built.

The city districts were colourful and different, the Chinese families eating with chop sticks and washing in the street, men carrying bamboo poles with their wares dangling at each end, washing lines strung from window to window, and a sense of frenzied activity.

In the Indian sections, the smell of spices and curries predominated. The red juice of spat out betel stained the pavements, men wandered about, some hand in hand, or squatted in the gutter.

But everywhere the steaming jungle made inroads into the suburbs, in places down to the water edges, where sampans were moored side by side, whole families living and dying on one boat.

In the white and business areas all was wide avenues, and beautiful cut grass; the Cricket Club padang with the tall spire of St Andrews Cathedral and the cupola of the Supreme Court made for an elegant city centre.

Everybody sweated continually, not helped by the dress codes — which were strictly upheld. These demanded collars and ties, dinner jackets or, for the military, bum freezers — the short white mess jackets.

She'd got books from Kelly and Walsh, medicine for her aunt from Maynards, the chemist, and shopped in the new big department store, Robinsons.

Everything was here in this lively city except one thing — *Tom.*

She pondered how to get a message to him, and decided to visit the Governor's

Office or, failing that, see if the RAF could help.

She knew of several airfields — the closest at Kallang just by the city, then one at Tengah and another at Sembawang, and of course, there was always the Cricket Club. She knew the chief Air Force Officer was an Air-Vice-Marshal Pulford who more than likely was a member, if not a visitor.

She finished another box, ran a towel over her sweating face and arms and lifted her dress away from her front to let the air pass over her skin. Tomorrow — she would start tomorrow.

He'd been on the squadron now for several weeks, doing dawn patrols out over the North Sea, only coastal shipping interrupting the endless grey waves. Not a dot in the sky, despite all the intense staring that eventually led to dots whirling all over the place — in his eyes.

He could still remember the first patrol, with the CO and a wingman. Tom had been keyed up, tense with the thought that he was going into battle, that Huns with live ammunition were going to try to kill him. His mouth had been so dry he'd got ulcers and had had to see the dental officer who'd given him a mouthwash and told him to suck lozenges. It was something to do with breathing near pure oxygen. Tom didn't believe him for one moment — he could still remember the fear.

But as the days passed and nothing happened, he grew used to the routine. The fear stayed with him, but was at the back of his mind, not the front.

And it wasn't only him getting used to the boredom. The populace in general seemed to have decided the war wasn't going to happen, despite the events at sea. 'Forget Hitler, and take your holiday' was one resort's slogan.

The news filtered in as Tom was sharing a pint in the local pub with the young Australian, one of the sergeants he'd joined the squadron with on the same day. They'd struck up an immediate friendship.

Tall, gangling George Hawksley was from Western Australia, and happened to have been touring Europe before going home to the family mining business.

Having seen the Nazi Party at first hand in Germany, when he'd arrived in London he'd immediately joined the RAF — much to his father's disappointment.

He was slow speaking, with a dry humour, often directed at pom bastards — especially anybody with a plummy accent.

Tom's problems which stemmed from his working-class origins naturally drew them closer together.

'My shout.'

George collared the glasses and went back to the bar to order a couple more pints, leaving Tom. He suddenly remembered, yet again, the phone call he'd made that morning to Codrington Hall. Fay's lack of contact was beginning to eat into him. Despite the dislike of doing it he hadn't been able to stop himself.

Wilson answered, and greeted him cordially enough, so Tom asked him if he knew about 'Miss Fay'. He said he didn't. Something about his voice made Tom suspicious. He asked if his Lordship was in, and he was not, so eventually Tom found himself waiting for Lady Rossiter.

When she eventually came on the line he was beginning to run out of time and money.

'Lady Rossiter, I'm trying to find out about Fay — has she been in touch?'

The voice at the other end was remote. 'No, she she has not.'

'Do you know if she's all right?'

'I really couldn't say. Can't *you* find out? After all you are her next of kin *now*.'

There was no doubting the implication

that she wouldn't help him even if she did know, and by the time he was sure that they had some idea, something in her voice and Wilson's, had made him feel that they didn't seem worried about her — that was something at least.

'Look, can I give you my address and forces post office number?'

The pips started up. As he struggled with getting more loose change from his pocket, the line went dead. He tried twice more, but it was always engaged. He got the message. He'd have to find some other way. Maybe the CO could help, after all, as her mother had implied, she was an RAF wife.

George came back with the pints and set them on the table.

'Hey, they're talking around the bar about a Reuters message — seems the Jerries may be attacking Norway.'

They looked at each other, downed their pints, and hurriedly left.

In the Sergeants' mess everybody was gathered around the wireless as the details started coming in. A massive German thrust through Denmark was already landing in Norway. Later that day Denmark surrendered.

And still nothing happened.

They all fretted about as the British force

in Norway ran into trouble. Apart from that débàcle all remained quiet.

The CO took Tom shooting — explaining that skills developed on the moors and estuaries could be transferred to air fighting. The highest scoring pilots of the Great War were the game shooters, well acquainted with the deflection shot.

So Tom shot birds as Norway fell. But his closeness to the CO did have one other benefit. He listened when Tom told him about his wife.

'I'll get on to old Tommy Parker. He's out there now.'

Happier, Tom blew a fast flying teal out of the sky. It plummeted at speed to earth.

'That's the way, Roxham.'

The CO clapped him on the back. 'Give the same medicine to the Hun when we meet him.'

Fay had just got up, showered and was at her dressing-table, combing her wet hair and enjoying the cool air from the overhead fan, when there was a knock on her bedroom door.

Pulling on a robe she opened it to find the houseboy standing there.

'Missie needed. Soldiers come.'

Puzzled, she hurried along the hall.

Her aunt was already up.

As soon as she saw the young flight-lieutenant she knew it had to be about Tom.

'What is it?'

The flight-lieutenant, who had his hat under his arm enquired, 'Mrs Roxham?'

'Yes.'

Her heart was banging so violently in her rib cage she thought they must all hear it.

'I have a message from your husband, madam.'

He held out an official buff-coloured envelope.

As Fay took it, her aunt was already inviting him to have a cold drink, and to have another sent out to his driver. Fay turned away, hands trembling, and tore it open.

Dear Fay
Hope this finds you in good order.
I am all right, no problems — other than your absence. Long for Sheringham again. Glad you are in a safe place. I will do my best to keep in touch.
Take care,
Your loving husband
Tom

She read it over again and then once more. Its shortness and lack of sweet sayings was disappointing. Then she realized that it had come through official channels — probably unofficially. He had had to avoid some jumped up little twirp stopping its transmission.

And the reference to Sheringham was his way of telling her he wanted to make love to her again. She ached for his touch.

'Is there any reply, madam?'

It was the young flight-lieutenant.

'I can reply?'

He grinned. 'I should say so. Apparently somebody knows somebody and is pulling strings.'

She raised a finger. 'Just a minute — I'll be quick.'

In the bureau she pulled a sheet of paper to her. It was then that she realized how difficult it was to write anything personal, knowing that she was going to give it to a stranger, who would read it and then others who would *also* read it. She thought quickly, and started writing.

Dear Tom
I'm very well and safe, living with Aunt Blanche in . . .

She looked up, said to the flight-lieutenant, 'Can I say I'm in Singapore?'

He nodded. 'Don't see a problem there. Anyway, if they don't like it they will erase it fast enough — black it out.'

'Thank you.'

Her pen scratched again.

. . . Singapore. Please keep safe and don't do anything silly for my sake. Shall always remember you at Sheringham — we must do it again as soon as we can.

Thinking of you every minute of every day.

Your loving wife
Fay

She folded it and put it into an envelope after kissing it quickly.

She gave it to him. 'There we are. When will he get it?'

The flight-lieutenant shrugged. 'Can't speak for the other end, Mrs Roxham, but that will be transmitted today as long as traffic is not too heavy. He certainly should get it in the next few days.'

When he'd gone she excused herself, saying to her aunt that she was going to get dressed. In her room, she sat on the bed and read the printed message again, then lay down holding on to it and cried.

■ ■ ■ ■

Tom had come back from another boring patrol over the North Sea to find the place a hive of activity. He'd asked his ground crew what was going on as he stepped out on to the wing and saw fuel bowsers and armourers buzzing all over the field servicing the aircraft.

'We're on the move, sir — don't know where.'

He grabbed a ride on a Hillman 10 heading for the hangars. The excitement in the squadron office was obvious, with saluting dispatch riders coming and going and clerks emptying filing cabinets.

The adjutant confirmed the news. 'We're off to Duxford, then across to France to support the BEF. By the way, the CO's asking for you — go on in.'

Tom tapped on the latter's door and stuck his head around.

'Sir?'

Although on the phone, the CO beckoned him in and, leaning forward, used two fingers to push a communication sheet towards him. Tom picked it up and read Fay's message. It was the most wonderful news.

The CO slammed the phone down and roared. 'Right, Sergeant Roxham, now perhaps we can get on with the war.'

But he was smiling.

They took off in threes, then lined up in 'V' formation over the sea and headed south.

It was only as the coastline of North Norfolk came up that Tom realized they were going to come inland again right over Sheringham.

He flicked the button on his mask radio.

'Blue 3 to Blue 1 — over.'

The CO acknowledged.

Tom asked him for permission to drop out of formation and fly low over the town.

Having received it, he eased the stick forward. At just over 200 feet he flashed in over the beach with its groins and newly laid barbed wire, then over the turrets and dome of the Grand Hotel.

It was gone in a flash and, as he climbed away from the pine trees on the ridge and slotted back into formation, he felt a deep sense of sadness. A lump came into his throat. Already it all seemed such a long time ago.

CHAPTER TWO

Churchill's grim voice came out from the wireless.

'The Battle of France is over, I expect the battle of Britain is about to begin.'

Lord and Lady Rossiter sat numbly in their beautiful drawing-room listening until Churchill finished — *'last for a thousand years, men will say this was their finest hour.'*

When Wilson switched off the wireless they sat in silence.

It had all happened so suddenly, so *violently.*

On 13 May, Hitler had launched a sudden attack on Holland and Luxembourg. Rotterdam had been bombed with 800 dead and thousands homeless. By the 15th the Dutch had surrendered.

But the main blow came from the Ardennes, the so called impassable route. The German Panzers were soon across the River Meuse, by-passing the Maginot Line upon which the French defence had depended so much.

By 25 May, the outflanked and retreating BEF was converging on Dunkirk; by the early morning of 4 June, the last British and French personnel had been lifted from the beaches, and a new word had entered the language.

Blitzkrieg.

Tom had been fighting continuously and moving his Hurricane hurriedly from one grass strip to another as the Panzers and Stuka dive bombers devastated all before them, overrunning airfield after airfield.

Over Ypres he'd had his first terror-stricken realization that he was being fired upon. He pulled his Hurricane around so hard that he momentarily blacked out, coming to as the blurred shape of a Messerschmitt passed before him. He fired his first ever burst in panic — and missed. Then his gun jammed, and thereafter he just ducked and dived to stay alive.

As they flew back he felt elated — he had survived.

But the elation soon turned sour. As they got back to their grass field they were told to refuel quickly and fly south as they were about to be overrun.

On taking off, they were jumped by low

flying ME 109s coming in with the sun behind them. He saw the CO go down in flames.

Maybe the capacity was there already, but from that moment on Tom Roxham became a ruthless predator of enemy aircraft.

His first kill came when they bounced some Stukas without fighter cover, diving on to roads clogged with civilian refugees as well as French Army trucks.

The first one he caught in his cross-wires as it climbed away leaving a tremendous column of black smoke rising from the ground. He swooped through it. The awkward slow Stuka was no match for the Hurricane. Tom released the safety catch, and watched as his tracer thumped into the wing root. It promptly folded up and plummeted to earth like a shot duck. There was a ball of fire and that was that.

He'd killed his first man — or rather two.

Somebody else got another one, but Tom managed to be in the right place at the right time as a third one tried to escape at ground level. He dropped down, following the black cross as it flew along a railway line. Tracers started coming up — he could see the terrified rear gunner's face despite his mask. He killed him first, then let his shells creep up the long canopy. With the pilot dead, the black gull-like shape flew along for a while, wobbled then veered away into a forest. Trees were still burning long after he left the area.

Now the squadron was back in Scotland, badly mauled and only sixty per cent strength.

He and George Hawksley were the only two sergeant pilots left. They sat in a pub with two pints of heavy, not talking — just too exhausted.

Lord and Lady Rossiter went to bed early.

The news of Dunkirk, when it reached Singapore seemed incredible, but for all that there was no increased anxiety, no building of air raid shelters or anything like that. Although Britain was now alone against the Axis powers, that applied to the rest of the world. Her Empire still stood shoulder to shoulder with her.

There was no rationing, hotels and bars dispensed as much drink as you wanted. Fay worried about Tom, but went swimming at the Targlin Club and on the beaches facing Jahore. Aunt Blanche's improvement had reached a plateau. On the really exceptionally humid days she looked awful, and stayed under a fan with a bowl of water and a wet flannel on her forehead. Fay realized that the old lady ought to be at home, in England, for the last years of her life.

The Japanese were acting belligerently, certainly towards the Chinese, but *The Prince of Wales* and the *Repulse* could still be seen in the Navy dockyards.

A reassuring presence of Britain's might.

The frustration of not being in the fight finally ended for the squadron when, at the beginning of August 1940, they were sent south from 13 Group to replace one of the badly mauled squadrons of Air Vice-Marshal Park's 11 Group which had been guarding the south-east of England and the approach to London.

The Battle of Britain was at its height.

Almost immediately, Tom found himself sent to intercept raiders approaching Margate, but before they could engage the formation, ME 109s appeared from cloud and dived on them.

In the mêlée that followed, he found himself on the tail of one and managed a perfect two-second deflection shot, watching as metal ripped off the side and black smoke poured from the engine. Remembering his CO and all the coaching on the shooting trips, he yelled in excitement, 'That's one for you, sir,' and put in another three-second burst. The Messerschmitt exploded into whirling pieces. For a split second he thought he'd been hit by some of the wreckage as the Hurricane shuddered and the stick flicked violently in his hand.

Then as an incendiary bullet flashed over his arm and blew the instrument panel to pieces, he realized he was being attacked. He'd made the classic error of not breaking away as soon as he'd carried out his attack. The fuel tank beyond the panel caught fire, white smoke, thick and burningly hot, instantly filled the cockpit. Panic gripped him. He jerked the hood back, released his straps, flipped the plane over, and fell out into a maelstrom of cold blasting air. At 12,000 feet above the coastline he counted three and pulled the rip cord.

Fay sat bolt upright, eyes wide in the dark, chest heaving, her body bathed in sweat.

It took a while for her to realize where she was — inside the mosquito net around her bed. Her heartbeat slowly began to return to normal. She'd had a nightmare.

Pulling aside the net, she swung around and set her feet down on the tiled floor, found her thermos of iced water and gulped down a glassful.

Fay tried to remember her dream, but

strangely she couldn't recall a thing —
except an overwhelming sense of fear.

It took a long time for her to doze off
and she never really went back to a deep
sleep.

In the morning Fay had a headache that
in the clammy rainy dawn would not go
away. She also couldn't shake off a sense of
dread.

It was November 1940 before Tom returned
to the squadron. He suffered a broken leg
and arm going through the roof of a railway
station; he'd then fallen further on to the
platform in front of staff and passengers
sheltering in the waiting-room.

Lying in agony, he realized just how lucky
he was when an engine hauling ballast had
made the ground quiver around him and
enveloped him briefly in steam. Two feet to
the left and he'd have been under the thing.
The irony of his being killed by a train did
not escape him.

Tom saluted the new CO who then shook
his hand, 'Glad to have you back, Tom and
congratulations on the commission.'

It was now Pilot Officer Roxham, and he
had seven kills to his name.

George Hawksley had also been promoted
having been awarded the DFC.

Tom was disappointed. He'd hoped there would be a message waiting for him from Fay, but the silence continued. It made him miserable but at least she was safe. Some of the boys worried about their wives and sweethearts, especially those living in the big cities.

In the next few months, and then on through the summer and autumn of 1941 he took part in the increasingly deep fighter sweeps over enemy occupied territory, especially the Pas de Calais, called 'Rhubarbs'. He added two ME 109s to his bag, catching them both with his cannon on their unarmoured bellies as they flew into his line of fire. Thick black smoke marked the end of both. A month after being back on the squadron he too was awarded the DFC and then a few weeks later was made a Flight-lieutenant; the citation listing his airmanship, combat skills and aggressive leadership.

He was now a Flight Commander opposite George.

Then, in mid November, one cold frosty morning he tightened his helmet strap, went through his pre-flight checks, felt the rudders and stick, and signalled for the engine start. Squadron Leader Tom Roxham led 'A' flight in a slanting climb over the white cliffs and out across the channel until they reached 22,000 feet, then moments later passed over the French coast.

He never stopped searching the skies, and it wasn't long before he saw several black dots, like angry bees, swarming down on them.

He flicked his throat button, informing his wing commander that he could see 'Bandits, eleven o'clock, coming down,' then slipped the safety off the firing button.

It was time to get to work.

Fay's war started in the early hours of Monday, 8 December 1941. Around four in the morning the bombs started to fall. She had stood with her aunt on the veranda, arms around each other as they had watched the flashes coming from the direction of Chinatown and the docks, followed by the thud of the bombs a second later.

Then came an even nearer orange glow, and it was only subsequently they were to discover there had been a direct hit on Robinson's new air-conditioned restaurant in Raffles Place. Throughout the air raid the lights of the city had remained on.

But as they sat down to breakfast, fearful of what had happened and about the news that the Japanese had landed at Kota Bahru, a coastal town near the Siamese border, the radio broke into its programme to announce something that halted Fay's spoon as it was about to alight on her egg.

The Japanese had bombed Pearl Harbour, no details, but many ships had been seen on fire. So, America was in the war. They both cheered up no end, and had a sherry at breakfast, a cheerfulness that was to evaporate slowly over the coming weeks. A black-out was imposed, though not adhered to. Because of the humidity people needed to be on their verandas, so a little light was allowed. More raids followed, and the town began to see boarded-up shop fronts and debris. Then came the stupefying news of the Japanese advance down through Malaya.

By the time Fay realized she should have made Aunt Blanche leave, despite the older woman's protestations that no Jap was going to chase her out of her home, it was too late. The radio interrupted its music with another announcement and she knew that there was no possibility of taking a boat to Australia.

They were in the cricket club, beneath a big ceiling fan turning lazily in the hot, stifling evening. What followed made her not only immeasurably sad at the loss of so many young lives, but it also shook her and all the British present as to the extent of the peril they were in.

The impersonal voice announced the loss of the *Prince of Wales* and the *Repulse* to enemy bombers.

There was absolute silence in the room, broken after a mere thirty seconds, by a glass hitting the tiled floor and smashing into a thousand pieces. Everybody drank up and went home quietly.

It was too late. Aunt Blanche had taken a turn for the worse. As Fay nursed her, changing her sheets and bathing her shrivelled old body, the Japanese had relentlessly advanced down the Malayan Peninsula until they were now at the gates of the city — or rather, on the other side of the Causeway which linked it to the mainland.

They had begun shelling the military installations, and a liner, the *Empress of Asia* had been sunk in the Straits. They could have been on it.

All was confusion. Desperate fighting was taking place as the Japanese ferried troops across the Straits near the Causeway. Nobody seemed to know what exactly was going on.

Continuous air raids, explosions and giant fires in the north and south festooned the doomed city with black oily smoke. Once immaculate lawns were now cratered and covered with blasted trees.

Fay had tried to do her bit with the Red Cross, but now she stood outside a hospital, almost dropping with fatigue, her face grimy and dirt streaked above a white uniform covered with soot and blood.

She smoked a cigarette as she stood by a huge trench nearly two hundred yards long that had been dug by a mechanical digger.

The corpses of Europeans were being put in one end, Asians the other, then sprinkled with lime.

The stench told its own story.

She knew they were doomed, no one who could see all this with their own eyes could think otherwise. There was a report of a smaller hospital that had been overrun, where the Japanese had bayoneted patients and staff alike — some still on the operating table.

She finished her cigarette and tossed it, still alight, away. If she was going to die, her only regret was that she had left Tom.

She should have followed her heart and rejected everything else; her parents; their backgrounds; her career; *everything.*

Now it was all irrelevant — too late. Would they ever meet again in this life?

What would she and Tom be like in the next?

CHAPTER THREE

As soon as Tom heard of the fall of Singapore he was inconsolable. Worried by his mental state, the group captain got the doctor to suspend him from flying duties.

'It's his wife — she's in Singapore. He's no good to me at the moment — positively bloody dangerous. Anyway he needs some leave.'

Tom was being eaten away by fear, unable to sleep, a pain in his guts like somebody twisting a knife in him.

He rang Codrington Hall. Whoever it was, it wasn't Wilson's voice that answered. He asked for Lord or Lady Rossiter.

The voice said, 'Sorry, can't help you I'm afraid, old boy, this is the Headquarters mess of the Fifth Division.'

'But they must be somewhere?'

'You'll have to ask the War Department Requisition Unit.'

No, he didn't know the number.

Tom was going mad. If anything had happened. . . .

If she was alive — he snapped out loud at himself. 'Of course she's bloody alive' — as a civilian she'd have been interned by the Japanese. It didn't bear thinking about. The newspaper headlines were painful reminders of the disaster that had befallen them all. He had to avert his eyes at the frightening pictures of the burning city.

He took a train to London and thence by Tube to Paddington. The Great Western terminus had already changed — for the worse. Most passengers seemed to be in uniform — from all over the world. The platforms were dirty, the posters exhorting people to 'Dig for Victory' and 'Keep Mum, She's Not So Dumb', already torn and defaced.

The journey was long and slow, with many stops, due apparently, to poor coal. The carriages were filthy, choking with cigarette smoke and troops with kit bags, boots scuffing the floor, jamming the corridors as he stood all the way by a toilet, with continually heaving and squeezing bodies always going in and out. He added to the smoke himself by lighting one cigarette after the other.

When he eventually got to Cirencester he

managed to get a room at the Fleece Hotel. Next day he went to the municipal offices. They referred him to the post office.

There, it was only due to his rank and the fact that he was looking for Lord and Lady Rossiter to tell them about his wife — their daughter, that they relented and gave him their address. They'd moved into town — a large house near the Bathhurst Estate.

He went straight around, stopping to look up at the handsome stone façade with its tall Regency windows, criss-crossed now with anti-blast strips of brown paper.

He knocked on the door. Slow footsteps sounded on the other side. When it eventually opened he didn't recognize the thick-set lady in a dutch apron.

'Yes?'

'I'm looking for Lord or Lady Rossiter.'

'If it's about them ARP wardens. . . .'

He cut her off. 'No — it's personal. Are they in?'

She gave him a hard look, and a begrudging, 'Wait here.'

He heard some muffled talking, then Fay's father appeared, in his First World War uniform.

The two men stood eyeing each other, one immaculate in khaki with riding breeches and a Sam Brown, the other in a crumpled

sky-blue uniform with the top button undone.

But Lord Rossiter's eyes noticed the rank
and the DFC — and the new DSO for
inspired leadership.

Tom spoke first. 'Have you any news of
Fay?'

'You'd better come in.'

Tom closed the door behind him and followed her father down the corridor and into
the sitting-room.

Lady Rossiter was sitting on a sofa with
her back to them.

'Is it to do with your Home Guard
review?'

'No, my dear, it's Tom.'

He noticed the use of his Christian name
as did his wife who whirled around.

She stood slowly, using a silver-topped
cane, face anxious. He was struck by how
much older they both looked.

'Do you know something about Fay?'

He glanced away from her, unable to bear
the sight of the pleading and worry in her
eyes.

'No — I'd hoped you had some idea. Did
she get out?'

Miserably, her father shook his head. 'Her
Aunt Blanche was very ill. I gather she
wouldn't leave her.'

They looked helplessly at each other. For the first time he felt sorry for them, their arrogant bearing of old now gone. They were just suffering parents — like thousands of others in this awful mess.

But they were *her* mum and dad.

Gently he asked, 'When did you last hear anything?'

As Lady Rossiter lowered herself painfully back on to the sofa, her father motioned for him to sit down.

'Nothing directly — I promise you. We've not held back any letters or anything. I know from the last war how word from family was good for the men.'

Tom bit back any retort about being seen as just one of the men. Her father had acknowledged that Fay was, for him, beloved. He realized that Lord Rossiter had probably been reading the *London Gazette* since the war had started, and must have seen his awards and promotions. He hadn't had any communication from them — perhaps that was asking too much.

Her father continued: 'No we haven't heard from Fay for a long time, but for a while I was able to get information through various channels.' He sniffed. 'They've gone now, of course.'

Guiltily he looked down at the floor. 'We

heard she was in touch with you awhile back. I'm sorry we didn't keep in contact.'

There was a pause before Tom roused himself. 'Well, there are a good many things all of us should, or should not have done. Let's just forget all that's gone before. Getting Fay back is all that matters — to all of us.'

He told them that, although he had been sad — agonizingly so — at not hearing from her day on day, he hadn't been worried. In fact, since the war proper had started, just the opposite. He was glad that she was somewhere *safe:* that was until the catastrophe and sudden surrender.

He tried to cheer them up, and by so doing, convince himself that all was well. 'She's a civilian; she'll be all right.'

They looked at him pleadingly. They so wanted him to be right. This old couple still dressed immaculately from an age that had already gone — *utterly.* Tom was aware of his rather crumpled uniform with the top button — defiantly undone, and Lord Rossiter in his beautifully turned out kit. In their uniforms, was reflected everything that had happened in the last several years; from a once great nation, the hub of an Empire on which the sun never set, to an island race fighting for its survival.

But all of them were sick with worry.

And one unspoken question hung over everything.

Was she even *alive?*

The last days had been horrendous, but now, with the short tough soldiers of the victorious Japanese army guarding bridges, with rifles and bayonets bigger than they were, and British soldiers patrolling the city centres armed with pick-axe handles to keep order, life was calmer after the hell that had gone before.

Fay had been out, trying to get some food — their houseboy had disappeared — and she had been amazed by the normality. Admittedly it wasn't like the Singapore of a week ago — that had died — but it was all strangely different from what she had been expecting.

And then the orders came through. Internment camps had been prepared. The district where they lived was to be cleared.

Now, on a Tuesday morning, at ten o'clock, she was with her aunt and several hundred women and children, standing in the blazing sun on the cricket club padang. Two thousand men were also lined up. There was no breeze, the sea which was so near, shimmered waveless like a mirror in the heat.

Fay's dress hung limp with wetness. The black patches of sweat extended from her armpits down her front and back. But her worry was for her frail aunt. Fay held a parasol over her. Once she'd slid to the ground, but a bellowing Japanese soldier had stormed over to them and made jabbing motions with his bayonet.

After two hours an officer climbed on to a wooden crate and addressed them. Women and children would get transport — the men would have to walk. Houses had been prepared as a temporary camp, but they would all go on to Changi jail after a few days.

When they got there, the women found the houses stripped of all furniture and mosquitoes swarmed like a living cloud everywhere. They lay down on the bare floor, Fay doing her best to make her aunt comfortable, wrapping her in a sheet to stop the mosquito bites, with a veil made from a piece of torn petticoat. The guards were sometimes helpful, sometimes indifferent, but water was provided and some food for the children.

They remained there in filth and squalor until, in early March, they were ordered to march the seven miles to Changi. To Fay's immense relief the infirm and very old, along with some pregnant women were given transport. The rest of them walked, in a column that stretched for over a mile, complete with prams, old rickshaws and trolleys piled with pots and pans. It took all day, and by the time they approached the walls of the jail, they were exhausted, bedraggled, trudging on blistered feet, shoulders drooped, dresses dirty and wringing wet with sweat.

Suddenly, a tiny woman at the head of the column began to sing and the song was taken up by others. Fay joined in, and soon over a hundred voices, hoarse and tired, were singing with a passion that lifted spirits and straightened backs. With the little woman leading the way, they marched through the gates, singing so loudly, that the men in their section, behind the high wall that divided the prison, heard them and joined in.

Fay sang away at the top of her voice, chin up as she passed the sullen looking guards.

'There'll always be an England
And England will be free.'

CHAPTER FOUR

With no news, Tom went to see the group captain and asked for a transfer to the Far East Air Force. His reason was blunt. The war there was his war. It had just become very personal.

George Hawksley also wanted to transfer, because as he said, it was nearer to his home. Their applications for transfer went off together. They then retired to the mess.

Over a couple of pints they talked about the way things were.

George played with his drink. 'I tell you Tom, I don't think I'm going to make it through to the end.'

Surprised, Tom looked at him. 'What's got into you?'

The Australian gave a wry smile. 'Just being rational. How many blokes have we seen off since the start of all this?'

'Oh come on, George, this isn't like you.'

George Hawksley took a good swig of his

beer and licked his lips. 'Did I ever tell you I'm an only child?'

Bewildered, Tom shook his head. 'Nope. So what? I am too.'

'Maybe that's why we get on.' The Australian grinned. 'You're the brother I never had.'

Embarrassed George finished his beer and stood up. 'Another one?'

Tom drained his glass and pushed it across. 'Too right if you're signing — *Brother.*'

A week later Tom's father was dead, his mother complaining that the fire watching on damp winter nights had done it. He attended in uniform, with a black band around his arm, and let his mother proudly show him off to help her through the day. He could see the look in Mrs Bars's eyes, the next-door neighbour. She had lost Jimmy on the *Hood* when she had been sunk by the *Bismarck*. As the vicar went through the service, and he held his mother at the graveside, he wondered if George's sudden revelation wasn't a sign of the times. Perhaps the euphoria at the idea of surviving alone had finally drained away from the country, perhaps they were all getting war weary.

But he wasn't. All he wanted to do was be nearer to Fay, to do everything in his power to get her out, back where she belonged, and as soon as possible.

And if anything unthinkable had happened to her . . . he would kill as many Japs as he could — until they got him.

His transfer was approved, as was George's. 'They must be desperate out there' was the laconic remark from the latter.

They were taken off flying duties, given a whole series of jabs at the station sick quarters which left him feeling really rough for forty-eight hours and then given embarkation leave. George came with him back to Cheltenham. For nearly a week they walked the hills in the daytime, saw a couple of films, talked most nights over a few pints in the Norwood Arms.

On their first day they went to Cirencester on the train. As they walked up the high street, Tom said, 'We're going to meet the in-laws. I want to see if they have any more news of Fay.'

George said, 'You mean their Lordships?'

Tom nodded.

The Australian grinned.

'Maybe they're descendants of the ones who sent my great-grandfather to the colonies for poaching.'

This time Lord Rossiter was in a dark

grey, double breasted suit, his wife out, with the WVS. The old man's face lit up when he saw him.

'Come in, come in. Just had a phone call from an old school chum in the office. I'm led to believe all the civilian women are in Changi Jail, that's on the island about fifteen miles from the city — but no names yet. The Red Cross are looking into it. The Japanese have a Red Cross, did you know that?'

Tom shook his head, digesting the news. Changi Jail — he'd never heard of it.

They had tea made by the formidable, stocky woman whom Tom had encountered on his previous visit, and were taking their leave, when Lord Rossiter suddenly offered his hand.

'Take care now, Tom, when this is all over we don't want Fay to be a widow.'

He took it, and they shook — just the once.

Lord Rossiter grimaced. 'She would have been if she'd married Jeremy.'

Tom looked at him, frowning as he took in the meaning.

Her father nodded and went on, 'Killed at Tobruk. Got an MC. We're going round to see his wife tomorrow. She's got a little boy.'

Tom shook his head. 'I'm sorry.'

Ten days later they left Southampton on a troopship bound for India. It was almost the same jetty from which he'd seen off Fay — that seemed like a lifetime ago. In the gloom at the end of the day, as they passed The Needles, he wondered if he'd ever see Old England again.

For the first few months in Singapore, they managed, but life was wretched, with not enough food. But slowly the Japanese indifference to them and to illness, began to take its toll, especially with the very young and the very old.

Denied medicines that people knew existed in the city, some quietly faded away. Others died in an agony of sweat and in their own filth from dysentery.

Aunt Blanche grew very weak, seemed to become just bones, her skin like yellow parchment on a frame.

Fay managed to scrounge a little bit of extra, watery fish soup which she spoon fed her. It was the last thing she did for her aunt who, without fuss, quietly went that night.

Fay watched as a couple of helpers wrapped her in a winding sheet and placed her on to a cart.

There were no tears — she didn't have any spare fluid — her eyes just burnt.

But against the awful hardships, a school was started for the children, and plays and concerts were produced. News came from some prisoners who were let out to go into the city to do vital work on the infrastructure. Some of them managed to deceive and, in some cases, bribe, their guards to turn a blind eye while they talked to 'friends' — who, in reality, were go-betweens, disseminators of information.

Short-wave radios concealed in the city received news broadcast from the British in India with morale boosting personal items from the wives and husbands of those inside the walls.

Fay waited in vain for any message for herself.

Tom and George found India a mixture of squalor and richness, excitement and depressing boredom. In the transit mess they drank far too much, and joined in with others in the game of sitting around, emptying their beer bottles then throwing them up into the ceiling. You were supposed to sit absolutely still, no flinching was allowed as the big fan batted them down again; there were a few injuries.

They'd been there for a month, when they were posted to a training squadron, learning the techniques of low-level jungle dog-fights, and the use of air-to-ground rocket projectiles against tanks, strong points, convoys and road and rail bridges.

At last, they were addressed by the CO.

'You are going to fight a tough, coura-geous but fanatical enemy, who will never give up. He is also ruthless, savage and barbaric. The Japanese Army in Burma just doesn't have to be defeated — it has to be *destroyed.*

'Our troops facing him in the 14th Army deserve all the support you can give them. They are fighting under the most difficult circumstances you can imagine, across steaming dense jungles, mountains, wide rivers and swamps.

'And when they meet the enemy they always engage at close quarters. It's virtu-ally hand-to-hand stuff all the time.

'If that wasn't enough, they also have to contend with the killer diseases of malaria, dysentery and scrub typhus.

'Our transport boys are doing a wonderful job servicing long, tenuous supply lines. Your job will be to gain air superiority, and give close support to the men on the ground.'

He paused, then the CO tapped his shaven head which had taken them all by surprise when they had first met him.

'I know some of you have wondered about this, and think it's just to keep cool. Let me tell you something: the 14th is made up of many races — Britons, Indians, Africans, Burmese — and of course, the Gurkhas. I doubt if the like of it will ever be seen again: shave your heads, gentlemen, in honour of the tough riflemen who are doing the dirty work. Now, the drinks in the mess tonight are on me.'

They arrived at their operational airfield as the monsoon broke, to find they were living in Bashas made of bamboo with overhanging eaves, tucked into the jungle alongside the strip.

They watched as a grey-blue horizon above the green jungle moved towards them, growing darker all the time, until they stood under a black sky. As new boys they were bewildered as everybody seemed to be running for shelter and laughing at them. When it came, they were completely taken by surprise. Suddenly, almost instantly they were in a gale, followed in seconds by rain heavier than anything they had ever seen in their lives.

But with it came no respite from the heat and the swarming flies that took shelter with them. Moisture was everywhere, camp beds and sheets were as wet as the air they breathed. Outside the flimsy huts, a blustery wind and sudden stinging downpours continued. Mildew was everywhere, even cigarettes were musty and covered in mould when they opened fresh packets. Nights were spent lying in pools of their own sweat under mosquito nets, playing cards and writing home.

Monsoon or not, the war went on. To begin with they just carried out defensive patrols, the Japanese hitting back with bombers and fighters, making sudden attacks against Allied airfields.

Despite the heat, they wore their Beadon flying suits at dispersal, complete with long trousers to protect against fire and the jungle leeches if they were shot down and lived. All pilots carried a survival kit of knives and screwdrivers strapped to their legs, plus a Mae West. They sweated like pigs until there was a scramble and then they got to the colder air at altitude, and shivered.

Tom got his first Zero and George got two bombers in these skirmishes.

After three months, they began to take part in fighter sweeps over Burma, the 'rhubarbs' they'd been used to over the Pas de Calais, flying east over the Arakan Yomas peaks, dropping down to tree to level over the rolling green sea of jungle to Shebo. Here, enemy supply convoys were concentrated.

Diving down he watched his rockets blowing supply trucks to smithereens, great columns of black smoke marking their success when an ammunition lorry erupted in flame and pyrotechnics. Afterwards they sprayed the roadside bushes where the drivers had flung themselves for cover — just to be thorough.

Once they'd climbed, at tree-top level, over a high ridge and on dropping down on the other side, they came across a whole regiment. They were lined up complete with reviewing officers and large flags of the Rising Sun carried over shoulders.

With his first cannon burst Tom took out the reviewing party, their flags rolling in the dust. As the troops ran for cover, the rest of the squadron followed in wreaking carnage. In less than thirty seconds nearly a hundred soldiers lay dead or injured on the ground. The Japanese reinforcements had only just reached the front.

It was one of the better days, and worth all the flies, the diet of bully beef and sausages made of soya beans. It justified kite hawks with their vicious razor-sharp claws that swooped down on anything neglected for a moment, and the prickly heat that went into red weals from the continuous sweat that poured from their ever thinner bodies.

It made it seem possible that in the seemingly endless days, months and finally years, that the war might one day be won, and they could all go home and leave this beautiful but impossibly hostile land forever.

And through it all, Tom, as he wrote home, and now to his in-laws as well, could only think of Fay, and what she might be going through. Never religious in his life, he prayed nevertheless to an unknown, unseen God that she was alive, and well.

Late in the autumn of 1943 he received a letter, in signal form, from the Air Ministry. It was one of many seen every day by the squadron. He tore it open, still talking to George as they walked out to their Hurricanes, freshly fuelled and armed with rockets and 500lb bombs for the latest rhubarb in support of the increasingly victorious Forgotten Army. He took it to be some annoying directive or censure from head office, so it took some time before his brain caught up with his eyesight.

To Squadron Leader Thomas Roxham

We have received information from the Japanese Red Cross that your wife, Fay Beatrice Constance Victoria Roxham is an internee at Changi Jail, Singapore. She is in good health and is being well cared for.

The strength went out of his body. Tom sank to his knees, as George carried on his way, before he realized what had happened. He rushed back, crouched down by his friend.

'Tom, what the hell is it? Are you OK?'

Then he noticed the tears streaming down his face. 'Are you in pain?'

Tom shook his head, wordlessly, holding up the letter.

George took it, expecting it to be a death telegram — the bloody orderly officer should have delivered it personally. Then, as he read it, he realized that his chum was overcome with relief and joy.

A turbaned mess steward ran up to him.

'Help me get him on to a charpoy.'

Inside the mess tent, they lowered him on to a coco-fibre couch.

Tom looked up at him, wiping a hand across his wet face. 'George, I'm sorry for behaving like an idiot. I just seemed to buckle at the knees.'

George beckoned to the mess steward. 'Get a brandy.'

He turned back to Tom. 'You stay here, you're not fit to fly today. Take the day off, Tom.'

When he started to protest, George shoved him back down into the chair,

'Don't be a bloody fool — there will be plenty of war to go around tomorrow, and the next day, and besides, your mind won't be on the job — and you know how dangerous that can be.'

Tom opened his mouth to say something but George was already on his way. Ducking, he paused in the entrance, 'And Tom,' he winked, 'good on you mate — you never lost faith.'

CHAPTER FIVE

Fay had been in a tiny cage at the Kemp-Tai Police Headquarters in the YMCA Building, the Japanese equivalent of the Gestapo, for several months now. She shared it with two other women and six men. They had no beds and no furniture of any type, just a lavatory which she had to use, as did they all, in front of everybody, including the guard who never took his eyes off them.

She had been beaten regularly, especially by one Major Imamura who always came for her at night. Her back was now as raw as liver. After each beating she was dragged, legs trailing on the ground, and thrown back into the cage. The other women tried to bathe her wounds with rags torn from their clothing, soaked in water from the lavatory, which was also their only source of drinking water. Lice were everywhere, and there was no protection from mosquitoes. Malaria was now rife.

Day after day they were all grilled and deprived of sleep, kept awake by the guards when they were not being interrogated. Sometimes there was no food for days.

It had all started on the infamous Double Tenth — 10 October 1943, when a large force of the Kemp-Tai and troops had raided the jail. It had been discovered that short-wave radios were operating in the city, now called Syonan, and information was being passed into the camps.

At first, Fay hadn't been arrested. She just got on with her daily routine of helping the doctors fight the diseases that always threatened the jail's population.

Amputations were carried out on a bamboo table kept under a mosquito net all day. Fay and other women acted as nurses, and met the men who whispered the latest news from the illegal radios, before scooping out their ulcers with spoons, poking out dead flesh and drawing the stinking pus before swabbing it out with boiled water, then applying bits of cloth soaked in acroflavine over the top and binding it up.

Malignant tertian malaria was also a worry, and could wreak havoc among the sick already struggling with scabies.

Despite some extraordinary feats of courage and endurance, the names of those involved in the relay of information were inevitably given up, together with those of many who were not. Such were the conflicting stories that the Kemp-Tai, paranoid at the best of times, began to believe. They became sure that the civilian camp harboured a major spy and a sabotage organization controlled from India.

And so more and more prisoners were taken in for questioning until finally, Fay was named.

She was dispensing quinine doses, and tablets from the scant supply of M&B 693 for beri-beri cases when they came for her.

At the first interrogation Major Imamura had slapped her hard around the face, causing her ears to ring and lights to flash, and when he'd got nowhere, she had been tied to a wooden bench and flogged by a corporal.

She'd gritted her teeth, but as it went on and on she had begun to scream. When they eventually stopped, they asked her questions, the interpreter sometimes whispering softly, at others screaming into her face. Fay just shook her head, again and again. Suddenly, she realized that Major Imamura was looking at her oddly. He started to remove his tunic, revealing a barrel chest and sweating smooth skin. He took the whip from the hands of the corporal, and told him and the interpreter to get out. He slammed the door behind them, and came over and brought the whip handle up under her chin, raising her head so that she had to look into his dark brown eyes and impassive face.

It was then that she realized he especially liked seeing *her* hurt, humiliated.

He began whipping her slowly, down her exposed back, and on to her buttocks. Whatever thrill that gave him didn't worry her, at least it took the blows away from her ravaged back.

She still refused to give any names, to say anything.

Over the weeks the battle of wills went on. Towards the end she was alternately left alone for long periods, then given no respite for days on end. It didn't take her long to work out that she was only interrogated when *he* was on duty.

The other people came and went as the months passed, but she remained.

The Japanese finally had too much information, most of it conflicting, and they seemed to lose interest. Everybody was released back to Changi, she was now the only one in the cage.

The day came when Major Imamura came

to see her, and nodded for the guard to open the door. He gripped her fleshless arm, forced her, stumbling, along the corridor to the room with the bench and straps.

Fay, expecting a beating, wondered in her near delirious state whether perhaps this was the end, he would beat her to death this time.

Instead he forced her down to her knees, and stood, legs apart, over her.

It was then that she saw his ceremonial sword lying on a side table.

So that was it.

Suffering as she was from dysentery, oedema and scabies, death would be a welcome release. She would never give in to Imamura. If she did, they, the enemy, would have finally won, triumphed over everything she stood for.

It was as simple as that.

He picked up the sword, all the time staring at her, and drew it slowly out of its scabbard. Its arc gleamed in a shaft of sunlight. Fay did her best to suppress a shiver.

He didn't ask her any more questions, or threaten her. With one hand he grabbed her hair, twisted it and brought her face up. For several seconds they stared hard at each other.

Angrily he bent her down, head nearly

touching the floor, and swept the hair from her bared neck. She felt the cold touch of metal on her sweating skin.

Eyes tightly shut she filled the blackness with a swift cavalcade of images — of her mother and father and her childhood; of Codrington and the Cotswolds, and, above all, of Tom. The coldness left her neck, and there was a swish of steel through air.

CHAPTER SIX

Tom lay on his mattress, staring up at the slowly moving fan. It was five o'clock, an hour till dawn. He had been thinking about the impersonal nature of God. On the day he had received news of Fay's safe internment, he'd waved goodbye to George — not knowing that he would never see him again.

The wing had returned without him — but someone had seen him bail out. They'd been coming out of a low level attack on a Jap position when he'd been hit by ground fire. He'd managed to get altitude and bail out.

Tom immediately got into his Hurricane and took off for the co-ordinates that had been given for the attack by a ground observer. He was racked with guilt. If he had gone as usual, it might — *should* have been him.

When he arrived over the jungle he'd quickly seen the parachute canopy draped among the trees. As he circled he looked in vain for any sign of movement — but there was none. There was no enemy fire coming up at him.

Tom racked the Hurricane hood back, and lobbed out several packs of food and survival kits attached to small message parachutes — just to feel he was doing something. The chances of George finding one were remote to say the least.

It took a month for news of his fate to come through. When it did, it turned Tom Roxham into a man of icy detachment, with only one thought in his head when he climbed into his cockpit. By May of 1944, when the squadron was withdrawn for rest and re-equipping, he had become one of the top scoring fighter pilots in that theatre of operation, and a ruthless, almost suicidal attacker of ground troops.

But he had changed. Tom now tended to remain aloof, spending time reading, and going through George's effects over and over again. The legal people at Group HQ had confirmed that George had left everything to him. Amongst these were his favourite books, a much thumbed copy of *The Coral Island* by R.M. Ballantyne, and Dickens's *A Tale of Two Cities*. He noticed the fly leaf had been inscribed with 'Love,

Mum and Dad, Christmas 1935.' There were also some papers relating to the family business in Australia. It took some time for him to write to George's parents, who knew already through official channels that their son was dead, but he wanted them to know how close they had become. He asked if he might visit them when the war was over. The one thing he didn't add was how George had actually died.

He'd made it down OK, but when men of 6th Gurkha's had advanced they'd found his body. He had been bayoneted fourteen times.

They were saying goodbye to the trusty Hurricane. It was renowned throughout the air force as a magnificent gun platform, capable of soaking up the punishment, and ideal as a fighter or a bomber at low altitude. Only in the higher skies was it eclipsed by the more glamorous Spitfire.

They were taking on a new machine, one that was well tried and tested in the European theatre and latterly the Pacific. It was a very large, pugnacious fighter-bomber, nicknamed Jug — short for Juggernaut.

He walked around the Republic P-47D Thunderbolt, a Yankee job.

It certainly was big, with a fuselage that was deep, ending in a blunt, cowled nose —

streamlined it was not. It was camouflaged in jungle green and grey, with roundels without the red centre — so that they could not be confused with the Rising Sun, symbol of the enemy.

Tomorrow he would fly one for the first time.

A truck dropped him off at the mess. There was a document waiting for him in the adjutant's office apparently.

Maybe God was feeling sorry for him, because he was informed that arrangements were now in place for messages to be sent to civilian internees through the Japanese Red Cross. He was warned that it would be heavily censored, by both sides, and could not be longer than twenty-eight words.

He spent nearly the rest of the day drafting it, tingling with the knowledge that he was writing to her, that she would be reading his *very* words — the first they had exchanged in years, and that he must pack as much information in it as possible for her.

He finally came up with:

Darling, your mother and father join me every day in thinking about you. You are not forgotten. Can't wait to be together again. Love you, love you, Tom.

He copied it, and wrapped it — together with the message he'd received telling him that she was alive — around her photograph. The latter was heavily creased, and had lost its gloss around her face where he had kissed it so much during the last four years.

He sank back in his chair, and wondered how much longer it would take? How much more could *he* take?

That night he went to a film show put on by ENSA entitled *Cover Girl* with Rita Hayworth. One song got to him so much so, that he found tears running down his face, mercifully in the dark. 'Long Ago and Far Away'. That summed up the way he felt. He'd only been happy a long time ago, and far away from this green, noisy, biting hell.

The Jug proved to be as good as they said. When the squadron returned to the fray they now flew 'cab-rank' patrols directed by ground, and sometimes airborne, observation posts. With their three 500lb bombs, or 0.50 calibre guns, or ten rockets they played havoc among Japanese troops and supply lines.

And they took the damage inflicted on them, and still kept on flying. Just before the war in Burma was finally over, Tom came back with 87 bullet holes in his wings and fuselage, one the size of a football. He invariably went right down on a target, totally ignoring the flak coming up. By now he had a bar to his DFC.

The fall of Rangoon passed almost unnoticed in Europe, where people were celebrating in the streets at the ending of the war against Germany.

The Japanese retreat continued. Wherever they fell into the hands of the Burmese villagers, they were shown no mercy; British forces following up sometimes came across scenes of ambushes where gold teeth had been hacked from the jaws of soldiers whilst they were still alive, and disembowelling of the sick and wounded had occurred.

Tom was spared all this, he just kept flying every minute, every second, of every day, blasting the Army of Nippon wherever it made a stand.

Ironically, one of his last acts was to attack a train, watching his rockets strike the engine and front carriages. Steam shot hundreds of feet into the air, and the wooden carriages piled up into a blazing pyre that could be seen twenty miles away.

Dazed survivors struggled out on to the embankment. Younger members of the squadron, fresh out from England, watched in horror as Tom went in so low that his prop flicked pieces off bushes, the .50 calibre machine-guns ripping up the earth, flesh and blood as he rubbed out as many of the survivors as possible.

On their arrival, they'd heard his views in the mess, as he'd downed a brandy.

'Sub-human buggers, unfathomable savages. They love inflicting pain — and death.' He'd coughed, then added 'Got to be exterminated.'

He'd straightened up and tossed back the rest of the drink.

'They've got their backs to the wall now — but don't expect them to give in — they'll fight like cornered rats. Take my advice, if you ever fall into their hands — take your cyanide pill — OK?'

With that he'd walked in to supper.

It was a different war.

And one that still had to be won.

CHAPTER SEVEN

The planning for the invasion of Malaya began in earnest, code name, *Operation Zipper.*

As Tom sat in the briefings he found he couldn't help thinking about Singapore — when would the army finally get there. If there was heavy fighting, would Fay be safe? Would she survive? It would be something he couldn't live with if anything untoward happened.

Not after all this time.

In Singapore the air raids had started, tiny silver aircraft high up in the clear blue sky rained bombs down on the docks and stores, and blew up ammunition dumps and airfields. The Japanese Air force always took off and disappeared before these raids. Enemy ships limped into the Jahore Straits badly damaged, and stayed there, unable to be repaired. Daily, rumours were rife in the prison: they were all to be shot; they were all to be released the next day; they were all going to be taken by the Nips to the 'Homeland'. Finally it seemed that if an attack started, they would be shot — not fed.

Fay, who had weighed 8st 1lb when she had arrived in the Colony, now weighed 4st 10lbs on the medical room scales. The doctors and nurses lavished all the care they could give, and even with extra food from the black market, it was still months before she could walk unaided.

Major Imamura had brought the sword slashing down on to the whipping bench, scything through leather and bloodstained wood. He had said nothing, sheathed the ceremonial weapon, and left.

When he'd gone Fay had pitched forward on to the floor, body convulsing as she vomited black bile. But she knew she had won.

Today she was sitting out by the vegetable plot, watching the more able-bodied working on the potatoes.

Suddenly she was aware of somebody standing beside her. She looked up, and saw a woman who did the internal postal rounds. Not once had she come to Fay, and now she was holding out a strange yellow-orange coloured envelope. Blankly she took it.

When she didn't immediately open it the woman prompted. 'It's from the Red Cross, dear, it must be from home.'

Fay looked at it. 'Home?'

The woman took it back from her, opened the flap and pulled out a single thin sheet of paper. 'There, now you can read it.'

Fay looked down noticing the badly printed scrolling and the illustration of a building — something about Tokyo Headquarters.

Then she read the message.

Tom? It was from Tom.

A wet spot landed on the cheap rice surface and spread out like on blotting paper. Then another. The woman looked up at the sky, but it was a clear blue.

When she looked down again the letter was splattered, the spots coalescing.

It was then that she realized that Fay was crying, soundlessly.

The first hints that the years of stifling captivity, deprivation, and horror were coming to an end, came through the secret radios. VE Day had passed, huge naval victories by the Americans in the Pacific, had followed, Burma was finally free and — the invasion of Malaya was imminent. Then something about a secret and massive bomb on a place called Hiroshima, followed by another at Nagasaki mystified and excited them.

On 15 August somebody listening to a radio heard the news first. The Emperor of Japan, Hirohito stunned by the awesome power of the bombs, and fearful of his country being systematically wiped off the face of the earth, had surrendered unconditionally.

To begin with nothing much happened, though the guards became less aggressive. After three days, food that was supposed to be unobtainable began to flow in. Likewise medical supplies came from nowhere, and in great quantities. No one was required to work, and prisoners from the military camp started to wander around. The Japanese didn't seem defeated, but they no longer had the swagger of old. Cigarettes were shared with the guards.

Fay, still very weak, tottered out and looked around. It didn't feel like freedom, until on 5 September the advance troops landed at the docks. British paratroops arrived at Changi, to be greeted politely by the Japanese. They were quickly disarmed and whisked away.

Some of the men walked into the city to see the official surrender ceremony when

Mountbatten arrived, standing fearlessly upright in his car, dressed in a white naval uniform as he was driven through thousands of wildly cheering Malays and Chinese.

On the steps of the civic hall General Seishiro Itagaki met him and formally handed over his sword, as Major Imamura, alone in his room, committed hari kari.

For Fay, and the thousands of internees and POWs it was finally over.

Tom had been in the crowded mess when someone started shouting out, 'Quiet, quiet you bloody heathens.'

In the silence they heard the BBC announcer's voice impart the news of the bomb dropped on Hiroshima with a complete lack of emotion.

In the silence that followed the details someone said, 'Christ Almighty.'

Three days later the same BBC man announced another bomb had been dropped on Nagasaki, and a week later the stunning news that Japan had surrendered.

So it had finally come to an end.

And to many of them it was an anticlimax, a weird vacuum. Suddenly there were no more sorties, no strain and anxiety, just a guilty euphoria and almost exotic laziness. When the fact that they had survived finally sunk in, the parties had started, wild and drunken. Frustrated, Tom had tried to get to Singapore, a compelling, overwhelming urge driving his every waking moment, pestering the Transport Section, getting nowhere. Until now.

He'd decided to make his own arrangements. As the celebrations continued around him he took his whisky out on to the veranda. A flock of green parrots swooped and climbed, screeching to roost in the banyan trees, preening and fluttering and bobbing their heads as the sky turned from violet to dark blue and the stars began to show. He stood looking at them, wondering, praying that she too was seeing them.

Tomorrow — he would do it tomorrow.

His SAC looked at him worriedly as Tom climbed on to the wing. 'Where you off to, Sir?'

He knew there were no sorties being flown now. Tom shook his hand warmly.

'Thank you for taking good care of me, Jimmy, we must have a pint in Civvy street I'd like to meet that young daughter you've never seen.'

Jimmy helped strap him in.

'You're not going to do anything silly are you, Sir?'

It took a second for Tom to realize Jimmy was worried that he was going to commit suicide — unbalanced perhaps by the guilt of surviving, when so many, including his close friend, had not.

He grinned. 'No Jimmy, I'm not. I wouldn't need external tanks for that, would I?'

With them he had a range of 1,800 miles — more than enough.

'But you're right in one way — I'm not coming back. Can't stand the diabolical insect life a second longer.'

They both laughed at that.

He slapped him on the back.

'Don't be around when they first start asking questions — but at the right time you can tell 'em I said something about going to find my wife, OK?'

Jimmy's eyes widened. He knew where the boss was going.

The two and a half thousand horse power engine coughed, then roared into life as the Pratt and Whitney engine fired up. He waved the chocks away. Jimmy suddenly stood to attention and saluted. Tom acknowledged with a gloved hand — touching his forehead, and then buttoned his mask across his face. He did his checks as he taxied at a fast rate out on to the strip, eager to get off before anybody in the tower, hopefully, nursing almighty headaches, realized what was happening.

He lined up dead centre on the strip, did one last instrument check, then gunned the engine.

Five minutes later, still climbing, he was at 24,000 feet and setting course for Singapore.

As white, fluffy clouds and a blue ocean passed by far below, he could only think of her, of that beautiful young woman who had so captivated him what seemed like a lifetime ago.

They had been apart for so long now, and so much had happened since then. He knew he was changed. Would Fay be the same girl he had been dreaming of, longing for, all these years?

In his heart he knew she couldn't be.

Both of them, like so many of their generation had had their youth cruelly and violently taken from them by a terrible war: and many their very lives — like George.

His mouth was so dry he couldn't even swallow, but tears blurred his sight. He raised his goggles, passed the back of his gloved hand across his face to clear them.

Automatically, he scanned the sky for any

461

sign of black dots.

It was still hard to believe that it was all over.

He checked his watch.

One hour to go.

CHAPTER EIGHT

Fay and all the others were now in the hands of an organization called RAPWI, which stood for the Rehabilitation of Allied Prisoners of War and Internees.

She had been moved to a large commandeered house near the city centre where there was better medical care. It had previously been a Japanese officer's happy home.

In the drive down, through almost deserted streets, Fay had looked out at the peeling paint, the wrecked buildings, the sky with kites lazily swinging around in circles in the currents of air. Even in the car you could detect the stink of broken drains. It was true, she thought, defeat does have a smell.

The jungle had grown around buildings that had been blasted in an act of hopeless defence all those years ago, the branches entering shattered walls to appear again in the roofless tops, curling over charred beams.

Weirdly, other homes were almost as if they had been left for the weekend.

The cricket club still stood, surrounded by rutted and yellowing greens, the administrative buildings across the padang, silent and abandoned looking.

Only the flame trees and jacaranda had added a colourful touch of the life of old.

She still felt as if she was in a dream — within the nightmare — and would wake up in it again.

With the aid of walking sticks she could get under a shower, but when she looked down at her body, at her yellowy scarred flesh, shrivelled breasts and protruding bones, she started to cry. Tom would find her hideous. She wondered when they would be united — or even if he was still alive. The letter from him was months old.

The RAPWI people had a lot to do, what with the thousands of exprisoners from up country joining those already there. Transports were waiting in the shipping lanes, but it was a massive undertaking. Already the troops, with the almost mandatory sense of humour that had helped them, and the amazing 14th Army survive and ultimately win, had dubbed it, 'Retain All Prisoners of

War Indefinitely'.

So she would not be a priority; she had been told so because of her poor health.

In fact, now the time had come, she was afraid — afraid of what she would find with her freedom. The world had changed, and so had she. It was time to face reality.

And that was the one thing Fay feared more than anything she'd been through in the past four years. Because what had kept her going was the thought of being with Tom again.

And now she was terrified of that prospect.

So much so, that she'd asked the RAPWI not to reveal her whereabouts. Not yet.

Perhaps not ever. . . .

Tom had flown into Tengah airfield, and into an unholy row. He cared nothing about threats to court-martial him, they could stick the bloody service up their jacksy.

Having checked into the mess he clipped on his sidearm — a reflex from the days of up country airstrips — and got a jeep and a driver from the pool.

'Where to, Sir?'

'Changi Jail.'

As they went through the outskirts of the city they passed working parties of Japanese prisoners, running in squads, naked save for

465

their boots, peaked caps and flapping loin cloths. How fallen were the ferocious, savage warriors of Nippon!

If somebody had stopped him and asked him to shoot one of them, he would have done so without a second's thought.

Tom realized he was damaged, dehumanized by an experience of a hell on earth and might never be the same again; the world, his world, had lost its innocence.

When they got there, Tom looked up, aghast at the sight of the huge block with the hundreds of tiny windows, each one marking a cell.

Had Fay been languishing there for years? It didn't bear thinking about.

He approached a temporary office in a hut and found a civilian who looked up from a desk blasted by a portable electric fan. Piles of documents were held down by various weights. Despite all that, he still had huge black sweat marks under his arms and up his back, and obviously hadn't been long out from Blighty.

Testily he looked up. 'Can I help you?'

Tom told him he was looking for his wife Fay Roxham.

The man reached for a pile of papers and began to work through them.

'Ah, here we are.'

He examined one, frowning.

'She was not well — had been inter-rogated by the Kemp-Tai — that's the military police — been transferred to a medical facility.'

The shock was as if he had been kicked in the stomach.

Despite the heat Tom felt such a coldness he shivered. 'Is she all right? What did they do to her?'

The man shook his head.

'I have no details — but it seems she was near death's door when they returned her to Changi, that's why she needs to be where she is.'

Tom could hardly breathe. 'Where is she?'

The man shook his head. 'I'm sorry, I'm not allowed to say.'

'I'm her husband — where is she?'

'I'm sorry —'

The man's eyes bulged as Tom released the clip on the flap of his holster and drew out his service revolver.

There was something in the wing com-mander's eyes — he'd seen it before. After what they'd been through a lot of them out here were deranged.

Hurriedly he scrambled for a pen, began to write.

'I shouldn't do this, but seeing you're —'

Tom snatched the paper away, glanced at the address.

'Thank you.'

He turned on his heel. At the jeep he showed it to the driver. 'You know where this is?'

'Yes, Sir.'

'Take me there.'

He swung into the front seat and looked back. The man was holding the phone, but dropped it like a hot potato when he saw Tom looking at him.

'And put your foot down.'

On the journey Tom was in a state of fear. Fay, his Fay. *Tortured.* He felt as if his head was going to explode.

Fay had walked, using her two sticks, out on to the veranda and settled herself into a wicker chair. One of the staff got her a cold drink. She closed her eyes, thinking of a time that seemed so long ago. She recalled the first moment she had seen him, playing the saxophone at that dance, of the weird shiver that had gone through her, and the strange urge to fend him off. It was as though something was telling her that this was the *one* — that she was no longer alone in the world, but would never be completely free again.

All so long ago, so far away, another time, another place. . . .

She dozed, feeling immeasurably sad.

They had been so in love. . . .

Tom leapt out of the jeep, looked up at the lawns to the long low house set among the trees. Frightened by what he might find, he walked, less resolutely, up the winding path to the veranda, then up the step to the wide open double doors. He entered the cool large lobby, the fans in the ceiling whirling almost silently above the marble floor.

'Can I help you, Sir?'

The young nurse eyed up the sun-tanned wing commander with medal ribbons.

'Yes. I believe my wife is here?'

'And the name, Sir?'

'Mrs Roxham.'

'Oh she's out on the veranda — just by the doors. You must have passed her.'

He shook his head. 'No, there was only an elderly lady asleep. . . .'

The nurse watched the agony on his face as realization dawned. He turned and slowly, fearfully, retraced his steps, his chukha boots making no sound on the marble. In the doorway he looked down on her, head bowed in sleep, at the woman he loved more dearly than life itself, and realized just how nearly he'd lost her.

Fay came out of her dreaming, fluttering her eyes in the brightness. A man was standing over her, a lean handsome RAF Officer, a *pilot.*

'Yes?'

He took his cap off and knelt down, gently taking her hands in his.

'Hello, Fay, I've come to take you home.'

OBITUARY
NATIONAL PRESS 2007

WING COMMANDER TOM 'ROCKY' ROXHAM

Wing Commander Tom 'Rocky' Roxham, who has died aged 88 was one of the RAF's most colourful and outstanding pilots in both the European and South East Asia theatres during WWII.

He began his war as a sergeant pilot during the Battle of France, flying Hurricanes, where he shot down two Stuka Dive Bombers. During the Battle of Britain he claimed a further ME 109 before he himself had to bail out, landing dramatically on a station roof and breaking both a leg and an arm.

On his recovery he was commissioned as a Pilot Officer and rejoined his squadron, carrying out aggressive fighter sweeps over Northern France and Occupied Europe. During this period he was awarded a DFC and later a DSO for inspired leadership. He became known for his superb shooting skills developed on the moors and estuaries of Northern England and Scotland.

In the European Theatre he had a final total of eight enemy aircraft destroyed — six of them ME109s.

With the fall of Singapore he volunteered for South East Asia, spending the rest of the war on Hurricanes and latterly P47 Thunderbolts giving close support to the 14th Army.

It was here that he earned the epithet 'Rocky', and a reputation for being as hard as nails and a ruthless fighter who gave no quarter.

He caused some consternation when he flew unauthorized to Singapore on its liberation, to find his wife, who had been an internee at the infamous Changi Jail.

After the war Roxham discovered that an Australian colleague, who was killed in the final months of the fighting in Burma, had left him his share in the family copper mine in Western Australia. Subsequently he became the sole owner and one of the wealthiest men in post-war Britain.

In memory of his comrade he founded the George Hawksley Foundation for the families of WWII Aircrew.

He fully refurbished Codrington Hall near Cirencester, his wife's family seat, which was in a state of near-terminal disrepair, turning it into a warm and comfortable home which became famous for its parties.

But Roxham never forgot his humble roots and by 1972 was disenchanted with life in Britain. He moved to New Zealand, settling in Devonport near Auckland.

With his huge wealth, Tom Roxham, a pre-war railway policeman, built his own railway for some fifteen miles through rolling countryside.

He bought, refitted, and shipped out two steam locomotives from the Western Region waiting to be broken up for scrap, together with several coaches, and could be seen working as a ticket collector on what came to be known as the Cotswold Line.

His wife, whom he taught to fly, predeceased him by one month. He is survived by two daughters, adopted when it was feared that Fay Roxham could not conceive after her wartime experiences, and a natural son and daughter.

ABOUT THE AUTHOR

David Wiltshire served his National Service in Aden and Singapore before returning to England. He is married with three children and seven grandchildren and lives in Bedford. His novel *Nightmare Man,* also published by Robert Hale, was adapted by the BBC as a four-part series.

We hope you have enjoyed this Large Print book. Other Thorndike, Wheeler, and Chivers Press Large Print books are available at your library or directly from the publishers.

For information about current and upcoming titles, please call or write, without obligation, to:

Publisher
Thorndike Press
295 Kennedy Memorial Drive
Waterville, ME 04901
Tel. (800) 223-1244

or visit our Web site at:

www.gale.com/thorndike
www.gale.com/wheeler

OR

Chivers Large Print
published by BBC Audiobooks Ltd
St James House, The Square
Lower Bristol Road
Bath BA2 3SB
England
Tel. +44(0) 800 136919
email: bbcaudiobooks@bbc.co.uk
www.bbcaudiobooks.co.uk

All our Large Print titles are designed for easy reading, and all our books are made to last.